"Kent Krueger keeps upping his game with each thriller featuring O'Connor. . . . Fans will not be disappointed."

—*Pioneer Press* (Minnesota)

"Krueger keeps up the tension and mystery . . . [with] taut storytelling and intricate plots."

—*Star Tribune* (Minnesota)

SULFUR SPRINGS

"Totally un-let-go-able, a can't miss for fans and a new obsession for new readers."

—*Globe Gazette* (Iowa)

"A blistering Wild West mystery."

—*Minneapolis Star Tribune*

"Realistic and believable. . . . Cork O'Connor is a worthy protagonist."

—*New York Journal of Books*

MANITOU CANYON

"Explores the tension between belief and truth, between protecting a sacred place and embracing technological progress, between having empathy for a cause and taking action to defend it . . . Krueger has crafted a gripping thriller . . . steeped in the mythology of American Indian tribes of Minnesota . . . [a] deeply spiritual novel. Read it with your heart."

—*Minneapolis Star Tribune*

"A mystery made up of several shiver-inducing levers . . . [with] a plot that keeps tightening around O'Connor and the granddaughter— and the reader's nerves. A first-rate addition to this series."

—*Booklist*

WINDIGO ISLAND

"Krueger demonstrates his penchant and ability for finding deep, rich and new veins of stories from the seemingly inexhaustive mine of the rural and deceptively peaceful northern Minnesota and its surrounding environs."

—*Bookreporter*

"William Kent Krueger . . . writes with fresh passion and purpose in *Windigo Island*."

—*New York Times Book Review*

"Krueger is skillful in many things—creating strong characters, building drama and conflict, braiding in Indian legend and spirituality, and spinning a good yarn—but sense of place may well be his forte."

—*Minneapolis Star Tribune*

TAMARACK COUNTY

"A winter's tale that will both break and warm the reader's heart. . . . Krueger's evident empathy for the Ojibwe and their traditions and values blends seamlessly with horrific violence played out against O'Connor's struggles to heal his family's wounds—and his own."

—*Publishers Weekly* (starred review)

"Hold-your-breath suspense, heightened by the isolating blizzards of a Minnesota winter and the eerie presence of a stalker. . . . Because Krueger works in the history of his characters' relationships in a clear and elegant way, this exceptionally scary suspense story will prove riveting for both newcomers to the series and readers who have followed Cork as he and his family have aged and grown."

—*Booklist* (starred review)

Also by William Kent Krueger

DESOLATION MOUNTAIN

A NOVEL

WILLIAM KENT KRUEGER

ATRIA PAPERBACK

New York   London   Toronto   Sydney   New Delhi

ATRIA
PAPERBACK

An Imprint of Simon & Schuster, LLC
1230 Avenue of the Americas
New York, NY 10020

First Atria Paperback edition April 2019

ATRIA PAPERBACK and colophon are trademarks of Simon & Schuster, LLC

For information about special discounts for bulk purchases, please contact Simon & Schuster Special Sales at 1-866-506-1949 or business@simonandschuster.com.

The Simon & Schuster Speakers Bureau can bring authors to your live event. For more information or to book an event contact the Simon & Schuster Speakers Bureau at 1-866-248-3049 or visit our website at www.simonspeakers.com.

Manufactured in the United States of America

20 19 18 17 16 15 14 13 12

The Library of Congress has cataloged the hardcover edition as follows:

Names: Krueger, William Kent, author.
Title: Desolation mountain : a novel / William Kent Krueger.
Description: First Atria Books hardcover edition. | New York : Atria Books, 2018. | Series: Cork O'Connor mystery series ; 17
Identifiers: LCCN 2018017327 (print) | LCCN 2018021101 (ebook) | ISBN 9781501147487 (eBook) | ISBN 9781501147463 (hardback) | ISBN 9781501147470 (paperback)
Subjects: LCSH: O'Connor, Cork (Fictitious character)--Fiction. | Private investigators--Minnesota--Fiction. | Ojibwa Indians--Fiction. | BISAC: FICTION / Mystery & Detective / General. | FICTION / Suspense. | FICTION / General. | GSAFD: Suspense fiction. | Mystery fiction.
Classification: LCC PS3561.R766 (ebook) | LCC PS3561.R766 D47 2018 (print) | DDC 813/.54--dc23
LC record available at https://lccn.loc.gov/2018017327

ISBN 978-1-5011-4746-3
ISBN 978-1-5011-4747-0 (pbk)
ISBN 978-1-5011-4748-7 (ebook)

For Randalyn Nickelsen Clark,
whose beautiful spirit is with us always

DESOLATION MOUNTAIN

AUTHOR'S NOTE

Many years ago, in a stand-alone thriller titled *The Devil's Bed*, I first introduced readers to the character of Bo Thorson, who plays a significant role in the following story. Over the fifteen years since that book's publication, I've received a consistent flow of requests from readers to bring Bo back. It wasn't until I conceived of the plot for this current novel that I saw a way to resurrect him. I always thought that Bo Thorson and Cork O'Connor were the kind of men who would appreciate each other and might look forward to cracking open a couple of brews and trading tales. I hope you enjoy his presence, and if he intrigues you, I encourage you to pick up *The Devil's Bed*, in which his full history is made clear.

CHAPTER 1

He watches the boy on the steep rise above him. He is that boy and he is not. The boy is intent on the sky, a witch's brew of swirling gray clouds. He is anxious, waiting. The boy. And him. For what, neither of them knows. The air smells not of the evergreen all around but of something foul. Diesel. Fire. A breeze blows across his face carrying a different smell, even more foul. Burning flesh. The boy holds a compound bow, complicated, powerful. An arrow is notched. The boy's stomach is taut. His body knows something his mind does not, something terrible. The boy watches the sky, and he watches the boy.

The bird appears out of the dark boil of clouds. Wings spread broad, catching the wind. Curling in a wide arc above the hill. The bird—clearly an eagle now—lets out a screech. High-pitched. Then another.

The boy raises his bow.

The eagle circles, near enough that the boy can see details. Golden irises, saffron beak, long, dangerous talons. The eagle cries again.

The boy draws back the bowstring. Calculates trajectory, wind speed. Leads the bird. Takes a breath. Eases it out. Lets the arrow fly.

The great bird twists in an explosion of feathers. Tries to right itself. Begins to plummet.

The boy lowers the bow. Watches an egg drop from the eagle. Watches the eagle in its fall, lost among the evergreens. The boy stands still as death. He feels uncertain, as if there is still more to be done, but what that is he doesn't know. He turns and stares down the hillside. At the young man who stares back. Him. And not him.

Neither of them understands.

Then the boy on the rise above him sees something, which he senses now at his own back. From the look on the boy's face, from the way his eyes grow huge, he understands that what is behind him is enormous and terrifying and threatens them both. He feels its breath break against him, hot and hungry. He should turn, face this beast whatever it is, but he's paralyzed with fear. The boy on the hill opens his mouth to cry out. At the same moment, he opens his.

The sound of their one scream wakes him.

The old man sat on the other side of the fire, listening. Old? He was ancient, with more years behind him than any living thing in the dark of that great forest—turtle, owl, deer, wolf, bear, all were children in comparison. The years, kind to no one, had done their best to weather his flesh, weaken his muscle, erode his bone. His body displayed none of the power and comeliness that had so marked it when the twentieth century was young. Time had etched lines long and deep into his face. His white hair hung over his shoulders in spidery wisps. The weight of ten decades of living had bent his spine, but only slightly. In the firelight, he appeared to be the ghost of a thing, not the thing itself.

And yet the young man who stared at him across the fire perceived only wisdom, only possibility.

"Many times you have seen this vision?" the old man asked.

"Many times," the young man answered.

"That is all of it?"

The young man nodded. "All of it."

"The eagle is sacred. Killing an eagle, that is a terrible thing."

The fire popped. An ember leapt from the flames, landed on the jeans the old man was wearing. The old man gazed up at the stars and didn't seem to notice.

"Your leg, Henry," the young man said.

But the ember had burned itself out.

"And so," the old man finally said, as if speaking to the stars. "Why now?"

The young man didn't understand the question. "Why now what?"

The old man's eyes came back to earth. "You tell me."

The young man knew better than to press this elder, his mentor. He considered his reply.

"Now, because it worries me. It's a portent, Henry. Something terrible is going to happen. My visions are always about terrible things. I've never had one that's hopeful."

"They have proven helpful," the old man pointed out. Then he asked again, as if it were a new question, "Why now?"

"If you mean why have I come to you only now, it's because I thought I could figure this out on my own. But I don't have a clue. I need help, before it's too late."

The old man closed his eyes, looked as if he were about to sleep. Then, "Too late for what?"

"If I understood the vision, I would understand that."

"Maybe so. Maybe not. Visions are tricky. They can be the thing itself, or the shadow of the thing."

"If it's only a shadow, why does it scare me so much?"

The old man took a stick from the fire, the end still licked by tongues of flame. He moved it toward the young man's face. The flames came nearer and nearer, until the young man could feel the heat on his cheek, the fire only inches from his flesh. But he didn't flinch.

"You are not afraid?" the old man asked.

"I believe you won't burn me. Or if you do, there's purpose in it."

"A vision is like that." The old man returned the stick to the fire. He stared deeply into the young man's face, his eyes dark, hard, gleaming in the flickering light. "Who is the boy?"

"I'm the boy," the young man answered. "And I'm not."

"What is this beast that frightens you?"

"I don't know. It's behind me. I never see it."

"And who is it you are afraid for, Stephen O'Connor?"

"For the boy," Stephen answered. "And for me." He leaned toward the old man. "And I don't know why, Henry, but for you, too."

CHAPTER 2

Anyone who knew Tamarack County, Minnesota, and the town of Aurora, in particular, knew Sam's Place. The old Quonset hut turned burger joint sat on the shoreline of Iron Lake. Behind it was blue water, a vast expanse. South rose a copse of poplar trees at whose center lay the ruins of an old ironworks. Aurora itself was a stone's throw west, just beyond the raised bed of the BNSF railroad tracks. A short, unpaved road crossed the tracks, connecting Sam's Place with civilization.

Corcoran Liam O'Connor stood in the parking lot, appraising the sign he had just affixed with sheet metal screws to the side of the Quonset hut. The sign read: TRY OUR NEW WAABOO BURGER! Cork had made the sign himself, at the workbench in his garage, with the help of his five-year-old grandson, Waaboo—legally, Aaron Smalldog O'Connor. The family nickname for the little guy was Waaboozoons, which, in the language of the Ojibwe, meant "little rabbit." It had been shortened to simply Waaboo. The exclamation point was entirely little Waaboo's handiwork.

It was late afternoon, late September. The leaves of the poplar trees were like gold doubloons. The air was cool, the sun a lazy yellow. There were no customers lined up at the serving windows. They would arrive eventually, Cork knew, closer to suppertime. He appreciated this quiet period, between the hustle of the lunch crowd and what would come.

A green Forester turned up the road, bounced over the tracks and into the lot. The driver parked and got out. She was tall, pretty, with hair the color of corn silk. She opened the back door and helped a child from his seat. They stood with Cork, looking at the sign.

"Me," little Waaboo said with great pride, pointing toward his name.

"A hundred people are going to eat you up tonight." Cork opened his mouth wide as if to take a bite out of his grandson. Waaboo danced back, happily.

"Any sign of Stephen yet?" Jenny asked. She was Cork's daughter, Waaboo's mother.

Cork shook his head. "He's with Henry. So who knows?"

"Has he said anything to you yet?" Concern shaded her words.

"Whatever it is, I'm sure he's sharing it with Henry." Cork stepped to the sign, brushed at a spot of what looked like dripped black paint but turned out to be a spider. "When he's ready, he'll tell us."

"He's a darkpoople," Waaboo said.

"Darkpoople?"

"We've been reading *The BFG*," Jenny explained. "Roald Dahl. Waaboo's creating his own dictionary of words."

Cork laughed. "Darkpoople. You nailed him, little guy."

"Waaboo and I can stick around until he shows," Jenny offered.

"Rainy's going to cover, if necessary."

"I want to stay," Waaboo said. "I want to help Baa-baa." His name for Cork. Not one of his new, made-up Roald Dahlish words. It was what he had always called his grandfather.

"For a while, then," she agreed.

Inside, the place smelled of deep-fry oil and of the meats that had sizzled on the griddle, decades of aromas soaked into the walls. The Quonset hut was divided into two parts. The front was Sam's Place, with all the food prep equipment, big freezer, storage shelves, stainless-steel sink. The back was an office Cork used for both the business of Sam's Place and his own work as a private investigator. There was a round table and four chairs, all of sturdy maple, old and worn. A little kitchenette with a small refrigerator, a microwave, a coffeemaker, counter space, sink. A couple of tall, gray file cabinets stood against the wall, one for documents pertaining to Sam's Place, the other for the files related to Cork's investigations. He didn't advertise that side of his business doings anymore. He had a reputation. Those who needed him found their way.

"Can I have an ice cream cone?" Waaboo asked, addressing his grandfather, not his mother.

"Whoa," Jenny said. "I thought you just wanted to help."

"Yes. But I'm hungry."

"Just a cone, Jenny," Cork said. "Won't spoil his dinner."

"A small one."

Waaboo sat on a chair at the serving window, licking his cone, a chocolate and vanilla twist. Cork scraped the griddle. Jenny sliced tomatoes.

"Are you going to the town meeting tomorrow night?" Jenny asked.

"I'm working here, remember? You put together this week's schedule."

"I'll get one of the kids to cover."

Cork had always hired high school students to staff Sam's Place in season. For many, it was their introduction to the working world. He tried to be firm in what he asked of them but patient in his oversight.

"That's okay. There'll be plenty of people attending. Senator McCarthy will get an earful without me."

Jenny said, "It's a chance to see the senator up close."

"I've seen Olympia McCarthy up close. She's a fine woman, but still just a woman."

"A lot of people are pinning a lot of hope on her. Daniel's agreed to put Waaboo to bed. Rainy's going with me."

"Then you two make plenty of noise for the rest of us."

An old Jeep rattled over the railroad tracks.

"The prodigal son," Cork said. "You and Waaboo are free."

A few minutes later, Cork heard the Quonset hut door open and Stephen appeared. He smelled of woodsmoke and evergreen sap. He shed his gray hoodie, hung his backpack on a hook. The backpack looked heavy, and Cork knew it was full of college text-books.

"Sorry I'm late. Hey, Waaboo!" He tousled the boy's hair. In appearance, Stephen more resembled his nephew than his father or sister. His Anishinaabe genes dominated—dark hair, almond eyes, broad, bold facial bones. He was twenty years old and walked with a limp that was becoming less and less noticeable with time.

"How's Henry?" Cork asked.

"Old." Stephen bent toward Waaboo. "You gonna eat that whole thing?"

"Yes."

"I haven't eaten all day. I could sure use a lick."

"Uh-uh."

"Come on." Stephen lunged toward the cone.

Waaboo swung away, protecting the treat with his free hand. "No-o-o-o."

"Grinch."

"Darkpoople."

"Darkpoople?"

"Grab . . ." Waaboo hesitated. "Grabgrubber."

"Don't know what you're saying, but it doesn't sound good."

"How about a Waaboo Burger?" Cork suggested.

"Waaboo Burger? I saw the sign. What is it?"

"Patty made of ground bison instead of hamburger."

"Named after me," Cork's grandson said proudly.

"When did we start offering that?"

"Today. Jenny and I have been talking about it for a while. Being a college man now, you've just had other things on your mind. What do you say? You can't sell customers on it until you're sold on it yourself."

"Sure."

Cork dropped a patty on the griddle, buttered two bun halves.

"We're out of here," Jenny said. "Come on, kiddo. You can finish that cone on the way home. I've got to get dinner going. Joining us, Dad?"

"No, I'll stay here and close tonight."

"I think I'm supposed to close," Stephen said.

"I'll take it."

Stephen didn't argue.

When the others had gone, Stephen stood at an empty serving window, staring toward the copse of poplars to the south. Stephen had been doing a lot of staring lately. Something had set a hook in him, snagged his senses. College, perhaps. Stephen was in his first semester at Aurora Community College, taking classes to fulfill his general requirements in preparation for an eventual degree in criminal justice studies. The same route Cork had taken long ago when he started on the road to becoming a cop. But he hadn't seen any real enthusiasm for the coursework, and in truth, he wasn't at all certain his son was cut out to wear a badge. So was it a girl, maybe? For a couple of years, Stephen had been in an on-again, off-again relationship with a young woman on the rez, Marlee

Daychild. During the past month or so, it had been in the off mode. Cork didn't know if this was Stephen's doing or Marlee's. His son had always been private, hesitant to reveal a lot about himself, and that had been especially true lately. What Cork had sensed, what all the O'Connors had sensed, was a growing restlessness in Stephen, which Cork told himself was natural in a young man. One of the thoughts he'd had was that maybe it was time for Stephen to leave Aurora. Maybe if he was away from all that was familiar, at least for a while, it might be easier for him to see the path he needed to travel. It was possible this was what Stephen had been discussing with Meloux, seeking the old man's advice.

But there was another possibility. Stephen saw things others did not. He had visions. And so Cork understood that what was weighing on his son, what held Stephen's attention while he stared at what appeared to be nothing, might well be something his eye couldn't see.

CHAPTER 3

"All the buzz on the rez is about the town meeting tomorrow night," Rainy said as she undressed. "Everyone at the clinic, everyone who comes in, Senator McCarthy is all they're talking about."

Rainy Bisonette, Cork's wife, worked at the tribal clinic in the town of Allouette on the Iron Lake Reservation. Trained as a public health nurse, she was also a member of the Grand Medicine Society, a Mide, a healer in the traditional way. They'd been married only since the previous April, not even six months. Still on honeymoon, Cork often thought, especially whenever he watched her shed her clothing.

"She's a safe raft in a stormy sea," Cork said. He was already in bed, his back against the headboard.

Rainy stepped out of her jeans and unbuttoned her blue work shirt. She was full-bodied, but not heavy, having spent the last several years before her marriage seeing to the needs of her great-uncle, Henry Meloux, living in a cabin without running water or electricity, with only a wood-burning stove for heat, fed with wood she'd chopped herself. She knew hard work. When she drifted her hands across Cork's body, he could still feel the calluses.

"She'll listen," Rainy said. "Everyone believes we'll be heard."

"And that she'll carry that message forward. Good thing to believe."

She'd slipped off her bra and had reached for her nightshirt, but she paused and studied him in the light of the lamp on the nightstand. "You don't?"

"I believe she'll listen. I'm not sure I believe it'll do any good."

"She's a U.S. senator. She has influence."

"The other side has more. And they hit harder and they don't play fair."

She slipped the long nightshirt over her head and down her body, then joined him in bed, where she leaned against him. "You sound like you believe the battle is already lost."

"Not lost. But I've been in battles like these before. There are always casualties." He changed the subject abruptly. "Talked to Stephen lately?"

"I've tried. He's burrowed deep inside himself."

"He's like a sleepwalker. I tell him something, and, poof, it's gone from his head."

Rainy flipped her long black braid so that it hung at an angle between her breasts. Her fingers slowly traced the strands of the plaiting, in a way that made Cork think of rosary beads. "I'm wondering if he's seen something."

"I've wondered that, too. But it could be just that he's getting used to college. Or maybe it's Marlee. There's nothing like a woman to addle a guy's brain."

"I'm going to ignore that remark," Rainy said. "He hasn't gone out with Marlee Daychild in weeks. And he just seems so unsettled. More and more I'm thinking he's had another vision, Cork. And I think this one scares him."

They both knew Stephen had a right to be afraid. Before the bullet that caused his limp was fired, Stephen saw the man who would shoot him in a vision. He saw his mother's death years before it happened. He saw the threat from a monster, a murderer of young women who'd called himself Windigo and who'd tried to kill Cork and Jenny. It hadn't escaped their notice that Stephen's visions had always foreshadowed terrible things.

Cork said, "I wish he'd share what he's seen."

"It would be an unburdening," Rainy said.

"Practically speaking, it might help us get ready for whatever's coming."

"Something to do with the proposed pit mine, you think?"

For years, a large corporation had been at work to secure the permits necessary to begin a huge open-pit mining operation that would extract copper, nickel, and a number of heavy metals from an area adjacent to both the Iron Lake Reservation and the Boundary Waters Canoe Area Wilderness. In Tamarack County, a region once wealthy because of the iron ore that underlay everything, the issue had been divisive. With the iron mines having closed or closing and good-paying jobs evaporated, there was a considerable element applauding the possibility of the return of industry. On the other side were the Iron Lake Ojibwe and many other groups who feared that the mine would ruin the pristine wilderness and the clean water. Their fears weren't unfounded. While iron mining had brought wealth, at least for a time, it had made much of the North Country resemble the barren surface of the moon.

"I'm thinking something more personal." Cork put his hand over hers as she worked her braid, stilled it. "He talks to Henry. Could you talk to Henry?"

"I can try. But what's between Uncle Henry and Stephen will probably stay between them, unless Stephen indicates otherwise."

"Maybe a sweat?"

"Until Stephen is ready to share, he'll be as hard to crack as a walnut."

"A sweat couldn't hurt."

"I'll suggest it. You smell good, by the way. Like French fries. How'd the new Waaboo Burger do?"

"A winner. Everybody loved the bison patty, and everyone who knows our grandson loved the name."

"Doesn't surprise me a bit. The world loves Waaboo."

Rainy picked up a book from the nightstand and prepared to read. It was a novel titled *Downwind of the Devil*. The author was Jennifer O'Connor. When she wasn't helping run Sam's Place or involved in all she did as mother and wife, Jenny wrote stories. *Downwind of the Devil* was her first published novel, a fictionalized account of the hunt for a missing Ojibwe girl, in which she and her father and the monster who called himself Windigo were deeply involved. It had done well enough that Jenny was under contract for a second novel. She wouldn't tell her family what it was about, but they all suspected it would be another telling of a story in which some of them played a part.

Cork picked up the book he'd been reading every night for a week, *To Kill a Mockingbird*, one of the many American classics he'd never read, but one that both Jenny and Rainy had insisted he should. Within ten minutes, his eyes fluttered closed. He felt Rainy slip the book from his hands, turn out the light, and he was wrapped in a blanket of sleep.

CHAPTER 4

Next morning, well before sunrise, Cork heard Stephen leave the house. He slid from bed and stood at the window, watching Stephen walk away in the blue, early light, and his heart twisted. His son was struggling and Cork didn't know how to help. Rainy had advised patience. Which was the same advice her great-uncle Henry Meloux might have offered. Good advice, Cork knew, but it didn't mean he wouldn't suffer along with his son. He dressed quietly, hit the bathroom, went downstairs to make coffee. A few minutes later, he stood on the front porch, sipping from the steaming mug in his hand and breathing in the cool air of approaching dawn. Gooseberry Lane was quiet, the neighbors still abed.

With the exception of a few years as a cop in Chicago, he'd lived in Aurora, Minnesota, his whole life. His roots on his mother's side went back to a time long before white men muscled their way into the North Country and began the destruction of the natural order, a ravaging that had never really ended. His Anishinaabe heritage might not show on his face, but it shaped his conscience. As he stood in the cool, evergreen-scented air, in the fresh feel of that fall morning, he understood the calm probably wouldn't last.

He was more and more certain that Stephen had had a vision, seen something, and the things that Stephen saw had always been monstrous.

He picked up the morning paper from where it had been thrown under the porch swing and headed back inside. Rainy was awake and up, pouring coffee from the pot he'd made. He heard footsteps coming downstairs, heavy, probably Daniel English, his son-in-law, ready for work. Daniel was an officer with the Iron Lake Ojibwe Department of Conservation Enforcement. When explaining, he generally referred to himself as a game warden. Like Jenny, he was a writer, a poet. Like his aunt Rainy, he was full-blood Ojibwe, an enrolled member of the Lac Courte Oreilles Band of Lake Superior Chippewa.

"That coffee smells good," he said as he entered the kitchen. He wore his willow-green uniform. Rainy poured him a cup of the brew.

"You're up early," Cork noted.

"A lot on the agenda today. We've had reports of a couple of poachers on the rez. We've tried tracking them, but they keep slipping away."

"Jenny tells me you won't be going to the town meeting tonight," Cork said.

"I'm on Waaboo duty. Putting our little guy down for the night." Daniel sipped his coffee and looked satisfied. "You're not going either, I understand."

"Somebody's got to sell the new Waaboo Burger."

Daniel dropped a couple of slices of bread in the toaster. "How'd it go yesterday?"

"Sold like hotcakes."

"Waaboo was excited last night. He kept saying, 'People are eating me.'"

Rainy laughed. "Everybody could use a little Waaboo in them."

After Daniel had gone, Cork put on his jacket and kissed Rainy. "You haven't had breakfast yet," she said. "Where are you off to?"

"To talk to Henry."

"About Stephen? I'm not sure he'll tell you much."

"Can't hurt to ask."

"I told you I'd talk to Uncle Henry myself."

"When will you see him next? Between your clinic work and the town meeting with the senator, your schedule's packed." He kissed her again. "Meet you in bed tonight."

He drove north out of Aurora, along a graveled county road that followed the shoreline of Iron Lake. The woods were a mix of broadleaf and needle in which autumn had created great islands of gold and red among the evergreens. The cabins along the lake, mostly resorts and summer homes, looked deserted now, but on weekends they were still alive with activity and would continue that way until the leaves had been stripped from the trees and the color was gone. Come winter, the population of Tamarack County would shrink significantly.

He parked at a double-trunk birch several miles north of town, locked his Expedition, and began the long walk through the forest, following a path familiar to him since childhood. The sun was just about to rise, and the strip of clear sky above the path was a pale red, the color of water mixed with blood. On either side of him, the birds, those who had not yet wisely headed south, cried to one another with harsh, territorial challenges. Squirrels chattered at his intrusion. He startled a doe and her two fawns, who bounded away and disappeared among the trees. Everything about the morning and the walk along this familiar path, which normally would have calmed him, felt unsettling. The blood-colored sky, the contentious birds, the angry squirrels, the startled deer, all seemed to signal threat. He thought maybe this was a glimpse of what Stephen must feel when he'd had one of his ominous visions.

A mile in, he crossed onto rez land. A mile farther, he broke from the trees onto Crow Point. He stood at the beginning of a broad meadow filled with tall grass and with wildflowers still blooming—marigolds and oxeyes and asters and Canadian horseweed. On the far side rose two simple cabins, between them an outhouse. The nearer cabin had been Rainy's for many years. Now its sole occupant was Rainy's aunt by marriage, a septuagenarian named Leah Duling. The far cabin had been on Crow Point for more than eight decades and during all that time occupied by Henry Meloux, who was Rainy's maternal great-uncle and more than a hundred years old.

Smoke came from the stovepipes on both cabins, but Cork headed toward Meloux's place. Before he arrived, the door opened.

"I've got oatmeal with walnuts and dried blueberries ready," Leah said from the threshold. "Henry told me you won't have eaten."

Without any forewarning, Meloux was expecting him, one of the many mysteries of the ancient Mide. Cork found the old man at his small table, a book opened before him. When he was young and a renowned hunter, Meloux's eyes were like those of an eagle. His vision, though no longer eagle-sharp, was still good enough that he didn't require glasses. Cork saw that the book was *Downwind of the Devil*.

"She tells a good tale, your Jennifer," Meloux said, looking up. He was a part of the events at the heart of the story. "But she has simplified much."

"Most readers aren't as astute as you, Henry." Cork removed his jacket and sat with the old man. "I want to talk to you about Stephen. I think he's had a vision, and I think he's shared it with you."

"First, we have some breakfast," Meloux said.

Leah dished up oatmeal for them all and joined them at the

table. Meloux gave a blessing in Ojibwemowin, most of which Cork didn't understand.

"Maple syrup?" Leah offered.

Cork knew she'd tapped the trees and boiled down the sap herself. She was well into her seventies, but seemed younger, the effect, Cork suspected, of life on Crow Point in the company of Meloux.

They ate in silence. The hot oatmeal sat well on Cork's empty stomach. When the meal was finished, Meloux said, "Let us build a fire, Corcoran O'Connor. We will smoke and talk."

Leah wasn't invited to join them, and she made no comment as Meloux gathered his tobacco pouch and pipe, eased on his old plaid mackinaw, and walked out the door.

"*Migwech*, Leah," Cork said in thanks.

She glanced where Meloux had gone. "He probably won't say anything to you, but he's worried."

"About what?"

Leah shrugged. "He doesn't say anything to me either."

Cork followed Meloux across the meadow along a path that ran between two rock outcrops. On the far side, Iron Lake stretched away, mirroring the morning sky, and near the shoreline was a stone fire ring. Sawed sections of hardwood had been spaced around the ring for sitting, and cut firewood was laid up against one of the outcrops. Cork had helped Meloux build more fires here than he could remember. He gathered wood and kindling, used his pocketknife to curl off dry tinder, built a small tepee at the charred center of the fire ring. Meloux handed him a wooden match, and Cork struck a flame.

While Cork fed the growing fire, the old man took pinches of the mixture—tobacco and red willow—from his beaded pouch. He offered these to the four directions of the earth, and to the center, then put a bit into the pipe bowl. Cork sat with him. Meloux lit the tobacco mixture and they smoked together, while the fire crackled before them.

"Something's coming, Henry," Cork finally said.

The old man replied, "You have visions now?"

"I feel it."

"What do you feel?"

"Unsettled. Watchful."

"Afraid?"

"That, too. Stephen has had a vision."

"He told you this?"

"No, but he's clearly troubled, and he won't talk about it. Except to you. He's shared the vision with you, hasn't he?"

"You ask a question I cannot answer."

Which Cork took as an answer. He leaned toward the old man. "It must be a frightening vision, because it worries you, too."

Meloux's eyes were soft brown and unreadable. "You see into my heart now?"

"Leah told me. What is it that you know?"

"Not the answer you are looking for. But I will tell you this. These woods are alive, and all that is living speaks. To a human who listens, knowledge is given. Stephen listens. Maybe the spirit of what is alive here has spoken to him. Maybe if any man quiets himself enough, he also can hear what is being said."

"You've listened, Henry. What have you heard?"

"I was talking about you, Corcoran O'Connor. I believe if you quiet yourself, what it is that you are looking for will become known to you."

"I've never had a vision." Cork heard the brusqueness in his voice and tried to calm himself, tamp down his frustration. "I doubt I ever will."

"A vision is not everything." Meloux's face took on a soft cast. "You have a keen mind, Corcoran O'Connor, and a warrior's heart.

You also have a warrior's impatience. Quiet yourself. Use your head and your experience and the quiet, and perhaps you will not need a vision."

"You listen, Henry, better than Stephen, better than anyone. Can't you just tell me what you know?"

Meloux took a good while to answer. The wind shifted. The smoke from the fire drifted across Iron Lake, casting a dark, gray shadow over the blue surface.

"There is a beast in these woods that does not belong here," Meloux finally said. "What exactly, I do not know. But it is huge and it is evil. And that is all I can say."

CHAPTER 5

At a quarter to three that afternoon, Stephen turned his steps toward Sam's Place. He was scheduled to work until closing with his father and with a high school senior named Naomi Burns. The day was warm but overcast, thin clouds muddling the sky. He walked along the streets of Aurora with his hands in his pockets, his shoulders slumped. Fallen leaves as colorful as pieces torn from a Mediterranean tapestry littered the sidewalks. Over the course of his twenty years, he'd been down these streets a thousand times, knew them like he knew the lines that crossed his palms. They were part of who he was and also part of what he struggled against. It was comfortable, this small, familiar town, this isolated county. Every day he slid into life there like a finger into a glove. More and more, he'd begun to think that to understand the man he was at heart, he would have to separate himself from all that was familiar.

His father had abandoned Aurora when he was a young man and spent nearly a decade in Chicago before returning. His sisters, too, had left. College took Jenny away for a long time before she returned and settled down to family life in Aurora. Annie had been gone forever—in Iowa and New Mexico and California and now in South America, for a second time. Stephen had seen only a little of the world, and he'd begun to hunger for more. He'd also started to wonder, if he were far away, would the terrible things he sometimes saw not be able to find him?

His father was inside Sam's Place, preparing for the dinner crowd, which would begin arriving in an hour or so. Naomi was there, small and quiet, with streaks of color like cotton candy in her hair. She stood at the prep table, tossing coleslaw in a big stainless-steel bowl. His father looked up from the burger patties he'd been preparing next to the grill.

"Where've you been?"

"Around," Stephen replied.

"I tried to call."

"I didn't feel like talking."

Cork wiped his hands on some paper toweling. "How about we talk now?" He led the way into the back of the Quonset hut, poured himself some coffee from the pot he'd made earlier, held the mug out in offering to Stephen, who shook his head.

"I went to see Henry," his father told him. "I figure you've had a vision, and since you won't talk about it to anyone except maybe him, I went to find out what he knows."

Stephen's first thought was that this was a trespass, that his father had stepped across a line. Then he realized that, in its way, it might be an unshackling. He couldn't share the vision himself because it felt too personal, too close, and was still too indecipherable. What good would it do to bring others in if it accomplished nothing except to make them as afraid as he was? Now that what he'd seen was in the open, he thought differently. He had no illusions that his father, who could sometimes be a stump when it came to sharing his own emotions, could help him understand the meaning and purpose of the vision. Even Henry had been unable to do that. But he felt as if a weight had been lifted from him, and now his father might help to shoulder some of the burden.

"So he told you?" Stephen said.

Cork shook his head. "But he admitted that he believes something bad is out there in the woods, and he doesn't know what it is. Look, Stephen, I don't want to intrude on a thing so personal to you as a vision. But if there's something out there, something really bad, don't you think it would be best to figure out what it is? Maybe together we can do that."

"Henry couldn't help me," Stephen said.

"I'm not Henry. I see the world in a different way. Maybe my perspective can be of some use."

Stephen considered this, considered also how good it felt, even for a moment, to have the burden of the vision off his shoulders. He made his decision, and he shared with his father what he'd seen: the boy on the steep rise who was him and not him; the eagle appearing from the sky; the boy with the bow in his hands; the arrow flying; the eagle falling; the dropped egg; staring at the boy, him and not him, and the boy staring back, both of them ignorant of the meaning in all this; and at the end, the sense of something monstrous looming at his back.

In the serving area, Naomi plopped a burger patty onto the grill, and the sizzle seemed inordinately loud.

"The boy is you and not you," Cork said. "I have dreams like that."

"This isn't a dream, Dad." Stephen heard the note of impatience in his voice and tried to soften. "It's so different."

"I understand. I'm just trying to get the lay of the land here. The hill, is it a place you recognize?"

"In that way, it's like a dream. It seems familiar, but not like a real place."

"The boy. Can you describe him?"

"Fourteen or fifteen, maybe. Dark hair. Dark eyes. A little shorter than me."

"You a few years ago."

"But not me, Dad."

"Native?"

"Maybe."

"The eagle. Is it like a real eagle?"

"Yes," Stephen said, thinking that this wasn't getting them anywhere. Then he realized something. "Not exactly like a real eagle."

"What's different?"

"The tail feathers should be completely white, but other colors are mixed in."

"What colors?"

Before Stephen could answer, Naomi called to them, "We've got incoming."

Through the doorway into Sam's Place, Stephen could see a couple of cars pulling into the parking lot. Behind them came two more.

"We'll talk later," his father said, and they turned to the business of a burger joint.

The town meeting with Senator McCarthy was scheduled for that evening. It was expected to draw a good audience, a huge number of Tamarack County residents with strong feelings on both sides of the mining issue. The dinner crowd came early and heavy. Cork had called in another of the kids on his roster, and he and Stephen and the high schoolers worked to move the lines at the windows. The Waaboo Burger continued to be a big hit, and the spicy fries, another recent addition to the menu, went fast.

Near six, while Cork was bent over the grill, the whistle atop the Aurora firehouse began a prolonged blast. Almost immediately, the phone on the wall in the Quonset hut rang. Cork handed the spatula to Stephen and took the call. The whistle, Stephen knew, was the signal for the volunteer firemen to assemble. His father wasn't a volunteer, but he was a part of the Tamarack County Search and Rescue team, and sometimes the whistle blast and the need for the team went hand in hand.

When Cork returned, he had removed his apron, and he threw it in the wicker basket where all the dirty aprons went.

"What is it, Dad?"

"A plane's gone down on the rez. Out on Desolation Mountain."

A brief image flashed through Stephen's mind. An eagle shot from the sky. "You're going? I want to go, too."

Cork opened his mouth, and Stephen fully expected to have to argue his right to be there. But his father simply nodded and said to the kids at the serving windows, "We're shutting down for the night."

CHAPTER 6

Tamarack County Sheriff Marsha Dross walked quickly up the old logging road where nearly a dozen vehicles had parked—deputies' cruisers, a couple of hook and ladders, an ambulance, and several civilian cars and trucks. Cork waited with Stephen beside the Expedition.

They were in the far east section of the Iron Lake Reservation, spitting distance from the Boundary Waters Canoe Area Wilderness. Before them rose Desolation Mountain, a great uplift of gray gneiss and greenstone, scoured clean by glaciers ten thousand years ago. The mountain stood several hundred feet above the crowns of the evergreens that grew around its base. Higher up, a grove of aspens ringed the formation. The very top was bare rock where only the most basic and tenacious plant life grew, patches of gold lichen that resembled ulcers on the outcrops. The dark mountaintop pressed itself against the darkening overcast of a clouded sky. A storm was coming.

Dross was in her mid-forties and had been sheriff for a number of years. Cork had hired her as a deputy when he wore the sheriff's badge, making her the first woman to don a law enforcement uniform in Tamarack County. She was experienced, tough. But Saturday nights she still put on cowboy boots, tight jeans, a snap-button western shirt, and the white Stetson her father once gave her as a birthday present, and kicked up her heels at the American Legion hall, line dancing. The lower pant legs of the khakis and the Wolverines she wore now were coated in mud.

Without prelude, she said, "It came down in a bog out there." She pointed toward the trees west of the logging road.

"Survivors?" Cork asked.

"So far nothing, but we just started looking and the debris is still burning."

"Know who was in it?"

As if a hand had pressed itself into her face, her eyes closed a moment, and all her features went flat. "We think it's Senator McCarthy. She was scheduled to land at Olson Field this afternoon. Her family was with her."

Olson Field was the small regional airport just outside Aurora.

"But you're not sure?"

"We're double-checking."

"Who called it in?"

"Monkey Love."

His real name was Jameson Love, but no one called him that. Monkey Love was a mixed-blood Shinnob who lived with his uncle Ned Love in an isolated cabin in the shadow of Desolation Mountain. Cork used to haul him in regularly, D and D—drunk and disorderly—at first, then for other offenses that had earned him significant jail time. But Monkey Love got clean and for the past few years had lived quietly, surviving thanks to careful spending of the allotment he received from the profits of the Chippewa Grand Casino and from the cutting and selling of firewood with his uncle.

"Monkey and Ned don't have a telephone at their place," Cork said.

"He hightailed it into Allouette, used one at the tribal office. Some guys from the rez came back out with him. They're up there now with my people. Daniel's one of them."

From out of the west came a crack like an enormous branch splintering, followed by a long rumble of thunder.

Dross's look went as dark as the sky. "Just what we need."

"Okay if we head on in to give a hand?"

"Foster's posted up the road a bit. He'll point the way. Check in with Azevedo. He's coordinating at the crash site."

Sirens screamed in the distance, although there was little need for a siren on the ill-traveled back roads of the rez.

Dross said, "State Patrol," and moved past Cork and Stephen to await these new arrivals.

They walked the logging road as it skirted the base of Desolation Mountain. Cork knew that in Alaska or Colorado or even Vermont they would laugh at the thought of calling this hump of gneiss a mountain. But it was the highest elevation in the county, a landmark that could be seen for miles. Although it was on the Iron Lake Reservation, it was a popular destination for photographers in the North Country, especially in the fall, when the view from the top was a stunning 360-degree panorama of color. Several small lakes were visible from the mountaintop. With binoculars, and if you knew where to look, you could see Ned and Monkey Love's cabin, hunkered among the pines on a lake called Little Bass.

Deputy David Foster waved at them from the side of the road. Cork could see where the undergrowth had been trampled and broken by the passage of many feet. The recently made trail led into mixed-growth forest of pine and poplar.

"How far in, Dave?" Cork asked.

"Couple hundred yards. Gets real mushy halfway there. After that, watch your step."

The trail wove a crooked course among the trees and between

great humps of rounded granite, miniature reflections of the bald mountaintop. A hundred yards in, just as Foster said, the soil turned wet underfoot and their boots began to make sucking sounds. The trees thinned out, and as the ground became softer and mushier, the pines and poplars gave way to tamaracks and tall ferns. Up ahead, from somewhere still out of sight, came the shouts of men. Also from that direction came another long roll of thunder.

They reached the scene, a boggy area, roughly circular and a hundred yards in diameter, full of reeds and cattails. The men already there were spread out across the marsh and around the edges. Those that had ventured into the reeds stood in brackish water up to their thighs. Close to the far side of the marsh, a group of the volunteer firemen had surrounded a large section of fuselage that was sending up a thick column of black smoke. Cork could see wreckage everywhere, but that one piece of fuselage appeared to be the only debris still burning. The firefighters wore yellow packs and were laying down a spray of suppressant foam where the smoke billowed.

Deputy Azevedo stood with a group of men Cork recognized from the Iron Lake Reservation, Daniel English among them. Cork headed their way, Stephen on his heels.

"Lots of debris in the woods," Daniel was saying as he pointed southwest of the marsh. "Looks like the plane clipped the treetops and began to break apart there."

"All right," Azevedo said. "Take your guys and see what you can find. But don't touch anything. Yell if you find someone alive."

When he saw Cork and Stephen, Daniel lifted his chin to acknowledge them, then turned toward the woods, the four Shinnobs from the rez trailing him. Cork knew them all. Ned and Monkey Love, Phil Hukari, who, like Daniel, was a tribal game warden, and Tom Blessing, who worked with Native youth.

Azevedo turned to Cork. "As soon as the fire's out, we'll check the fuselage. Cockpit's over there, sunk in the mud." He nodded toward a section of debris shaped like a white bullet and almost hidden by reeds. "We broke the windows out. Two bodies inside. I don't figure what's in that burning fuselage is going to be any more hopeful."

"Any idea how many passengers?"

"We think the two pilots, Senator McCarthy, her husband and son, and McCarthy's personal assistant. If this was McCarthy's plane. We've radioed in the registration number but haven't received confirmation yet."

"What do you need us to do?"

"The plane broke up pretty good. Hit the trees back there, like English said, then plowed into the marsh. If you're willing, follow the line it took coming down through those trees and across the marsh." He eyed Stephen and hesitated before going on.

"Looking for bodies," Cork said.

"Yeah," Azevedo acknowledged. "I've already got some guys on it, but I could use more."

Someone already in the marsh called to the deputy, and Azevedo waded in.

When he wore a badge, Cork had been on the scenes of dozens of brutal accidents—car wrecks, lumbering mishaps, explosions, fires. He'd seen life wrenched from the human body with nightmarish violence and in unimaginable ways. But that was far outside Stephen's experience, and the father in Cork hoped that they wouldn't find what might remain of the passengers from the destroyed plane. Yet Stephen was ahead of him, already wading into the reeds and the black water and the suck of the mud beneath it all.

CHAPTER 7

Moments after they entered the bog, brilliant tendrils of lightning crossed the sky to the west, and only a second passed before the air seemed to shatter. Roy Berg, the fire chief, hollered to everyone to clear the water. Although the broken section of fuselage still smoldered, Berg and his men abandoned their work and made quickly for the shoreline. Cork called to Stephen but got no response. Cork thought he understood. Stephen wanted to press forward, take the risk, find what there was to find, answer the questions. This fallen plane was part of his son's vision, and he had to know why.

"Stephen," Cork called sharply.

Another bolt of lightning, then thunder like the end of the world. Reluctantly, Stephen followed his father to safety.

A driving rain descended. Cork and Stephen hunkered beneath the trees a good, safe distance from the marsh water. After a while Daniel English joined them, along with the other men from the reservation.

"Anything?" Cork asked.

"Tail section and wings. Sheared off as the plane clipped the treetops," Daniel replied. "Everything's pretty torn up."

"You called it in, Monkey? What did you see?" Cork asked.

Monkey Love looked like the Devil had walked all over him, the result of years of addiction to booze and drugs. He was emaciated. His face bore scars from drunken fights in bars and alleyways, and his damaged right eyelid was beset with a persistent droop. He had unusually long arms and fingers—he'd been called Monkey all his life—and more often than not, he could be found puffing on a cigarette hand-rolled from American Spirit tobacco. When he spoke, it was like a rasp over metal.

"Was sitting on the crapper with the door open." Monkey and Ned Love had no running water at their cabin. They used an outhouse for taking care of business. "Got a good view of the mountain from there. Saw the plane come over it. They all do when they're headin' toward the airport. But this one was strange, kinda cockeyed and real low. Going way too slow, seemed. I lost it, then heard a lot of popping, like gunshots or somethin'. Then whump. I swear I could feel it hit. Got out of that crapper, and there was Uncle Ned, lookin' at the trees west of the cabin."

"Did you locate it right away?"

"Wasn't hard," Ned Love said, taking up the story. "Could see where the smoke was coming from. Got there pretty quick."

Ned Love had always been a quiet man, a lifelong bachelor and hermit, content to live in basic isolation. He was tall and thin, like Monkey, but with a vibrancy that Cork had always attributed to Ned Love's connection with the land he called home and his decision, long ago, to draw his life from it. A good deal of the man's sustenance came from trapping and hunting and fishing. Aside from Henry Meloux, Cork couldn't think of another human who knew more about harvesting food from what grew in the Northwoods.

"See anybody alive?"

"Just pieces of that plane and the fire. Figured Monkey and me couldn't do nuthin' but we oughta let somebody know, so I told him to hustle his butt to Allouette."

"And you guys came back with him?" Cork addressed this to the others from the rez.

"It was like Ned says," Phil Hukari replied. He didn't look Native. Young, blond, balding, he was mixed-blood from Oregon, his Native heritage Nez Perce. Much like Daniel, he'd come to Minnesota because of a woman. His wife, Sue, taught early childhood education on the rez, and everyone loved her. "The fuselage piece was in flames when we got here. Nothing we could do about that. Did a quick perimeter search just in case somebody got thrown clear. Then the first responders showed up, started hitting the fire with foam. Then you and Stephen." He looked at the sky. "Then this damn storm."

Finally it happened, exactly the reason Berg had cleared the marsh. A searing electric bolt hit the water. As if a bomb had gone off, the flash was blinding, the sound deafening. Even where he stood among the pines and tamaracks, many yards from the edge of the bog, Cork felt the jolt of the current rip through the ground under his feet.

"That's all she wrote," Tom Blessing said in a stone voice. "If anyone was still alive somewhere in that bog, they're dead now."

Blessing was full-blood Iron Lake Ojibwe. Like a lot of Native youths, he'd gotten into trouble young. He'd belonged to a gang on the rez called the Red Boyz and still bore the brand that was part of the initiation ritual. A set of bloody circumstances had tied him and Cork together in a way that changed them both, and after that, Blessing had abandoned the Red Boyz and now counseled troubled Ojibwe teens.

Moments after the flash, Cork got his first glimpse of the men in olive-green ponchos, a half dozen of them, spread out around the marsh along the shoreline, moving slowly. They held boxes in their hands, electronics of some kind. Cold rain cascaded down his face, and he had to wipe his eyes to see the men clearly. They were like wraiths, dark, silent figures, ignoring the dangers of the storm.

"Who're they?" Daniel asked.

Cork squinted but could see nothing that would be helpful in answering Daniel's question.

Deputy Azevedo intercepted one of the figures. They talked. The deputy stepped back. The men in the ponchos continued on their way. After they'd completely circumnavigated the marsh, they sifted among the trees and were gone.

Although the storm was violent, it was also brief and passed quickly. When the lightning was far to the east, well beyond Desolation Mountain, the fire chief gave the all clear and the search resumed, along with the dousing of what flames sent up smoke from inside the broken fuselage.

Cork realized that Stephen was no longer with him. He did a scan of the dark woods at his back and saw Stephen standing by himself, arms hanging at his sides, staring down at something. Cork jumped brambles and quickly made his way to where his son had become a statue with a bowed head.

There it was. A plane seat. Torn from its moorings. Bolt holes empty. Padding exploded from the ripped upholstery. Cork wondered if the passenger still strapped in the seat, a young teenager judging from his size, was the kid from Stephen's vision. It would have been hard to tell. The face resembled raw meat loaf.

Stephen turned to his father and asked a question Cork couldn't even begin to answer.

"Why?"

Rainy and Jenny had dinner waiting, macaroni and cheese and peas. It was one of Waaboo's favorites, and also Stephen's. The men stripped off their muddied clothing, cleaned themselves, and took their chairs at the table in the dining room. Stephen sat next to Waaboo, who loved his uncle and made grunting noises at him, like a pig. Stephen returned the grunts, but his heart wasn't in this play.

When they'd finished the meal and Waaboo had been read to and taken upstairs to bed, Stephen removed himself from the others and sat in the porch swing, rocking and processing. The night air felt clean after the storm. The sky had cleared, a waxing moon had risen, and the front yard under the elm was a complex tapestry of moon shadow and silver light.

Rainy joined him on the swing. Like Meloux, she had been nurturing Stephen in his own desire to become Mide, though nothing formal had begun. It was all preparation.

"You're struggling to understand," she said.

"Why do the visions come if there's nothing I can do about them, if they don't help prevent the horrible things that happen?"

"I've never had a vision, so I can't answer that."

"I don't want this. I don't want to see these things."

"I understand. But do you have a choice?"

He stared at the complex pattern of light and shadow on the lawn. "I tried to stop it from coming. I tried to close my mind."

"Even if you don't understand, maybe you should open yourself to acceptance, believe there's purpose, although what that might be isn't clear, at least at the moment." She looked up at the sky. "The Great Mystery."

This was one of the more poetic interpretations of Kitchimanidoo, which was also translated as the Great Spirit or sometimes the Creator. Stephen, in his efforts at spiritual understanding, had come to believe that whatever you called this spirit—God, Allah, Kitchimanidoo—it was an integrated consciousness on a cosmic scale, the interconnectedness of all creation. When he was grounded, centered, he understood and, exactly as Rainy was counseling, worked at acceptance. But at that moment, all he felt was frustrated, cut off, full of anger and rejection.

"If I'd understood, maybe all those people would still be alive."

"Or maybe not. Who can say? It seems a lot to take on your shoulders, responsibility for this."

"If I'd only understood in time."

"Stephen," she began.

"I'm going for a walk." He shoved himself out of the swing and rushed headlong across the yard and down Gooseberry Lane.

Cork stepped onto the porch. "Where's he going?"

"To be with himself."

"Maybe I should go after him."

"I don't think he's ready to talk." She watched the figure growing small and dark. "He feels responsible."

"For the plane crash?"

"For not keeping it from happening. He believes he failed because he didn't understand his vision."

Jenny and Daniel joined them.

Cork asked, "Waaboo's down?"

"Sound asleep." Daniel leaned against the porch railing. "I was just listening to the radio. It's all over the news."

"Do they know how many were on the plane with Senator McCarthy?" Jenny asked.

"Her husband, her son, an aide, and the two pilots. That's the working count. NTSB is on the scene now. I suppose we'll know more tomorrow."

"Do they have any idea what caused it?"

"They're still looking for the black box."

Cork shook his head. "I wish to God they hadn't hustled us out of there. I can't help feeling there was more we could have done."

At the same time Stephen had discovered the boy's body still strapped in its seat, another influx of searchers had arrived. Among them were FBI personnel, agents from Minnesota's Bureau of Criminal Apprehension, and first responders from other communities in Tamarack County. Control of the scene moved into the hands of the FBI, and all the others were asked to stand down and clear the marsh. Floodlights were brought in. Cork, Stephen, Daniel, and the others made their way back to the logging road, the lights behind them glaring and unnatural. And within Cork, maybe within them all, a disturbing sense of something important left undone.

"Could you have saved anyone?" Rainy asked.

"I don't think so. But maybe some questions could have been answered."

"Like what?"

"Monkey says there was something odd about the plane, how it was flying, low and slow and canted. No one talked to him about that. Not Dross's people, not the FBI. He and Ned were first on the scene. But no one bothered to question them." He looked at Daniel and added, "Or you and the others who weren't far behind, for that matter."

"We spoke with Azevedo, but just briefly," Daniel replied. "He was the one doing all the talking with the FBI, but I don't know if he said anything about us."

"The sheriff?" Rainy asked. "Where was she?"

"Marsha stayed on the logging road, coordinating the flow of the other responders," Cork said. "I didn't see her at the scene until the FBI was telling the rest of us to stand down."

Jenny looked puzzled. "That seems unusual. Shouldn't she have been in charge?"

"Azevedo's been her go-to incident commander for a long time now," Cork explained. "Marsha trusts him with a scene. I'm guessing she was in communication with all the other agencies, making quick decisions, trying to keep a handle on things. Situation like this, it can be chaos, explode in your face."

"Mom!"

"Thought Waaboo was down," Cork said.

Jenny rose. "Probably picking up all our unsettled vibes." She and Daniel headed inside.

On the porch, alone with Rainy, Cork stared at the sky, where the glow of moonlight outshone the stars. "I don't know how to help him."

"He'll find his way."

"I understand where he's coming from. What good is a vision if it saves no one? Just makes you feel useless."

"You're both wishing you could have done something more."

"Moot point. What's done is done. I'm going inside. Coming?"

"I think I'll wait out here a bit longer," Rainy said.

Cork studied the empty street. "He may not be home for a good long while."

Rainy continued to rock in the porch swing, and Cork called it a night.

The house wasn't completely dark when Stephen finally returned. A light had been left on in the hallway. He shed his jacket and climbed the stairs to his bedroom, where he lay fully clothed on top of the covers. He'd found no answers on his long, solitary sojourn. Moonlight slanted through his window. Shadows invaded his room. He stared at the ceiling, seeing a body full of shattered bones strapped in a plane seat, a face no longer human. He was certain he wouldn't get any rest. But sleep stole over him with surprising suddenness.

And in the night, the vision came to him again.

CHAPTER 8

"Pilot error."

Cork was reading the *Duluth News Tribune*. It had been nearly a week since Senator Olympia McCarthy's plane plowed into a bog near the base of Desolation Mountain, killing everyone on board.

"That's what they're calling it. Not officially yet. Not until they've sifted through everything, which'll take weeks. But at this point they don't have a better explanation."

Rainy was at the kitchen counter, pouring her first cup of coffee that morning. "They still haven't talked to you or to Daniel. Have they talked to anybody who was out there?"

"According to the article, the investigation is ongoing. God only knows what that means."

In the first days following the crash, the world had become glaringly aware of Aurora, Minnesota. The hotels, normally filled with leaf peepers at this time of year, had filled instead with journalists and television reporters. Every day, the main street carried traffic equal to that of a busy summer weekend. The road to Desolation Mountain was a constant stream of coming and going, although the authorities had blocked access to the crash site itself.

That area was still cordoned off while the NTSB continued documenting the scene and collecting debris. But Cork knew that news was only news if it was fresh, and it was fresh only for a heartbeat. After a few days, if nothing sensational came to light, people's interest moved on. Aurora would soon be back to normal. Out of the limelight. He hoped.

"The funeral is tomorrow in the Twin Cities. A private affair," Cork said, relaying what he'd learned from the newspaper story. "Then a public memorial at the cathedral next week. They're expecting thousands."

Rainy joined him, propped her elbows on the table, sipped her coffee. "Minnesota lost a senator. The little guy in America lost a champion."

"Speculation is that our governor is going to arrange to have himself appointed to fill her seat." Cork folded the newspaper. "So for the next four years, the little guy in America will still be lacking a champion. And the question becomes, what do you do now?"

"What do I do now?"

"About the mine."

"Cork, you talk about that mine as if you have nothing at stake. It could ruin a lot of the water on the rez, to say nothing of the Boundary Waters."

"I'm well aware of the potential."

"Then why aren't you angry, like the rest of us?"

"Rest of us? There are a lot of folks in Tamarack County who'd be overjoyed to see that mine begin operation. Jobs coming back. It's been a long time for some of the men who worked the iron mines."

"But it's so shortsighted. In the long run, all I see is devastation."

Jenny entered the kitchen, Waaboo trailing behind her, still looking sleepy. Jenny wasn't looking so bright-eyed herself.

"Raised voices this early in the morning? Honeymoon's over, I guess."

"I had a bad dream, Baa-baa." Waaboo sat on his grandfather's lap and laid his head against Cork's chest. "It was scary."

"What was it?"

"A monster. He was chasing me."

"Did he catch you?"

"I hided."

"You hid," Jenny said, pouring herself a mug of coffee.

"It had lots of heads, Baa-baa. Monster heads."

Cork hugged his grandson. "Only a nightmare, buddy."

"Did you see Daniel?" Jenny asked.

"Already gone when I got up this morning," Cork told her. "Why so early?"

"He's still trying to track down those poachers. He keeps getting reports, but he can't nail the guys. I thought I heard Stephen leave early, too."

"Gone at first light."

"Did you talk to him?" she asked.

"Nope."

"Know where he was going?"

"No idea. Tight-lipped as ever."

Waaboo slid from his grandfather's lap and trotted to where Trixie, the O'Connors' ancient pooch, lay on a blanket near her food dish. Trixie lifted her head, and her tail swiped back and forth across the linoleum. In her old age, her pupils had gone cloudy, and there was some concern about her sight going altogether. But her ears and nose still worked well enough, and right now everything about her became suddenly alert as she let out a woof in warning. Only a moment later, the front doorbell rang.

"I'll get it." Jenny left the kitchen.

"A little early for visitors," Rainy remarked.

"Probably John O'Loughlin." Cork was speaking of the neighbor across the street. "Out of coffee again."

"Dad," Jenny called from the front hallway. "Someone to see you."

Although the man standing with her at the front door was a stranger, Cork knew immediately that he had a badge somewhere on him.

"Agent Able Gunderson, FBI." The stranger showed his ID. "Can I speak with you a moment, Mr. O'Connor? And your son and son-in-law as well."

"Is this about the plane crash?"

"Yes, sir."

"Stephen and Daniel are out, but I'm happy to talk with you."

"Can I get you some coffee, Agent Gunderson?" Jenny offered.

"No, thank you." He smiled, polite but steely.

"I'll leave you two to talk then."

"Have a seat." Cork led the way into the living room, and Gunderson took the easy chair.

He was nondescript. Fortyish, medium height and build, sandy hair kept short, eyes whose color was hard to discern or remember. He wore a light leather jacket and jeans.

"Finally getting around to this then," Cork said.

"A lot to be done, Mr. O'Connor. You understand." He took out a small notepad and pen. "What time did you arrive on the scene?"

"Must've been about six-fifteen."

"Who else was there at that time, do you recall?"

"Roy Berg, he's our fire chief." Cork gave the names of the volunteer firefighters he could remember. "Roy would have the full list, I'm sure. Have you talked to him?"

"We have. Any others?"

"Deputy Azevedo. He was coordinating things at the site. Alf Morgan and Joe Riley, they're search and rescue guys, like me."

"I understand there were men from the Iron Lake Reservation."

"Monkey Love, of course. That's Jameson Love. He reported the downed plane. His uncle Ned Love. Daniel English, my son-in-law. Another game warden from the rez, Phil Hukari. And Tom Blessing. He works at the tribal office."

Gunderson wrote down the names. "What was going on when you arrived?"

Cork told him about the flaming fuselage and the firefighters.

"Where were the men from the reservation?"

"Just about to head off to search the woods where some of the debris had come down."

"But they'd been there awhile, searching the area before anyone else arrived, is that correct?"

"Yes."

"And when they went into the woods, you went with them?"

"Not right away. But after the storm began, with all that lightning, Roy made us clear the bog and we joined them then."

"Did any of you find anything?"

"Senator McCarthy's son, still strapped in his seat."

"Did any of you pick anything up?"

"Like what?"

"You tell me. Did you pick up anything?"

"Not that I recall. But as you already know, Daniel and the others were in the woods before us. Have you talked to them yet?"

"We will."

"I have a question for you," Cork said. "Why is the FBI involved?"

"I beg your pardon?"

"I didn't think you guys stepped in unless this was a criminal investigation."

"Senator McCarthy was a national figure, Mr. O'Connor. In these times, when acts of terrorism are possible anywhere, we have to take a close look."

"You think terrorists might have been responsible?"

"I didn't say that. Just that we have to look carefully at a situation like this. I'm sure you understand. These men from the reservation, what's the best way to get in touch with them?"

"Phil Hukari and Tom Blessing live on the rez. Check with the tribal office. They'll point you in the right direction. It's clear you already know that Daniel and Stephen live here. Ned Love and his nephew are a little more difficult. They have a cabin not far from the crash site, but it's pretty hard to find." Cork sat back. "I can't believe nobody's talked to Ned or Monkey Love yet. They were eyewitnesses to the plane going down. The only ones as far as I know."

"We'll get to them, Mr. O'Connor. Is there anything else about the crash site you think we should know, even if it seems inconsequential?"

"To tell you the truth, as soon as your guys showed up on the scene, we got hustled out of there pretty fast, so we weren't a part of the search for very long."

"Our people were preserving the integrity of the site," Gunderson said, as if by rote. He put his notepad and pen away and stood to leave. "Thanks very much for your help. If you think of anything more, feel free to call me." He held out his card.

After the agent had gone, Cork returned to the kitchen.

"What did he want?" Rainy asked.

"Whatever I could tell him about the search at the crash site. But get this. We're almost a week out and nobody's interviewed Ned or Monkey Love. Christ, they saw the plane go down." He took his jacket from where it hung on a peg near the back door.

Rainy gave him a questioning look. "Where are you going?"

"I want to talk to Marsha Dross and George Azevedo."

"Why?" Jenny asks.

"Something doesn't feel right."

Waaboo got up from beside Trixie and hugged his grandfather around the waist. "Watch out for monsters, Baa-baa."

CHAPTER 9

The entrance to the old logging road along the base of Desolation Mountain was blocked by a wooden barricade. Stephen drove his Jeep slowly past. Two vehicles were parked beyond the barricade, both dark blue SUVs, no official logo of any kind visible anywhere. The plates were U.S. government issue.

Stephen continued two more miles down the main gravel road until he was on the eastern side of the mountain. There was no easy way to the top from there. Photographers and others interested in the view always took a well-worn path that led up from the now-barricaded logging road. He pulled the Jeep off the shoulder and into a flat area among the trees and parked behind a blackberry thicket. He circled the Jeep, satisfied that between its scratched-up, dull olive paint job, the coat of dust and dried mud that it wore, and the leaves of the blackberry thicket it was fairly well hidden. He had no clear idea who he might be concealing it from, but his recurring vision made him cautious.

On official maps, Desolation was the name of the mountain, but the Ojibwe called it Majimanidoo-oshkiinzhig, which meant, more or less, Devil's Eye. Traditionally, it was thought to be a cursed place. Rez elders told children stories about it meant to give them chills. Most modern Shinnobs laughed at the dark tales. Still, Desolation Mountain wasn't a place you were likely to find folks from the rez taking in the view.

Stephen worked his way quietly through the woods to where gray-green rock outcrops, smaller versions of the mountain, began to appear. He wove among the rocks and around a small bog, where the ground began a sharp incline. There was no clear path up the eastern side of Desolation Mountain, and he chose his way carefully. He was in no hurry. Time wouldn't change what drew him to Majimanidoo-oshkiinzhig.

He entered the aspens that ringed the mountain just below the crown. The white trunks around him felt like a host of markers in a vast graveyard, testaments to the dark reputation of the mountain, and Stephen tried to shake the sense of dread that shadowed him.

He broke from the aspens onto a broad, barren stretch that formed the granite apron of the mountaintop. From the edge of the aspens to the crown, the only life-form was simple lichen, which looked like cancer on the rocks. It was a desolate landscape, the reason for the name the whites had given it was easy to see. Above the apron, atop the crest, rose a circular outcrop darker than any of the rock around it. Stephen had seen aerial photographs of the formation and, in them, the justification for the Ojibwe name—Devil's Eye—became clear. That crowning outcrop resembled perfectly a dark pupil set in a gray-green iris, a never-blinking eye staring skyward.

He climbed to the base of the outcrop, a roughly circular formation ten feet high and thirty feet in diameter. If he'd scaled the rock all the way to the top, he would have had a full view of the mountain slope. The landscape was familiar, but not just because he'd been there many times over the course of his twenty years in Aurora. He understood now that each time the vision came to him, this was the place where the scene played out. He looked up. The sky was blue, with a few cotton ball puffs of white. In the vision, the sky was always a boil of dark clouds. The air around him was redolent with the fragrance of the Northwoods, of evergreens and fallen aspen leaves and the mineral smell of the hard rock beneath his feet, and even the clean scent of the lakes he could see from the mountain's crest. In the vision, the air stank of burning fuel and seared flesh.

Stephen was still struggling to understand.

From his vantage, he could make out the bog where the broken wreckage of the plane had come to rest, a bare, circular area among the distant trees. On previous days, he'd tried to make his way there, but the woods continued to be alive with men still searching the crash site. From a case on his belt, he took out a pair of field glasses, put them to his eyes, and adjusted the lenses. The bog came clearly into view, and he saw a few searchers crawling like insects along the edges of the reedy water. The fuselage and other wreckage had been removed. Just a hair to the south were the trees where he'd stumbled upon the boy still strapped in his seat, his face obliterated, all the bones of his body shattered. He lowered the glasses, remembering the horror, the helplessness he'd felt. Time and again since that day, he'd imagined what it might have been like for the boy, his mother, his father, the aide, the pilots, as the plane fell. Through tiny windows, a view of the earth racing at them, the trees looming. The terrible realization, too fleeting to be spoken, of what would happen in the next instant. He'd imagined the mother—not the senator but the woman behind the title—turning her head toward her child, knowing that all she'd hoped for him, had dreamed his life might be, was gone. Worse than her own fate was what she must have understood of his.

Every time Stephen imagined this, he felt anger at the uselessness of his vision.

He put the glasses to his eyes again and moved the lenses to the north. He spotted the oval of blue water that was Little Bass Lake, where Monkey Love and his uncle Ned lived. He could make out the rustic cabin and even the tiny outhouse through whose opened door Monkey had watched the plane go down.

Then he became aware of movement among the aspens ringing the mountain a hundred yards below him. He shifted the field glasses, adjusted the focus. The men who came into view wore military fatigues. They seemed to be conducting a quadrant search, an evidence-gathering technique described to him by his father, in which an area was divided into squares and covered methodically.

A couple of other men in fatigues appeared on the worn path that came up the western slope from the barricaded road. They carried powerful-looking rifles and joined the men conducting the search among the aspens. Stephen couldn't understand why they were searching the mountaintop when the plane had crashed far below. They seemed out of place, especially with the heavy weapons. Something felt terribly wrong.

He continued to scan the trees below. Except for the quadrant where the men in fatigues disturbed the peace, it was a lovely scene. The aspen leaves were shivering gold, the trunks stark white, sunlight breaking among the branches, the ground below dappled with shadows.

Then he spotted the boy. Standing very still. Another shadow among the many shadows beneath the trees. The boy watched the men. Stephen watched the boy. A gentle wind rose up. The shadows of the trees shifted. The sunlight between them danced.

In the next moment, the light faded as a brooding shadow crossed the mountain. Stephen glanced up. The sun had been obscured by a sudden convergence of clouds. When he put his eyes to the lenses again, the boy had vanished.

He moved quickly off the mountaintop and risked a dash down

the bare rock apron, across open ground toward the trees where he'd last seen the boy. As he ran, he heard a shout from the direction of the search area. To his right, two men with rifles rushed from the aspens. His gimp leg was on fire, and the burn ran up his back to the place where a bullet had once entered and lodged against his spine.

The cloud passed and sunlight returned, a dazzle that once again laid down shadows among the trees. He caught a glimpse of something moving there. The boy? *Run,* he wanted to shout. *Run.*

Instead he stopped dead still and turned to face the men with rifles. A decoy so the boy could escape. A sacrifice that deep inside him felt right.

CHAPTER 10

Sheriff Marsha Dross sat in her office, looking up at Cork with eyes so tired they made him want to lie down.

"I'm not running for reelection next year," she said.

"Believe me, I understand."

"Sit."

Cork took the vacant chair on the other side of her desk.

"I thought I'd been through it all. But the senator's plane crash?" She raised her hands in surrender.

"I understood you were out of the investigation."

"We are. Officially. I've still got a line of guys from a zoo of federal agencies coming in constantly, looking for assistance, local info. FBI, NTSB, Homeland Security. The wording I'm supposed to deliver to the media goes something like this: The investigation is out of my hands, but I see nothing to make me question the preliminary determination that the cause of the crash was pilot error."

"A lot of interest among a lot of agencies for a crash caused by simple pilot error."

"In the political environment today, a terrorist is behind every tragic event."

"I was finally interviewed by the FBI this morning."

Her eyebrows lifted. "Only just?"

"They've been busy, the agent said."

"Yeah, fighting among themselves. I can't tell who's in charge."

"Nobody's talked to Monkey or Ned Love yet."

She closed her eyes in frustration. "Is it any wonder we still don't know who really killed Kennedy?"

"Margaret told me at the contact desk that George Azevedo requested a leave."

"Asked for two weeks off. Claimed he couldn't stand the badgering from the feds and the media. They were camped out at his house, following his family. He had to get out of Dodge."

"Not you, though?"

"The buck stops here."

"How would you like to piss off the feds, Marsha?"

"I'd like that quite a lot."

"Put your badge on and follow me."

"Where to?"

"I think it's time somebody talked to Ned and Monkey."

Because Marsha Dross had never been to the Loves' cabin, Cork drove. Also, he liked the idea that his unmarked vehicle wouldn't attract as much notice. They skirted the southern end of Iron Lake and headed east onto rez land, where Cork took back roads he'd traveled all his life. Dross was in her second term as sheriff, but she wasn't native to the area. Like a lot of white folks in Tamarack County, even those born there, when she was on the Iron Lake Reservation, she might as well have been in the Australian outback. Cork kept off the main route to Desolation Mountain, figuring that one or all of the interested federal agencies would still be monitoring the traffic. He eased through a couple of iffy bog areas, and finally Desolation Mountain came into view above the tops of the trees.

"What do you know about Monkey Love?" he asked.

"I heard he was trouble around here when he was a kid, but I've never had a problem with him."

"Nobody's sure who his father was. His mother died when he wasn't much more than a toddler. His uncle took him in, raised him for a long while. Ned Love's a good man, but he's always kept to himself out here in the woods. Monkey grew up comfortable not being around people."

"I can't recall seeing either of them in Aurora more than half a dozen times in the last few years."

"Like I said, comfortable in their isolation. When Monkey was twelve, his aunt, Beulah Love, that's Ned's sister, decided he wasn't being raised right, got Social Services involved. They took Monkey from Ned and placed him with her. She lives in Allouette. A well-meaning woman, I'm sure, but one hell of a Bible thumper. Monkey was an odd kid. Odd looking and socially backward. Threw in with a bad crowd, despite all the preaching of his aunt Beulah. He started using, committed a bunch of petty crimes. Shoplifting, boosting cars, a string of B & Es. Got himself sent to the juvenile detention center in Bemidji. Once he came of age, I ran him in a lot for D & D. Then he tried armed robbery using a pellet gun. Did a couple of years in Sandstone."

"Serving time straightened him out?"

"Not exactly. A guy in Sandstone introduced him to the White Bison program. It's a movement that, among other things, helps incarcerated Native men and women get sober. The program didn't take when he was inside, but it finally clicked for him after he was released. Henry Meloux had a lot to do with that. Monkey moved back in with his uncle five years ago, been there since. Still odd, but he seems a lot more comfortable with who he is."

Cork was following two barely visible ruts. Low-hanging tree branches and the wild undergrowth scraped audibly along the sides of the vehicle.

He finally pulled to a stop in front of the old, one-room cabin that had been home to Monkey Love when he was a kid, and was home to him again.

Dross peered through the windshield. "So, just Monkey and Ned out here?"

"Got themselves an old bluetick hound they call Cyrus, in honor of Monkey's grandfather. Used to be a good hunting dog, but he's old now, years past his prime, arthritic. Mostly he lies in the shade and barks a warning when anyone comes around."

"I don't hear him barking."

Ned Love's old pickup was parked next to the cabin. Beyond it lay the road the Loves took when they came and went, a narrow lane that in winter could be snow-choked and impassable. In the spring melt, when the ground was often nothing but a wet, black mire, it could be just as difficult to traverse. When either Ned or Monkey wanted to go into Allouette, they were often forced to walk, taking the path Cork had just followed, a five-mile trek each way.

Cork and Dross got out of the vehicle and approached the cabin.

Ned Love was a hunter, and beside his front door lay a pile of jumbled deer antlers. Cork knocked, a little surprised that no one had stepped out to see who'd come calling. Cork was pretty sure the Loves got few visitors. At the very least, Cyrus should have been barking up a storm.

"Ned, Monkey, it's Cork O'Connor!"

He glanced at Dross and reached for the door. Few people on the rez used locks, and the door swung open. Inside, the place was furnished simply: an old woodstove at the center, two bunks with their heads against the far wall and between them a chest of drawers, a small table next to the single eastern window with two chairs shoved under, two kerosene lanterns—one on the table and one on the chest of drawers. A wooden counter ran along the south wall; the shelves above it held dry and canned goods and cooking utensils. On the counter itself sat a hand mirror, a white enamel basin, a straight razor. Considering it was the home of two bachelors, the cabin was neatly kept. And empty. Just that. Empty. Nothing sinister. Yet Cork felt something wasn't right.

"Where do you suppose they've gone off to?" Dross spoke just above a whisper, as if their presence was a trespass. Which, technically, it was.

"Hunting maybe. That's mostly how Ned keeps the larder filled."

"They must have taken the bluetick with them."

Outside they checked the shed, which was empty except for the axes, saws, splitter, and other tools Ned and Monkey used to gather and prepare the firewood they sold. The only other structure was the outhouse. Cork walked to it. The door was closed, but he heard a scratching on the other side. He reached for the wooden latch and paused. The scratching ceased. Dross had come up next to him, her sidearm out and in her hand. Cork yanked open the door.

A squirrel shot past them, a blur of gray fur that darted up the nearest pine.

A wooden dock, rickety-looking, jutted out into Little Bass Lake a few yards from the shoreline, just enough to tie up a boat or land a canoe. There was nothing tied at the dock, but Cork strolled out to its end and stood gazing across the lake, which was oval-shaped and only a few hundred yards wide. Reflected on the still, silver-blue surface was the upside-down image of Desolation Mountain, which rose beyond the trees on the far shoreline.

"I didn't see their rifles anywhere," he noted. "So maybe they did go hunting."

Dross bent down and inspected the warped, weathered dock boards. With the tip of her index finger, she touched a spot that had caught her interest, one of a spattering of dark spots at the edge of the dock.

"I wouldn't bet the farm, but I'd wager this is blood," she said.

She stood and looked across the lake, which was as empty as the cabin, and took in the sight of Desolation Mountain, its crown bare and gray against the blue wall of the sky.

"Marsha," Cork said quietly.

She looked where he was looking, into the water just off the end of the dock. The lake was four feet deep there and crystal clear. From the bottom, Cyrus, the bluetick hound, stared up at them with open, dead eyes.

CHAPTER 11

Stephen sat in a chair in the lodge of a resort on Iron Lake, south of Aurora. The resort—North Country Cabins—had been closed for three years. Stephen wasn't sure what the issue was, why exactly it had closed, except that during the recession a lot of resorts in the area had suffered. The cabins had stood empty since. Until now. The lodge room where Stephen sat with a good view of the lake was full of electronic equipment and bankers' boxes containing file folders. Topographic maps of Tamarack County and the Iron Lake Reservation hung on the walls, with pins of various colors stuck in patterns Stephen couldn't decipher.

He was afraid, but not with the kind of fear that always accompanied his vision. It was broad daylight, and the men who'd brought him there appeared to be with the government and bound, he believed, by laws. It wasn't like he was a terrorist.

He'd been questioned, twice. First by the men on top of Desolation Mountain. Hoping they would let him go, he'd told them he was just curious. Instead, they'd brought him down to the lodge. Since the plane crash, there'd been a great deal of activity in Tamarack County, lots of official outsiders poking around. Nobody seemed to know much about the nature of all that effort, beyond trying to get to the bottom of what caused the crash. Which, if you believed the NTSB briefings, had already been pretty much determined to be pilot error.

But if that were the true reason for the crash, Stephen asked himself as he sat, what was it they were looking for among the aspens on Desolation Mountain?

He wasn't alone in the room. A man who called himself Gerard was with him. Gerard was military, Stephen had guessed—because of the man's bearing, which was stiff, his clipped way of talking, the hardness with which he eyed Stephen. Also the camo and the crew cut.

They'd stopped conversing. Stephen had stuck to his story about just being curious. You know, a kid. He'd smiled when he said that. Gerard's reply had been that twenty years old was not a kid. Younger men were in uniform, dying for their country.

In his questioning, Gerard had kept hammering at Stephen about a camera. Was he taking pictures? Stephen had maintained that he wasn't.

In the empty silence after the questions had ended, a woman entered the room. She was tall, blond, and carried herself with the same kind of bearing as Gerard, very military. They spoke in low voices, and Gerard turned to Stephen.

"We've brought your Jeep down. It's parked outside. You're free to go. But, Mr. O'Connor, if we find you in that restricted area again, there will be charges. Do you understand?"

"Yes, sir."

"Show him out, Craig."

Before Stephen left the room, he asked one final question: "Who exactly are you?"

"We are the dead. Short days ago, we lived, felt dawn, saw sunset glow, loved and were loved, and now . . ." Gerard stopped and waited, as if expecting something from Stephen. Then he looked disappointed. "Don't know that poem? 'In Flanders Fields,' a great piece about sacrifice. You want to know who we are, kid? We're the ones willing to put it all on the line so you sleep safe and warm in your bed at night. We stand between you and the enemy."

The woman accompanied Stephen to his Jeep and waited while he got in and turned the engine over. Before he drove away, he gave her a long, deep look. "Craig? Is that your first name?"

She didn't respond for a long time, but just when Stephen thought she never would, she said, "Sandi." From the look on her face, he could tell that she believed he was powerless to use the name against her.

He put to her more or less the same question he'd put to Gerard: "Who are you, Sandi Craig?"

A smile crossed her lips, one as cruel as Stephen had ever seen. The answer she gave him was much more succinct than Gerard's had been. "Your worst nightmare, kid."

It all felt otherworldly to him. As if Tamarack County had been invaded, occupied, and no one could say why. He returned to a deserted house. Daniel and Rainy were at work and Waaboo at preschool. He figured Jenny was at Sam's Place, preparing to open. Maybe his father was with her. In half an hour, Stephen was supposed to be in class, Introduction to Philosophy. He was also on the schedule at Sam's Place that day, from three to closing. If he skipped class, he calculated, there would be plenty of time to do what he believed needed to be done before he went to work.

When he broke from the trees and stepped onto Crow Point, he could see Henry Meloux sitting cross-legged in the middle of the meadow. Only the old man's head and shoulders showed above the tall grass and timothy and wildflowers. The Mide faced him, as if he'd been waiting for Stephen to appear. The sun hung almost directly overhead, and Meloux sat on his own shadow. As he drew nearer Stephen could hear the old man singing softly. At first, he thought Meloux must be singing a prayer, but when he came very close he discerned the lyrics: *Where seldom is heard a discouraging word* . . .

Meloux smiled broadly. "Sit," he invited with his hand held out.

Stephen settled beside him in the grass, which, when he was seated, reached nearly to his chest.

"It is a beautiful moment, is it not, Stephen O'Connor?"

"Henry, we need to talk."

"There is time. For the moment, enjoy this." The old man opened his arms, embracing the beauty of the meadow.

Stephen knew the old Mide would listen only when he was ready.

"Who among us knows how many of these moments we have left? I try to gather them, like a squirrel preparing for a long winter."

Meloux closed his eyes, lifted his lined face to the sun, breathed deeply.

In his presence, in this old man's vast enjoyment of a simple moment, Stephen felt an easing of the tightness in his chest. He breathed, closed his eyes, and like Meloux lifted his face to the warm sun.

"That is all of life," the old Mide said quietly.

"What?" Stephen asked.

"Letting go of the questions. Letting go of the fear that there will be no answers."

"Will there be answers?"

"What we believe we want is like knocking on a closed door. Better to open ourselves to what we have and what we know. The beauty of this moment."

Stephen understood the truth in Meloux's words. But his brain continued to knock at closed doors.

At last the old man gave in with a sigh. "What is troubling you?"

"My vision, Henry. And Dad says you've sensed something bad, too."

"They are different, what you have seen, what I have sensed."

"The vision terrifies me. Dad told me what you sensed frightens you."

"It has concerned me."

"My vision keeps coming back, Henry. I thought with the crash it would stop, but I've had it twice since."

"Is it the same?"

"Exactly. The boy, the bird, the beast at my back. The terror at the end. They have to be connected, what I see and what you sense. Here's another thing. I saw the boy. I saw him on Desolation Mountain."

Stephen related the events of that morning.

"Was he flesh and blood?" the old man asked. "Or like a vision?"

"He was there, then gone. Like a vision, I suppose. But he seemed real enough."

"Have you told anyone this?"

"Only you."

"You should tell your father. And then we will do a sweat."

"You and me?"

Meloux had passed the century mark. Sweats were hard on his body, so Stephen wasn't certain it was a good idea.

"We are the ones who have seen and sensed whatever the spirits of these woods are offering," Henry told him. "Perhaps what they are trying to tell us will become clear. Or we can wait and perhaps time will do the same."

Stephen's chest grew taut again. Time didn't feel like an ally.

"A sweat," he agreed. "But maybe just me."

The old man smiled. "You are afraid my spirit might abandon my body. Let go of that fear. I am not ready yet to walk the Path of Souls. Maybe what I sense and what you see are the same. Maybe they are different. The answer is a closed door now. Maybe a sweat will open it."

CHAPTER 12

"A dead dog and a few drops of blood," Marsha Dross said. "That's not enough to launch an official investigation, Cork."

They were on their way back from Ned and Monkey Love's cabin. Cork burned with a sense of outrage. "The Loves didn't shoot Cyrus."

"It could be the FBI finally sent someone out to interview them. They're off hunting. Only Cyrus is there, and Cyrus does what a good watchdog does. The agent or agents feel threatened and shoot."

"And dump the dog's body in the lake? Come on, Marsha."

"We've both seen stranger things. All I'm saying is that I'm not going to throw a lot of resources at this right now. I'll get those blood samples I took from the dock tested. If they're human, that's different."

"It'll take a while to get results. I'm not waiting."

She leveled a gaze on him, coldly professional in its scrutiny. Her voice was all law enforcement. "What exactly do you intend to do?"

Cork offered no answer. Partly it was because since he'd given up wearing a badge his methods hadn't always been within the letter of the law. But also partly because he wasn't sure how to answer her question.

"When I know about the blood, I'll let you know," she promised, when she got out in the parking lot of the Tamarack County Sheriff's Office. "And if you find out anything, you'll let me know. Right?"

He didn't look at her. "I'll see what turns up."

He drove directly to Allouette, the largest community on the Iron Lake Reservation. When Cork was growing up and hanging out with relatives and friends on the rez, Allouette had been a mixed bag. Like in a lot of reservation communities, unemployment was high, there was poverty and the ills that came with it. Most of the roads in town were still gravel then. The majority of the housing was BIA built, or trailers. Cheap, flimsy. Water and sanitation systems were not always in good operating condition. Tourism was nonexistent. White people kept their distance from Allouette and the rez in general, and complained about old treaties that gave the Ojibwe greater access to fishing on Iron Lake and oversight of areas that still had first-growth pine.

When the tribe built the Chippewa Grand Casino, things changed a good deal, both in Aurora and on the rez. The casino hotel and golf course made Aurora a destination for people who weren't just looking for a gateway to the Boundary Waters. The tribal coffers filled with gambling money. The roads in Allouette were paved. Updated water and sewer systems were laid. A new tribal office complex and a clinic were built. New stands were erected for the powwow grounds. A modern marina was constructed on the lakeshore at the edge of town, and because the cost of mooring was set a good deal less than at the marina in Aurora, a lot of white folks dock their boats there in season. A café had opened, the Wild Rice, with a view of the marina and the lake and the islands. There was a coffee shop in town, the Mocha Moose, and a couple of galleries that offered pieces by Native artists.

The revitalization of Allouette didn't mean that everyone cut their grass regularly. There were still cars up on cinder blocks and some trailers that looked as if a perpetual yard sale was going on, but most folks on the rez seemed to feel a sense of pride in their town, their sovereign nation, and the future they were creating for their children and grandchildren.

On the way, he'd tried the phone number for Beulah Love, Ned's sister, but got only her voice mail greeting: *Hello. This is Beulah. I can't answer the phone, so just leave a message and I'll get back to you. Have a wonderful day and remember that the good Lord's grace and my name end in the same way—with Love.*

Her house was small and yellow, with marigolds still blooming along the foundation. Almost nobody in Allouette had a fence around their yard, but Beulah did, built of little white pickets. Beulah had a head for numbers and worked in the accounting department of the Chippewa Grand Casino. She spent every Wednesday night and most of every Sunday inside the old Cenex building south of Aurora, which had become the Church of Holy Fire, where she was the organist. She had never married, but there had been rumors about her relationship with Rev. Alvin Doyle, the pastor at Holy Fire.

Beulah Love was among the last children from the Iron Lake Reservation to be sent to a government-run boarding school. Cork, who was only a year or two older, could still remember what she was like before she left—a quiet girl, pretty, with a long black braid and fluttery eyes, helping her grandmother make fry bread at tribal gatherings. She'd returned years later, hard, cold, with coiffed hair and a head for calculations. She didn't talk about her experience at the boarding school, but Cork had heard enough horrendous stories from others who'd been torn from their families and forced to go to such places that he understood what her silence concealed.

He stood at the front door and could hear her playing the piano inside. He didn't know much about classical music, but he recognized the Moonlight Sonata and hesitated a moment or two before knocking, reluctant to interrupt the lovely, quiet flow. When he finally put his fist to the door, the music stopped. She opened up and stared at him with eyes like black beetle shells.

"Morning, Beulah."

"Cork." A cold greeting.

"Wonder if I could talk with you a minute."

She checked the watch on her wrist. "I have to be leaving for work soon."

"Like I say, just for a minute."

She stood aside and let him enter.

The unofficial credo of the Indian boarding school system was "Kill the Indian, save the child." Beulah's home reflected nothing of her Native heritage. The paintings on her walls were pastel and pastoral, exactly the kind someone might find in a room at a Comfort Inn. She wore nothing beaded, didn't go to powwows. He believed she was the only Native member of the Church of Holy Fire. As he stood in the sanitized atmosphere of Beulah's home, Cork couldn't help thinking sadly that, in the first part of its mission at least, the boarding school had succeeded.

"What is it?" She crossed her arms over her chest, reminding him of a schoolteacher impatient with a child.

"Have you heard from Ned or Monkey in the last couple of days?"

"I never hear from my brother. I haven't spoken to that wild man in years. Since he took Jameson away from me."

In Cork's understanding, this had worked the other way

around. So he assumed Beulah was speaking of Monkey's decision, once he was grown and sober, to move back in with his uncle.

"What about Monkey? Have you heard from him?"

"I hate that name."

"Jameson then."

"Not since Sunday dinner, after church."

"Sunday dinner with you, is that a regular thing?"

"Yes. We eat, we pray."

"Monkey—Jameson—prays with you?"

"I do the praying."

"Has he talked to you this week?"

"No, but he doesn't need to. We both know he'll be here."

"He might not be here this Sunday."

"Oh?"

Cork explained what he'd found at the cabin. Beulah's face went from dour, its usual cast, to deeply concerned. She sat in a hard, straight-backed chair, staring at one of the pastels on her wall, thinking.

"It's got to be that wild man."

"Ned?"

"When we went to the boarding school, they couldn't keep him there. He'd run away, return to the reservation. They'd send him right back. He'd run away again. We weren't allowed to speak our language. But Ned did anyway. They beat him. Made no difference. He became like an animal. Wild."

But Cork thought the word *free*.

"When Jameson was a boy and I saw that Ned was making him just as wild he was, I took him away, tried to give him a Christian upbringing. But the wild was already there, too deep." For a moment, Cork thought she was going to cry. Instead, her face turned hard. "That wild man has finally gone crazy. Killed his dog and done Lord knows what to Jameson."

"Ned didn't kill Cyrus."

"Who then?"

"I can't answer that, at least not at the moment. Listen, Beulah, if Ned or Jameson contacts you, tell them it's important that I talk to them. Will you do that?"

"Talk to them about what?"

"There's a lot of strange things going on around here since the senator's plane went down. I think Ned and your nephew might know something that other people want to know."

"Like what?"

"That's what I'm hoping Ned or Jameson might be able to tell me."

"They're in trouble? Real trouble?"

"They may be."

"Ned can take care of himself." It was spoken with a grudging assurance. "But Jameson?" She looked up at Cork, her eyes soft and fearful. Family, he understood. Blood love. Even the white boarding school couldn't kill that.

"Let me know if you hear anything, all right, Beulah?"

She nodded. "And I'll pray for them."

He left her in that chair and, before he closed the front door behind him, could hear her supplication.

CHAPTER 13

The clinic was next to the tribal office complex, which housed a number of the enterprises of the Iron Lake Ojibwe, including the Department of Conservation Enforcement, out of which Daniel and the other game wardens operated. Cork dropped into the clinic first to see Rainy, but she was out making some home calls. In the Conservation Enforcement office, he found that Daniel was out, too.

"He's still trying to chase down them poachers," Clyde Kingbird, the senior game warden, told Cork. "We keep getting reports, and them poachers keep slipping away."

"Native?" Cork was thinking of Monkey Love and his uncle Ned, who hunted on the rez year-round, even though there were restrictions.

"White, nearly as we can tell." Kingbird had a dark mole on his upper lip that had always reminded Cork of a fly, and he'd always had an urge to shoo it away. "But pretty damn smart for *chimooks*. They don't leave nothing behind."

"Poaching deer?"

"Like I said, don't leave nothing behind, so hard to tell what they're poaching."

"How do you know they're poachers?"

"Who else'd be skulking around out there?"

"Where exactly is 'out there'?"

"East." Kingbird waved a hand. "Other side of Devil's Eye."

"Wildlife photographers, maybe. Beautiful, empty country."

"Maybe. They keep coming around, Daniel'll catch 'em eventually. Good man, your son-in-law."

Cork wandered over to the Youth Mentor Program office, where Tom Blessing was the sole employee. The door was closed and locked, no lights on inside. He returned to the Conservation Enforcement office.

"Seen Blessing this morning?"

Kingbird looked up from his desk, where he was reading some kind of official notice. "Nope."

"As far as you know, has anyone interviewed him since the senator's plane crashed?"

"Haven't seen any strange faces around here lately. Unless you count the guy who fills the Coke machine. Reminds me of a bigmouth bass, that one."

Cork had Tom Blessing's number among the contacts on his cell phone. He tried the number, got the message that the user wasn't available.

Tom Blessing shared a house with his mother, Fanny, on a back road a couple of miles outside Allouette. Cork drove down the narrow gravel lane. Marshland lay on either side, full of cattails. Cork had a great respect for the reeds, which his Anishinaabe ancestors had used in dozens of ways—the fluff to line moccasins, waterproof mats woven from the leaves, marmalade made from the roots, bread from the pollen. He pulled into the dirt drive, parked, and waited.

Like many folks who live rurally, the Blessings owned a dog, as much for security as for company. Cork expected Tornado, a bulldog, to come bounding out, woofing a warning. The dog never appeared.

The morning was sunny, but with a few patchy clouds. As Cork sat waiting, the house and the ragged front yard were engulfed in shadow, and a wariness crept over him, a sense that things weren't right. He listened to the red-winged blackbirds calling among the cattails, and he wondered where the hell Tornado was. Which was the same question he'd had about the bluetick hound at the Loves' cabin, and he hadn't liked the answer he'd found there.

He went to the front porch, mounted the three steps, knocked at the door. He tried to peer through a window, but the curtains were drawn. Although Tom Blessing's pickup truck was gone, his mother's big black 1998 Buick LeSabre was parked near the garage.

"Fanny!" he called at the front door. "It's Cork O'Connor."

He considered leaving, but reached for the doorknob instead, gave it a turn, and eased the door open.

"Fanny, are you here? You okay?"

Fanny Blessing had smoked all her life. She suffered from emphysema, and everywhere she went, a little tank of oxygen on wheels followed her. But she hadn't given up her habit, and the odor of cigarette smoke permeated the house, coming off the furniture upholstery, the rug, the curtains. Fanny Blessing had given up housekeeping a while back, about the time the oxygen tank began following her like a puppy. Tom wasn't the neatest of guys, so the place had a messy look. Cork proceeded carefully, as respectfully as possible for a trespasser. All the rooms were empty.

Back outside, he checked the LeSabre. The keys were in the ignition. He wondered if, in addition to everything else, Fanny had

become forgetful. He walked to the old garage, where the side door
was ajar, and stepped inside. The garage had no windows, and he
waited a moment for his eyes to adjust to the dark. When they did,
he saw Fanny sprawled on the dirt of the garage floor, the oxygen
tank upright on its wheels beside her, like a loyal pet waiting for
its mistress to awaken.

"Heart attack, maybe? Stroke?" Bob Arnold, one of the paramed-
ics from the clinic in Allouette, was talking with Cork while they
awaited the sheriff's people. "This isn't the first time we've been
out here. Fanny's been walking a thin line for years. Refused to
give up her coffin nails."

They'd lifted the garage door, and a rhomboid of sunlight fell
across the floor and Fanny's bare legs. She wore a housedress,
nothing on her feet.

"What was she doing out here?" Cork said this more to himself
than to Arnold.

The wood shelves of the garage were filled with cans of power
steering fluid and brake fluid, containers of antifreeze and motor
oil, a few miscellaneous tools. A couple of tires leaned against one
wall. In a corner was an old power mower.

Arnold replied, "Looking for Tom, maybe."

The crunch of tires approaching on gravel pulled Cork to the
opened garage door, and he watched Sheriff Marsha Dross arrive in
her TrailBlazer, Deputy Dave Foster following in his cruiser. Dross
greeted Cork, shook hands with Bob Arnold and Karl Renwanz,
the other paramedic, who'd been on the radio, communicating with
the clinic.

"You found her and called it in?" she said to Cork.

"Yeah."

She knelt, studied the woman's gray face.

"She's not wearing the oxygen tube," Dross noted. "Why would she take it off?"

"Got me," Cork said.

"Is Tom around?"

"Haven't seen him."

She rose, took in the scene of the woman's death. "What was she doing out here in a housedress and barefooted?"

"Ran out of Wesson oil and was maybe going to cook breakfast with a little ten-thirty?" Arnold offered.

It was clear Dross didn't appreciate the paramedic's black humor. "I gave Tom Conklin a call," she said. Conklin was the county's medical examiner. "He'll be here soon. I want him to have a look at her before we move the body." She turned to her deputy. "See if you can get hold of Tom Blessing."

"I already tried his cell phone," Cork told her. "No answer. And he's not at his office in Allouette."

"Next of kin?"

"Beulah Love is her cousin. I spoke with her this morning. She was just about to head to work at the casino. Could probably reach her there."

"Ned Love must be a cousin, too, then."

"On the rez, just about everyone's a cousin."

"Did you find out anything from Beulah?"

"She hasn't heard from Ned or Monkey in a while. That's about it."

"Check the house," Dross told her deputy.

"Already have," Cork said. "Empty."

Dross looked around, then at Cork. "They have a dog, right?"

"A bulldog. Tornado."

"Where is he?"

"Could be with Tom."

"Like Cyrus was with Ned and Monkey Love? Foster, check the property. See if you can find the dog."

"If he was here, wouldn't he be barking, Sheriff?" the deputy offered.

"Just look."

"Check the marsh," Cork suggested.

Dross studied Cork, then nodded and said to her deputy, "Check the marsh."

CHAPTER 14

It was ten minutes to opening, but his father wasn't at Sam's Place.

"He said he had things to do," Jenny told Stephen. "That's why I called Judy." She swung a hand toward the woman preparing to open the serving windows.

"What things?" Stephen asked.

"Dad found Ned and Monkey Love's dog shot and dumped in the lake at their cabin. The Loves weren't around, so he headed to the rez to see what he could find out. Where have you been all morning?"

"Tell you later." Stephen turned to leave.

"Where are you going?"

"To catch Dad at the rez."

"You don't know where he is out there."

"It's the rez. Somebody'll know."

"Be back at three. You're on the schedule and we'll need you."

Luck was with him. He'd just swung around the southern end of Iron Lake and passed the turnoff to Desolation Mountain when he spotted his father's SUV approaching from the direction of

Allouette. He waved Cork down, pointed to the side of the road, and parked on the shoulder. His father made a U-turn and pulled up behind him.

Stephen was out of his Jeep in a heartbeat and spoke to his father through the lowered window. "Jenny told me about the Loves' dog. Did you find out anything on the rez?"

"Whoa. Hold on a minute. Where've you been all day?"

"You're not going to believe this." Stephen related the details of his morning on Desolation Mountain and his interrogation by the man named Gerard.

"FBI?" Cork asked.

"Military, I think. Did you find out anything about the Loves?"

"Nothing. I went out to see Tom Blessing. He wasn't there, but I found his mother dead in the garage."

"Fanny? What happened?"

"Looks like it could have been a heart attack or maybe a stroke. We won't know until the ME's had a good look at her. But there's a lot not right about it. Any idea what the guys on Desolation Mountain were looking for?"

"None."

"Don't take this the wrong way, Stephen, but the kid you say you saw up there, was he real or another vision?"

Real, Stephen had thought at the time, but as the moment receded, he'd begun to wonder if it wasn't something else, another kind of seeing, not exactly a vision but akin. "He was pretty far away. I saw him through my field glasses. A lot of shadow involved."

"What was he doing?"

"Same thing I was. Checking out the guys in military camo."

His father looked past him, staring at where the lake was visible through a thin line of pines on the other side of the road. Stephen understood that the sparkle of the blue water probably wasn't what his father was seeing.

"I want to check out the mountain," Cork finally said.

"Not without me."

His father shook his head. "They picked you up once and let you go. The next time they won't be so lenient."

"You're not going without me."

Stephen stood with his hands on the vehicle as if intending to hold it there until his father agreed.

"They know your Jeep. We'll take the Expedition."

Three miles up the cutoff to Desolation Mountain, a good mile shy of the logging road that had been blocked that morning, they came to another barricade that hadn't been in place earlier. The two sentries posted there were dressed in military fatigues and wearing sidearms.

"One of them was there this morning with Gerard," Stephen said. "The woman. She'll recognize me."

"Pull the bill of your cap down, turn up your coat collar, and drop your head like you're sleeping. Don't let her see your face."

The woman approached and spoke through Cork's open window. "Road's closed, sir." Except for her sidearm, she wore nothing that signified authority and had no ID badge.

"Because of the plane crash?"

"I can't say, sir."

"Closed for how long?"

"Again, I can't say. You need to turn around and return the way you came."

"Thank you, Sergeant . . . ?"

"Have a good day, sir." The woman stepped back and gave Cork room for a U-turn.

Stephen sat up as they drove off. "What now, Dad?"

"There are other ways to get to the top of that mountain."

He took old logging roads, some so ancient the forest had almost entirely reclaimed the cleared ground. It was slow going, but
eventually they found themselves on the far side of Desolation
Mountain. Cork parked, and he and Stephen began to make their
way through a mix of evergreen, then gradually up the mountainside.

They crossed through the aspens that ringed the mountain
near the top. Cork paused before they broke into the open, with
a hundred yards of nearly bare rock between them and the dark
outcrop that crowned Desolation Mountain. Devil's Eye. For
several minutes, he waited to be certain no one was there to see,
then moved swiftly up the final bare face of the mountain. They
were both breathing hard from the sprint and took a moment
to catch their breath. The sky was an azure sea with islands of
white cloud drifting across. The wind was gentle, out of the
south, cooling their faces. The air smelled of the sun-heated rock
against which they rested. To the east, forested hills rolled all
the way to the Sawtooth Mountains, sixty miles distant, and
beyond that was the great flat blue of the Shining Big Sea Water,
Kitchigami, Lake Superior. It was a beautiful vista, and Cork
understood why the mountaintop was a favorite destination for
photographers. But the stories he'd heard on the rez all his life
twisted his perception and he believed he could feel the evil in
the place.

He nodded to Stephen, and they went to their knees and eased
their way around the wall of the outcropping. What greeted them,
Cork could never have predicted.

The man lying there was dressed in camouflage, not military
but that of a hunter, the pattern all branches and leaves. He wore
a sage-green stocking cap. On the rock beside him lay a firearm, a
Sig Sauer, Cork could tell. The man had binoculars to his eyes and
was studying the activity in the aspens below.

Stephen looked at his father. Cork put a finger to his lips and motioned for retreat.

Before they could move, the man grabbed the Sig, rolled to his back, and leveled the barrel at them. Then a smile spread across his lips.

"Cork O'Connor," he said quietly. "It's been a long time."

CHAPTER 15

"Best you lie down," the man said. "We don't want them to spot us."

Stephen followed his father's lead and lay on the flat rock beside the man in hunter's camo, who offered his hand. "Bo Thorson."

"This is my son, Stephen," Cork told him. "What are you doing here, Bo?"

"Same as you, I'm guessing. Trying to figure out what's going on down there."

"How's Secret Service involved?"

"I haven't been an agent for a long time, Cork. Went private like you, a few years ago." He put the binoculars to his eyes again. "So, Stephen, when they took you in this morning, did they give you a hard time?"

Stephen was amazed. "How'd you know?"

"Watched it happen. I didn't know who you were then."

"Where were you?"

"In the trees down there." Bo pointed to the aspens where Stephen had seen—or thought he'd seen—the kid from his vision.

"Did you spot anyone in the trees near where you were?" Stephen asked.

"Didn't see anybody up here but you and the searchers."

"Have you been on the mountain all day?" Cork asked.

"A couple of days now. Tried to get close to the crash site, but they've got that bottled up tight. Came up here thinking I might be able to get some kind of view, and that's when I stumbled onto those guys down there. They've been going over the mountainside inch by inch."

"Looking for what?" Stephen asked.

"That's the question, isn't it? I thought maybe the black box."

"There wasn't any black box," Stephen said.

Bo smiled. "You believe everything you read in the papers?"

"There *was* a black box?"

"I can't say for sure. But it's one of the possibilities."

Cork said, "Why would they be looking for it up here?"

"Why would they be looking for anything up here? But clearly they're after something. Whoever they are."

"Maybe it doesn't have anything to do with the plane crash," Stephen offered.

Bo gave Cork a wistful look. "Raised him on fairy tales?" He put the glasses to his eyes again. "We're going to have to move our position pretty soon. They've just about covered the west side of this mountain."

He slid himself back, behind the cover of the crowning rock outcrop, and stood in its lee. Cork and Stephen followed.

"I don't think staying here is going to accomplish anything," Bo said. "And I haven't eaten since before sunup. What say we head somewhere, grab some lunch? We can fill each other in."

Single file and in silence, they descended the eastern slope of Desolation Mountain. Bo had parked his Jeep ridiculously near the place where Cork had hidden his Expedition.

"I had a hell of a time getting here," Bo said. "Hope you know an easier way out."

"Follow me," Cork told him.

Allouette was the nearest town, and they gathered at the Mocha Moose for coffee and sandwiches. Before casino money had helped with the revitalization of the rez community, the building the little eatery now occupied had been a run-down bait and tackle shop. Sarah LeDuc, who owned the Mocha Moose, had completely renovated the place, and instead of fish and worms and leeches, the air was redolent with the scent of fresh-brewed coffee, hot soup, and baked goods.

As they sat waiting for their sandwiches, Stephen took stock of this Bo Thorson. At just over six feet tall, he wasn't imposing, but there was a tough feel to him that made Stephen think of leather. His eyes constantly swept the room, as if scanning for threats. His mind seemed to be constantly calculating, and although he had a ready smile, his face betrayed little of what was really going on in his head. His cheeks were heavily stubbled but his fingernails carefully manicured, which made Stephen wonder if the shadow of the beard was meant to roughen his appearance, make him seem more like a man who might naturally wear hunter's camo.

Cork said, "So, if you're not Secret Service anymore, you must be working for someone."

Bo winked at Stephen. "Your father was always a quick study."

"Who's your client?"

Bo gave Cork a pained look.

"Okay, what can you tell us?"

"The people I'm working for aren't ready to buy the pilot error story."

"What do they believe?"

"They don't want to jump to any conclusions. Right now, they just want more facts."

"And they're getting nothing from the official sources?"

"Is anyone getting anything from the official sources? It's the same story over and over and always shy on details. There are rumors of terrorism, but every time someone advances that possibility, the people in charge crush it like a bug. They continue to pump out the pilot error theory."

"NTSB is supposed to be in charge, but the FBI is definitely involved," Cork said. "Which would make sense if we're looking at some kind of terroristic threat."

"Those men on the mountain weren't FBI," Stephen pointed out. "At least they weren't wearing anything that identified them that way."

"They're very careful about not saying who they are," Bo acknowledged.

"They're the ones who stand between us and them." When his father and Bo looked at him oddly, Stephen explained, "That was the line Gerard fed me this morning when I asked who they were."

"Gerard?"

"The guy in charge. Or one of them anyway," Stephen replied.

"Movie dialogue," Bo scoffed. Which was exactly what Stephen had thought.

"But they probably believe it," Cork said. "You stood between the First Lady and death, Bo. You must have believed in what you were doing."

"I was sworn to protect the First Family. A noble calling, I still believe that. But the downside of that whole affair was that it opened my eyes to what a government really is."

"And what's that?"

"Do you know the Hydra in Greek myth? The many-headed monster?"

Cork didn't, but Stephen, the college kid, nodded.

"The government's just like that. Each head has its own agenda, and God help you if you get in the way."

"That's why you left Secret Service?"

"One of the reasons." He changed the subject, focusing abruptly on Stephen. "Why were you up on that mountain in the first place?" Then his eyes took a swing at Cork. "And why did you go back with him?"

Between them, Stephen and his father explained things: the vision, their time at the crash site, the missing Loves, the missing Tom Blessing, the slain dog, and the woman dead in her garage.

They'd just about finished when their sandwiches arrived, brought by Sarah LeDuc herself. Sarah had been married to George LeDuc, a hereditary chief of the Iron Lake Ojibwe and a longtime friend of the O'Connors. George and Cork's first wife, Jo, had both died under the same black circumstances, a tragedy that had bound Sarah LeDuc and Cork O'Connor ever since. She was a few years younger than Cork, late forties, gone a little plump, filled with a goodness that shone in her broad face and mahogany eyes. But she was clearly concerned when she delivered the food. "I heard about Fanny Blessing. So sad. And I heard that you found her, Cork."

Not much time had passed since his father discovered Fanny Blessing's body, but already word was abroad. The rez telegraph in action, Stephen knew.

She drew up a chair. "Was it a heart attack or something? Her health hasn't been good for a long time." Her eyes took in the stranger. "I'm Sarah," she said to Bo. "I own the Moose."

"Bo," he replied. "Old friend of Cork." His smile was gentle through the rough stubble on his face. "A nice establishment you have here, ma'am."

She looked back at Cork for an answer to her question.

"We won't know for a while, Sarah."

"There wasn't any . . ." She searched for the right words. "Foul play, was there?"

"Why do you ask?" It was Bo Thorson who put the question to her.

"It's just that . . ." Again, she seemed at a momentary loss of words. "It feels like there's something not right out here, ever since the senator's plane went down. I see guys here and all over the rez who aren't tourists and it gives me the willies."

"What do they look like?" Again, Bo's question.

"I don't know. Not abnormal or anything. Just . . . intense. And they're never alone. There's always at least two of them. Sometimes more."

"Where do you see them?" Stephen asked.

"They've been here, around town. And I see them coming in on back roads from the direction of Desolation Mountain. Sometimes they're just parked out in the middle of nowhere. Creepy." She made a shivering gesture with her whole body. "What about Tom? Does he know?"

"I tried calling him," Cork told her. "He's not answering his cell phone."

"Not in his office? You might try Bourbon Lake, there where the Coot River flows out. I heard he's been after a couple of otter poachers. Phone reception is pretty iffy that far out."

"Poachers? Did he report them to Daniel?"

"I don't know. It's just what I heard."

"Thanks, Sarah. I'll give it a shot."

She eyed Bo. "Get your deer yet?"

"Beg your pardon?"

"I figure you must be a bow hunter. That's the only season open at the moment."

Another smile appeared in the rough stubble. "I'm a hunter, Sarah. But not of deer."

As soon as they left the Mocha Moose, they checked at the tribal offices, but still no Tom Blessing.

"Where's this Bourbon Lake?" Bo asked.

"East, along the edge of the Boundary Waters. Not all that far from Desolation Mountain."

"Hard to get to?"

"Follow me," Cork said.

Chapter 16

"You seem to know him pretty well, Dad."

They were following a series of logging roads abandoned long enough ago that nature had reclaimed the ground. Scrub brush clawed the sides and undercarriage of the big vehicle as they maneuvered through. They crossed threads of water, streams nearly dry now, but during the next spring melt they would be impassable. Bo Thorson trailed in his Jeep.

"I met Bo when I was sheriff. This was when Tom Jorgenson was vice president."

Tom Jorgenson was a name probably every schoolkid in Minnesota knew. He'd been a popular governor and then vice president.

"The Jorgensons had a vacation home on Iron Lake for decades. Whenever the vice president was in residence there, I worked with Bo on security. We got on well, and let me tell you that wasn't always the case when I had to work with federal agents of one kind or another."

"So you trust him?"

"Why wouldn't I?"

Stephen shrugged. "Everything feels off. Me, I'm not sure what I can trust."

"Or who? You trust me, don't you?"

"Come on."

"And I trust Bo. Good enough?"

Stephen eyed the trailing Jeep, considered, finally said, "For now."

Cork slowed to a stop and peered through the windshield, studying the ground in front of the vehicle. "Somebody's been this way recently."

"Tom Blessing," Stephen said.

"A lot of damage to the ground cover, more than a single vehicle would have caused."

"He's probably been this way before. Sarah said he's been trying to track down otter poachers out here."

"Maybe."

Cork continued on, but he watched the forest more carefully now. Meloux's cautionary words echoed in his thinking: *There is a beast in these woods that does not belong here. It is huge and it is evil.*

"Over there," Stephen said a few minutes later. He pointed toward two vehicles parked among the pines. Beyond them, thirty yards through the trees, blue water sparkled. Bourbon Lake.

Cork parked near the other vehicles, one of them a big pickup, and Bo pulled alongside.

"That's Tom's Tundra," Cork said.

"What about the other?" Bo asked.

"I don't know. But it has rez plates, too."

They walked over a soft carpet of pine needles to the rocky shoreline. The reason for the lake's name was pretty evident: water the color of bourbon, the result of both the iron content of the soil and the bog seepage along the creeks that fed the lake. Except for the water itself, which shivered a little in the afternoon breeze, making the sunlight on the surface dance, nothing moved.

"Where are they?" Stephen's voice was hushed.

Cork backtracked, carefully eyeing the ground and the bed of needles that covered it. "Here." He went down on one knee and pointed to impressions left in the soft bedding. "They went east, toward the Coot River outlet."

He led the way, one eye to the ground and the other to the trees around them. Stephen and Bo seemed to have sensed his concern. They all walked carefully and didn't speak.

"Hold it right there!" The command came from the trees at their backs.

Cork stopped dead, silently berating himself for leading his son and Bo into this ambush.

"Turn around slowly."

They obeyed.

The man rose from behind the trunk of a fallen pine, a rifle in his hands, the barrel trued on Cork. He wore a green ball cap whose bill shaded the upper part of his face. But a smile slowly spread across his lips and he lowered the rifle. "*Boozhoo*, Cork. Hey, Stephen. What are you doing here?"

"Looking for you, Tom," Cork replied. "What's with the hardware?"

"Poachers," Tom Blessing said, as if the word were dirty. "Otter poachers. You gotta be one heartless son of a bitch to poach a creature as delightful as an otter."

"Good warm fur," Bo noted. "Brings a pretty penny, I bet."

Blessing eyed him with suspicion. "Who're you?"

Another figure rose from behind the blind of the fallen pine. Cork recognized Harmon Goodsky, who was a professional photographer with a gallery in Allouette. His right hand held a camera, to which a powerful-looking lens was affixed.

"*Boozhoo*, Harmon." Then to answer Blessing's question, Cork said, "This is Bo Thorson. A friend."

"Well, friend," Blessing said, "there's more to an otter than its fur."

"I understand," Bo replied. "Just talking about motivation. For some people, it's all about the money."

"Those kind of people we don't need."

"I couldn't agree more," Bo said.

Cork glanced at Goodsky. "I know why Tom's here. What are you up to, Harmon?"

Goodsky was huge, towering. In an earlier time, he'd been an imposing, powerful figure. Now, in a way, he resembled the fallen pine in front of him, a great trunk slowly rotting. He was a veteran of Vietnam and a victim of Agent Orange. He had Parkinson's and was riddled with cancer.

Goodsky held up his camera. "Tom wanted me to document things."

"How do you know they're poaching otters, Tom?" Cork asked.

"There's an otter lodge near the Coot River outlet. With field glasses, you can see it from here. I spotted a couple of guys there a few days ago. I hollered at them and they took off. I've been hanging around since. They came back yesterday and I ran 'em off again. No other reason to be here than those otters."

"Have you mentioned this to any of the game wardens? Daniel's looking for a couple of poachers, too."

Blessing gave a little croak of disdain. "Game wardens'll just hand 'em a ticket. I get hold of these guys, they won't be walking right for a while. I'll make sure they understand the real cost of poaching otters on Shinnob land." A woof came from the other side of the log. Blessing said, "Easy, boy."

"Is that Tornado with you?" Cork asked.

"He's not really a hunting dog, but I brought him along thinking he might help us sniff out these poachers. Or I could sic him on 'em if I had to."

The bulldog showed himself, appearing around the end of the log, his body tensed, as if prepared to attack should Blessing give the word.

What Cork had to do next, he didn't relish. "Look, Tom, I've got some bad news." He gave it a moment, then added, "About your mom."

Blessing waited, but even before he received the word his face reflected an anticipation of the worst. Which is to say, all his features became stone, unreadable. And when he'd heard, his response was a simple nod.

"I'm sorry, Tom."

Blessing's dark eyes searched the woods, the sky, the lake, as if looking for the answer to a question as yet unasked. "All right," he finally said, gathering himself. "We're done here, Harmon. Come on, Tornado." He slipped the rifle strap over his shoulder and began the long journey home.

Goodsky let him walk away a bit, then said to Cork, "Just like in Nam."

"How's that, Harmon?"

He scanned the woods. "You know they're out there. You just don't know when they'll hit you." He followed Blessing and the dog, walking slowly. At every other step, he faltered, as if afraid the bones in that leg might crack under his weight.

Stephen watched him limp away. "It's not just his body." In answer to Cork's questioning look, he explained, "What's eating him doesn't just feed on his flesh and bone, Dad. That man is sick in his soul."

"Think Henry could help him?"

"I'm not sure Harmon wants to be helped."

Cork understood. Some people fed on their anger or their bitterness or their resentment for so long that even though it was poison, it was what they craved.

"Interesting, don't you think, that these poachers seem to have appeared about the same time the senator's plane went down?" Bo said.

"Coincidence?" Stephen suggested.

Bo smiled. "And do you believe in the tooth fairy, too?"

"I think I'd like to talk to Daniel about those poachers he's been chasing," Cork said.

He turned to leave, but Stephen didn't move. He stood at the edge of the lake with his eyes closed. So Cork waited in the quiet of the Northwoods. This was familiar territory to him: the bourbon-colored water, the evergreen-scented air, the rustling bulrushes, the yielding needles underfoot. But something was off.

"Waiting," Stephen said, opening his eyes.

"Who's waiting?" Bo asked.

"The *manidoog*," Stephen replied. "The spirits here."

"Waiting for what?"

On his son's face, Cork saw the shadow of confusion and defeat, which had darkened it so often since he'd first received the vision.

"Hell if I know." Stephen turned and walked away alone.

CHAPTER 17

Bo followed Cork's big SUV west through the woods in the direction of Allouette. He was thinking about the question Stephen had put to him, which was essentially this: Could the appearance of the poachers and the crash of Senator McCarthy's plane be a coincidence? Although he'd sloughed off the question, he knew that due diligence meant he had to eliminate the possibility absolutely. He was hoping once they'd talked with this game warden, this Daniel English, he could put the question to rest.

They weren't far from town when his phone gave a chirp, signaling a text message. Driving along the rugged back roads required his full attention, so he couldn't check it immediately, but he was pretty sure who'd sent it and pretty sure he didn't want to respond just yet.

It wasn't exactly a stroke of luck that Cork O'Connor had stumbled onto him. Bo would have gotten around to him eventually. He remembered Cork from his days with Secret Service, and when he'd agreed to take this assignment, one of his early thoughts was that if he had to, he might be able to tap Cork's local knowledge. Luck came into play when it turned out that the kid he'd seen Gerard's people grab was Cork's son.

Stephen O'Connor was an interesting case. This vision thing. Bo didn't buy into it, but he could see that the young man's father was invested. Maybe it was because of the O'Connors' Native heritage or maybe the man wanted to believe simply because that's what fathers did, supported their children. Bo didn't have children. He'd never really had a father. So what did he know about that kind of relationship? He understood teamwork, however, and that when you've partnered with someone, as he had with Cork that day, you didn't double-cross them. He hoped that in all that might occur going forward, this would be a tenet he could stand by.

Cork parked at the tribal offices. Bo pulled up beside him and took a moment to check the text message he'd received: *Report?* He decided to wait until the day was over before responding. That would be soon enough.

Daniel English wasn't in the Conservation Enforcement office, but the head game warden, a colorful coot with a mole like a tick on his lip, pointed them toward the Mocha Moose, where English had gone for an afternoon break.

They found him sipping coffee and eating a blueberry muffin at the same table where they'd sat earlier.

English was tall, clearly Native, with black hair, dark eyes, high, fine cheekbones, and a steadiness in his gaze, the frank assessment of a law enforcement officer, which Bo could appreciate. Cork introduced them, and they joined English at the table. In an instant, Sarah LeDuc was there with them.

"Did you find Tom Blessing?"

"Out at Bourbon Lake, like you said, Sarah," Cork replied. "Harmon Goodsky was with him."

"Harmon?" Her face showed some pain. "That poor man. What was he doing there?"

"Documenting." Cork looked at Daniel English. "Tom says there are some guys poaching otters at Bourbon Lake. You hear anything about that?"

"Nothing about Bourbon Lake. How does Tom know they're poaching?"

"He spotted them near an otter lodge and put two and two together. He's pretty burned about it."

"Was Harmon there to document the poaching or document the beating Tom was going to give the poachers?"

"Maybe both. And maybe provide a little backup, too."

English looked skeptical. "He's big, but he couldn't provide much backup these days."

"A year to live," Sarah said. "Maybe two. That's the word anyway. Agent Orange. What were those people thinking?"

"People who make that kind of decision think only in the moment," Bo offered. "In my experience, it's an unfortunate hallmark of governments."

"Sarah told me about Tom's mother," English said. "Does Tom know?"

"Yeah." Cork wiped the perfectly clean tabletop with an open palm, as if there was something there that needed to be brushed away. "It's not like it was totally unexpected. She hasn't taken care of herself."

"But something's eating at you," English said.

"If it was just Fanny, that would be one thing," Cork replied carefully. "But add to it the shooting of Cyrus at the Loves' cabin, and it begins to feel questionable."

Sarah finally pulled up a chair. "You think these things are tied together? How?"

Bo said, "I can think of at least one important way. The Loves and Tom Blessing were among the first on the scene of Senator McCarthy's plane crash."

"Why is that important?" Sarah asked.

Although the woman couldn't see the connection, a look of understanding came to O'Connor's face. Then to the face of Daniel English.

It was young Stephen O'Connor who said what they were all thinking. "You were also one of the first out there, Daniel."

English's only acknowledgment of this truth was a slight nod. "Phil Hukari was out there, too."

"Where is he?" Cork asked.

"We came in from poacher chasing because he got a call from his wife," English said. "She was having some pregnancy-related difficulty." He pulled out his cell phone and made a call. He waited, finally spoke into the phone. "Phil, it's Daniel. Give me a call when you get this message."

"Where does he live?" Bo asked.

"They have a small place on Badger Creek, a mile or so outside of town," English replied.

As if of one mind, they all rose, except Sarah, who looked up at them with confusion. "What am I missing?"

"Thanks for the coffee and muffin," English said to her and quickly led the way out.

The caravan sped northeast with Daniel English in the lead. They took the main road for a mile before turning onto gravel and following a stream that threaded among pines and aspens. Bo wasn't a man much given to intuition, but a palpable sense of menace had descended on him. From the glove box, he took the Sig he'd placed there earlier and put it within easy reach.

The cabin was set among pines on the bank of the creek. No

vehicles were visible. English was out of his truck and already at the front door, Cork and his son with him, before Bo had killed the engine on his Jeep. Bo gripped his Sig and stepped from his vehicle, but he didn't join the others. The situation felt precarious to him, and he readied himself to provide cover fire, if necessary. He watched as English knocked, called out, finally opened the door, and disappeared inside. Cork and Stephen followed.

Bo scanned the whole scene. A small garage-like structure stood to the right of the cabin, against which several cords of wood had been stacked. To the left was a big white propane tank. Something moved in the tall grass under the tank. Bo lifted the Sig.

English and the O'Connors emerged from the house and stood talking.

"The propane tank," Bo hollered to them, nodding where they should look.

They saw it then, the movement in the grass. English moved to investigate.

"Easy," Bo called out.

English drew his own sidearm and approached the tank cautiously. When he was very near, the game warden holstered his weapon, knelt, and signaled for the others to join him.

"Noggin," English said, cradling the dog's head.

It was a golden retriever. Dark blood matted the fur on its side, but the animal wasn't dead.

"Easy, boy." Stephen slid his arms under the dog's body and gently lifted. "We need to get him to a vet."

Bo saw the look of indecision on Cork's face, which he interpreted as compassion for the dog competing with an investigator's compulsion to stay with the scene.

"You two go," Bo told him. "Daniel and I will secure things here."

"Keep us posted," Cork said.

"One more thing, Cork. As much as possible, I need to stay off the radar up here. You understand?"

Cork considered his request, then gave a firm nod. He moved ahead of his son to the Expedition, where they laid the dog in the back, then took off.

English eyed Bo. "Cork didn't say what exactly your interest in all this is. I'm guessing you're a cop."

"Former Secret Service," Bo replied. "I do private security work now."

"And you're here because?"

"Representing the interests of a client."

"A client interested in . . . ?" English waited for an answer that never came. "Well, Cork trusts you. That's good enough for me." He studied the scene. "Phil drives a Dodge Ram. Let's check the garage."

It was empty.

"How did things look in the house?" Bo asked.

"Nothing obviously wrong."

English swung his gaze back to the tall grass where they'd found the dog. "I don't think Noggin was shot under the tank. They probably dumped him there thinking he wouldn't be seen." He began to walk a spiral out from the propane tank. After a couple of minutes, he knelt in the wild grass beneath a crab apple tree.

"Here," he said.

Bo joined him. At their feet was a spattering of blood.

"This is where he was hit." English studied the ground and walked slowly toward the stream that ran behind the house. "They came in from this way. Two of them, looks like." At the stream, he paused, then waded across. The water was swift but reached only to his calves. On the other side he knelt, pulled a handkerchief from his back pocket, and picked up something, which he brought back to Bo. Nestled in English's handkerchief was an expended cartridge casing.

"Savage," English said. "Small caliber, probably two-fifty. Mostly for hunting small game or varmints."

"Or watchdogs," Bo said. "When Hukari got that call from his wife, what exactly did he say?"

"Just that she was having trouble, something to do with the pregnancy. She wanted him to come home right away. He said she sounded scared, but he chalked that up to this being their first child." English looked at the blood in the grass. "I'm guessing something else was scaring her."

"Or someone else. Someone who wanted to talk to her husband and wanted leverage."

"Why? What could Phil possibly have that would be worth this?"

When Bo had been with Secret Service and charged, on occasion, with ensuring the safety of someone important, he'd learned to read faces quickly, even in a crowd. He studied Daniel English. What he saw was a man truly at a loss for an explanation, a man hiding nothing.

"Something about the scene of the plane crash," Bo said. "Something these people want, and they believe that you or one of the others who got there early has it."

"Like what?"

Bo looked the whole scene over. The lovely setting at the edge of the stream, the young crab apple tree, the cozy cabin, the pines. All of it idyllic. Except for the splash of blood at his feet.

"That's the question, isn't it?" he said.

CHAPTER 18

Cork pulled his vehicle to the side of the road where Stephen had earlier parked his old Jeep. Just as he got out to help with the wounded dog, his cell phone rang. It was Daniel calling, his voice tense.

"Do you know where Jenny is, Cork?"

"She opened Sam's Place, then she was going to pick up Waaboo from kindergarten. Why?"

"She's not answering her cell phone."

"Did you try the landline at the house?"

"Yeah. No luck."

"What's your worry?"

"We think somebody snatched Phil and Sue. Bo thinks they might go after Jenny and Waaboo, too."

"Why?"

"Still working on that. But I need to know they're safe."

"I'm on my way to the house. You keep trying Jenny."

Stephen was still with the dog, comforting the wounded animal. "What is it?"

"I have to get home, make sure Jenny and Waaboo are okay.

You take Noggin to the vet in the Expedition. I'll take your Jeep."

Driving fast, it was twenty minutes to the house on Gooseberry Lane. Cork was relieved to find Jenny's Forester parked in the drive. He hightailed it inside, called out, received no answer. He checked the first floor, then the second. The house was empty. One of the things that worried him was this: Trixie, the nearest thing to a watchdog that the O'Connors had, was also gone. He thought of Cyrus dead in the lake and Noggin lying shot in the tall grass under the propane tank. He knew that silencing the dogs had made whatever happened to their owners possible. He called Daniel on his cell.

"Have you heard from Jenny yet?"

"Nothing," Daniel replied. "Where are you?"

"At the house. Her car's here, but she's not."

Cork stood in Waaboo's bedroom, staring at his grandson's bed. On the pillow lay a stuffed wolf, a gift Cork had given him on his fifth birthday, a reminder that Waaboo and the O'Connors were Ma'iingan, Wolf Clan. Protectors. Cork closed his eyes.

"I'm ten minutes away." Daniel ended the call.

Cork's heart beat like a fist against his chest, rage and fear battling to control him. He wanted to explode at someone, do something physical and decisive. He grabbed the stuffed wolf and threw it across the room, a useless gesture.

Then he heard the squeak of a hinge as a door opened—or closed—downstairs. He went to the top of the landing, listened, heard only the sound of his own fierce breathing.

"Jenny? Waaboo?"

No answer, and he began to take the stairs, descending slowly, pausing halfway to listen. Outside, a car passed on the street, the soft whoosh like the sound of someone hushing a child. He heard something, or thought he did, coming from the office off the downstairs hallway. He quieted his breathing, crept toward the door, which was slightly ajar, hesitated at the edge of the threshold, and listened again. Someone was inside.

His body went hard, taut. He readied himself, then shoved the door open fully and entered the office, prepared for battle.

"Boo!" His grandson jumped at him and wrapped his little arms around Cork's waist.

"Jesus!" Cork shouted.

"We scared Baa-baa!" Waaboo cried with delight.

Jenny's laughter died when she saw the look on her father's face. "I'm sorry, Dad. Waaboo wanted to scare you. Are you okay?"

She held Trixie's leash in her hand, the old dog sitting on her haunches, tongue lolling.

"Just surprised," Cork managed.

Waaboo released his grip and did a little dance of celebration around his grandfather.

"Where were you?" Cork asked his daughter.

"Taking Trixie for her afternoon walk. What's wrong?"

"Hey, little guy," Cork said. "Trixie looks thirsty. How about putting some fresh water into her bowl?"

"Okay. Come on, girl." Waaboo happily led the dog away.

"Call Daniel," Cork said as soon as Waaboo had gone. "Let him know you're safe."

"What—" Jenny began.

"Just call him, then I'll explain."

She turned to the desk, where one of the landline phones sat.

"What about your cell?" Cork asked.

"It's charging in the kitchen."

She made the call, told her husband that she was fine, listened, then eyed her father. "All right. I'll see you in a few minutes." She set the phone in its cradle. "What's going on?"

As Cork explained their concern, Jenny's face grew pinched. Her eyes moved from her father to the doorway where her son had disappeared with Trixie. She stepped out and down the hallway to where she could see Waaboo in the kitchen.

"What do these people, whoever they are, think Daniel or the others might have picked up at the crash site?"

"Good question. If, in fact, that's what this is all about. At the moment, the only thing we know for certain is that the Loves and the Hukaris are missing."

"And their dogs have been shot and Fanny Blessing is dead," Jenny added.

"We don't know yet what caused Fanny's death. It might have nothing to do with whatever's going on. But it's clear that everyone who was on the crash scene early has been targeted. That means Daniel and you and Waaboo might well be at risk."

The back door opened and Daniel swept in. Waaboo abandoned Trixie and ran to him. Daniel lifted his son and swung him around, and Waaboo shrieked with delight.

Jenny and Cork joined them in the kitchen. Daniel immediately embraced his wife and held her tight for a long while. "I was so worried, Jenny."

"Dad told me." She glanced down at Waaboo, who was watching closely, clearly perplexed, as if he understood that this was far more than a simple display of affection. "What do we do?"

They'd put on a video for Waaboo, *The Jungle Book*, one of his favorites. Now they sat at the kitchen table, talking in low voices, Cork and Daniel explaining everything they knew so far.

"Phil Hukari still isn't answering his phone," Daniel said. "I called the clinic in Allouette and the Aurora Community Hospital, where he might have taken Sue. Nothing. Not that I expected anything."

"Aside from Noggin, there's really nothing to indicate something worrisome has happened to them," Jenny pointed out hopefully.

"Add it up," Daniel said. "The Loves, Fanny Blessing, Phil and Sue. It's a pattern."

"We don't know what happened to Fanny Blessing," Cork reminded him. "We don't know what's going on with Ned and Monkey Love. And, as Jenny says, we don't really know about the Hukaris."

"Are you blind, Cork?"

"Easy, Daniel." Jenny laid a hand on his arm.

"I'm just thinking like the sheriff right now," Cork told him. "We don't have enough evidence for any kind of official investigation. Nobody's been gone long enough yet to be officially missing. As far as we know, nobody's been harmed."

"So we're on our own?"

"Pretty much. At the moment, anyway."

Stephen walked in the back door, took stock of the council going on at the table, and pulled up a chair.

"Noggin?" Daniel asked.

"He'll pull through."

"Thank God for that." Daniel gave Cork a sharp look. "And don't tell me because it was just a dog there's nothing official to be done."

Cork didn't reply. He understood his son-in-law's frustration, which was, he knew, rooted in a very big, very reasonable seed of concern.

"I'll let Marsha know the situation," Cork said. "But we need to canvass the rez, relatives, friends of Sue and Phil, make sure they're really missing before we assume anything."

"Where's Bo?" Stephen asked.

Daniel said, "He told me he had some checking to do on his own. Didn't say what it was. I have his cell phone number, if we need to contact him."

"So once again," Jenny said, looking in the direction of her son, "what do we do?"

"For starters, I'm not letting either of you out of my sight," Daniel told her.

"I'm not sure that's such a good idea," Cork said.

Jenny smiled. "I kind of like it."

"If he's with you," Cork explained, "he's not going be able to get the answers he wants and that we need."

He watched as Daniel weighed the truth of this against the concern for his family's safety. "You have a suggestion?" Daniel asked.

"We get Jenny and Waaboo to a safe place."

"Where?"

"Maybe we could stay with Aunt Rose and Uncle Mal," Jenny suggested.

She was speaking of Cork's sister-in-law and her husband, who lived in Evanston, Illinois.

The idea didn't sit well with Cork. "That's a long way, and I wouldn't feel comfortable unless one of us went along with you. But I don't think we can spare anyone here."

"And they have a new baby," Daniel pointed out. "I'd hate to think we put them all in danger if trouble followed you."

It was Stephen who ended the silence of the next few moments. "Crow Point," he said. "With Henry."

CHAPTER 19

The cabin sat on a rise above an inlet of Iron Lake, isolated. Bo left his Jeep and unlocked the cabin door. There were no luxuries inside, but the place was well appointed, with a fine view of the lake from its small back deck. Bo took a beer from the refrigerator, stepped onto the deck, leaned against the cedar railing, and breathed deeply.

He was alone, a comfortable state of affairs. For most of his life, he'd been alone. Growing up, he'd spent time homeless, living for a while in an abandoned school bus in a copse of trees on the Mississippi River, within sight of downtown St. Paul. He'd been well on the road to juvenile detention and beyond that, probably, a life that would eventually lead to hard time in a real prison. He'd been saved by a woman, a judge in juvenile court, who'd seen something in him, an ember of goodness, which all the crap that had been piled on him couldn't smother. The road after that had led him into the army, then to college, and finally into the Secret Service, where he'd nearly been killed by an assassin's bullet intended for the wife of the president.

That incident had been a sensational story but one that, for many reasons, had compromised his career. When he left the Secret Service, he'd begun his own agency, a one-man enterprise. He'd never lacked for clients, most of whom were high-profile and demanded total discretion, their interests primarily political. He wasn't sure the juvenile judge would see the same ember of goodness in him now. He often found himself walking a difficult line, one he wasn't always certain of himself. He'd come to understand that there was weakness in even the stoutest of hearts, and that the smallest flaw could be used to crack the moral resolve of the best of human beings. He sipped his beer, drank in the beauty of Iron Lake, thought about the O'Connors and the mess they were in the middle of. And he hoped that what might be asked of him before this whole affair was over wouldn't require that he throw them to the wolves.

He heard the vehicle pull up, set his beer on the railing, and slid his Sig from the belt holster. He entered the cabin and took a position covering the front door. Nothing happened. He edged to the window. Outside, a man stood beside a black SUV, arms crossed.

Bo opened the door.

"Waiting for an invitation?" he called. "That's a new wrinkle."

Gerard approached the cabin porch and paused in the grass at the bottom of the three steps, eyeing the Sig in Bo's hand. "Just wanted to make sure I wasn't going to be shot. You haven't been particularly accommodating lately."

"When have you ever found me accommodating?" Bo holstered his sidearm. "Why the visit?"

"Do I get an invitation or not?"

Bo stepped aside. "Be my guest." Inside the cabin, he closed the door and said, "I was just having a beer. Care for one?"

"I'll pass." Gerard stood in the center of the cabin's living room, assessing the place. "Cozy."

"So," Bo said. "Why the visit?"

"Just wondering whether you're working for me or not."

"I'm doing what I'm being paid for."

"Not exactly an answer."

"The best you're going to get."

"You know how this works. You give me regular updates. You let me know what you know when you know it. I get irritable if I have to track you down to ask."

"Clearly you know where to find me."

Gerard reached into his shirt pocket and drew out a cigar. "Mind?"

"Let's take it outside."

They moved to the deck, where Gerard unwrapped and lit his cigar. As he smoked, he took in the view. "Who gave thee, O Beauty, the keys of this breast, too credulous lover of blest and unblest?"

Bo waited, knowing Gerard would tell him soon enough the source of that poetic line. Quoting poetry and smoking good cigars were two of Gerard's favorite indulgences.

"Ralph Waldo Emerson." Gerard blew smoke toward the sky. "All right, let's have it."

"The men who were first on the scene, most of them Ojibwe, are being hunted," Bo reported. "I don't know why or by whom."

"The black box?"

"They're actually orange now. And according to NTSB, there was no flight recorder on board."

Gerard ignored him, shook his head. "Someone thinks the Indians must have it."

"It was the Indians who searched the woods where the tail section of the plane broke off. So, yeah, maybe it's the flight recorder they're after. Or maybe it's something else."

"Like what?"

"I don't know."

"It's the black box, Thorson. It holds the answers."

"Why would the Indians be hanging on to it?"

"Leverage," Gerard suggested. "Isn't that what everyone wants in a negotiation?"

"Who would they use this leverage on?"

Gerard had no reply.

"If it is the flight recorder, and if, as you say, it holds the answers, and if I'm able to get it for you—a lot of ifs, by the way— what will the people you're working for do with those answers?"

"Not my concern. Or yours."

"Just keeping the lid on things, is that what they're paying you for?"

"That," Gerard said, "and making sure you stay in line."

Bo lifted the beer he was holding in a sign of peace. "No trouble here."

"Let's keep it that way."

"Did you get anything out of your interrogation of Stephen O'Connor?"

For a moment, surprise showed on Gerard's face, then the look vanished. He puffed on his cigar. "How'd you know about O'Connor?"

"Part of what I'm being paid for, knowing that kind of thing."

"Just a curious kid. I reminded him that curiosity killed the cat."

"A lesson I'm sure he took to heart," Bo said wryly.

Gerard ashed his cigar and scraped off the ember along the deck railing. He put what was left in his shirt pocket. "I want to hear from you regularly, understood?"

"I read you loud and clear, Colonel."

Gerard walked back through the cottage and out the front door. Bo remained on the deck, waiting for the sound of Gerard's SUV to fade into the distance. On the lake, just beyond the mouth of the inlet, a boat drifted past, a man trolling. Bo considered what he might really be fishing for. In his life now, he never assumed that anything was what it seemed.

He wondered, were Gerard's men the ones hunting the Indians, or was someone else involved in this game? He shook his head at that thought. It might be deadly, but that's what it was, a game. Like chess, only without the luxury of seeing the whole board or knowing all the players. NTSB. FBI. Gerard and his ghost command. Homeland Security? DoD? Maybe even NSA?

What Bo told Cork O'Connor had been the truth. The government he'd worked for as a member of the Secret Service had never been of one mind. It was, and clearly continued to be, a fractured, barely contained conglomerate of little kingdoms, at war with one another just as often as they were at war with the enemies who threatened. In this isolated county in the North Country, who knew what kind of battle might result and which innocents might be caught in the crossfire?

Bo finished his beer. The sun was dropping and there was still work to be done before the day ended.

CHAPTER 20

Cork held out the baggie into which he'd put the expended cartridge Daniel had found at the Hukaris' cabin. "Same MO as the Loves, Marsha. Shot dog, people missing."

The sheriff took the baggie and studied the contents. "Not a large caliber." She looked up. "How's the dog?"

"He'll make it."

"Any sign of struggle, resistance, a fight? Anything at all at the cabin besides the shot dog?"

"Nothing obvious."

"So it could still be that Sue Hukari was having difficulty with the pregnancy and Phil took her somewhere to be seen. And . . ." She eyed the spent cartridge. "Someone's got a jones on for shooting dogs in Tamarack County."

"Daniel checked at the clinic in Allouette and at the hospital here in town. They didn't show up at either place."

Dross set the baggie on her desktop. "I know it doesn't look good, Cork, but really, what do we have to go on? I need something more than shot dogs."

"I'm not asking you for help, Marsha. Just keeping you in the loop."

She walked to the window. The view beyond was one Cork knew intimately from his own tenure as sheriff: the park, Zion Lutheran Church, the businesses along Oak Street, everything festooned in the red and gold of autumn.

"Something's going on in our county, Cork, something big. I hate to admit it, but I'm feeling helpless against it. Alex Quaker paid me a visit just before you came."

"Should I know him?"

"The number two man with the National Security Branch."

"Which is?"

"Responsible for the FBI's Counterterrorism Division. A courtesy call, diplomatically letting me know that I wasn't to interfere or involve myself in any way with the investigation of Senator McCarthy's plane crash."

"Counterterrorism? So they think the crash wasn't caused by pilot error?"

"He didn't say that. His explanation was simply that in these unsettled times and with someone as highly placed as a U.S. senator, eliminating terrorism as a possibility is essential. He was sure I understood. I told him that we would cooperate in every way we could. To which he said, and I quote, 'Just stay out of our way.'" She turned back. "What I wanted to say to that imperious blowhard was, how would you like it if I invaded your backyard and told you to go screw yourself?"

"Stephen got hauled in this morning and interrogated by someone who wasn't FBI."

"Who?"

Cork related Stephen's story of the men searching the aspen grove on Desolation Mountain and of his questioning by the man called Gerard.

"Military?"

"Certainly military trained. And clearly with authority. But nothing to identify any specific branch."

The sheriff stared at the floor, thinking. "Ned and Monkey Love. Blessing. The Hukaris." She lifted her eyes. "Daniel's next, Cork."

"That's what we figured, too."

"What are you going to do?"

"Put Jenny and Waaboo in a safe place, so they're out of harm's way. That's already happening."

"Daniel's with them?"

Cork shook his head. "I need him with me."

"Risky."

"Maybe so, but he understands."

"Does Jenny?"

That was a question Cork left unanswered as he departed the Tamarack County Sheriff's Office. It was late afternoon, the shadows growing long. He drove a couple of miles out of town to Olson Field, where, in a previously empty hangar, the experts from NTSB continued their business of sorting through the debris from the crash, looking for answers.

Supposedly looking for answers, Cork thought. Because he'd come to understand that at this moment in Tamarack County nothing might be as it seemed. There was plenty of activity at the airfield, vehicles arriving, leaving, NTSB personnel perhaps, but hard to tell because nothing was identified except by government license plates. Cork parked near the airfield entrance and spent an hour writing down the vehicle plates as they passed.

He was just about to wrap up when his cell phone rang. As soon as he answered, he heard the terrified voice of Beulah Love on the other end.

"Someone's after me, Cork. Help me. Please."

———

She met him at the old Quonset hut, having kept to main, well-traveled roads, as he'd instructed over the phone. When he greeted her at the door, her face was ashen, her hands shaking.

"They're following me everywhere," she said without preamble.

"Sit down and tell me about it, Beulah. Can I get you something? Coffee?"

"Nothing, nothing," she said in a pitched voice. "Just get them off me."

"Sit down," he said again and pulled out a chair for her at the table. He sat, too, and leaned toward her. "I want to know everything. From the beginning."

"After you left this morning, I headed to work at the casino," she began. "The whole way I had the feeling I was being followed."

"You spotted a car?"

"No. Just a feeling. I told myself it was because I knew about Ned and Jameson and poor little Cyrus and I was being silly. But when I got to the casino, I spent a moment in my car, trying to pull myself together, and I saw this pickup truck drive in and park not far away. It just sat there. I finally got out and went into the casino. As soon as I was inside, I looked back through the glass doors. Two men got out of the truck and went to my car, Cork. Right to my car."

"Did they do anything to it?"

"Not while I was watching. They started toward the casino and I took off, hurried up to the office."

"Did they follow you into the casino?"

"I don't know. I thought they would, but I didn't see them. Like I said, I went straight to the office. But I couldn't work. I couldn't concentrate. So I left early. The pickup wasn't there anymore."

"Where'd you go?"

"To church to practice on the organ. I hoped it might settle my spirit. But they followed me there."

"You saw them?"

"After I parked and went inside, I looked out the front window, just to be sure. The pickup drove past."

"The same vehicle, you're certain?"

"It looked the same, big and black."

"Did it stop?"

"Just drove past. I kept watching, but it didn't come back. I was scared, so I didn't stay at the church. I started home, but I stopped at the IGA to pick up a few things first. When I got inside the store, I checked the parking lot, and within a minute, that black pickup was there, parked a couple rows away. That's when I called you."

"What did these men look like?"

Her eyes went distant as she concentrated. Then she shook her head. "Just men."

"How were they dressed?"

She looked down at her hands, which had stopped shaking. "Jeans," she said vaguely. "Flannel shirts. Down vests."

Which could have described half the male population in Tamarack County.

"White, not Native?"

"Yes."

"Did you see any firearms?"

She hesitated. "No. But that doesn't mean they weren't going to hurt me."

"You're safe now, Beulah. Coming to me was a good move."

"Who are they, Cork? What do they want with me?"

"I can't tell you who they are yet. But I think they're looking for something they believe Ned or Jameson might have. Because you're family, I think they're surveilling you, hoping your brother or nephew might try to contact you."

"What can I do? Where do I go? I don't want to be alone."

"Is there someone on the rez you can stay with?"

Her eyes wandered the room. She looked back at Cork, clearly at a loss. The boarding school experience had killed the Indian in her, and she'd burned too many bridges on the rez. Ned and Jameson were her closest kin. She had nowhere to go.

"Let me make a couple of calls," Cork told her. "Are you hungry? Would you like something to eat?"

She gave him a silent nod.

"How about a Waaboo Burger?" To her blank look, he said, "A bison burger. It's good."

In Sam's Place up front, he gave Judy Madsen the order. Judy had been with Cork forever, and she sometimes stepped in to manage when none of the O'Connors were available. "Getting low on the bison patties," she informed him. "That Waaboo Burger's a winner. Will you or Stephen or Jenny be working tonight, or should I bring in some other help?"

They settled things, and Cork returned to Beulah and made a phone call to Sarah LeDuc.

"I have a favor to ask." He explained the situation. When he'd finished, he turned to Beulah. "I'm going to take you back to Allouette, but you won't be alone there. Sarah has agreed that you can stay with her."

Beulah looked even more concerned. "Won't that put her in danger?"

"I don't think you're actually in any danger, Beulah. They're just watching you, hoping to catch Ned and Jameson."

"What if I hear from Ned?"

"Let me know. But don't try to meet him or Jameson anywhere, okay?"

She needed no convincing.

Outside in the parking lot, Cork did a cursory check of Beulah's car, looking for a tracking device the men might have planted. He found nothing obvious but knew that didn't necessarily mean the car was clean. He led the way out of Aurora, Beulah following. He watched the road behind, keeping an eye out for the black pickup, or any other vehicle that might be tailing them. He was pretty certain that despite his best efforts, whoever it was tracking Beulah would know where she'd gone. What he'd told her was what he believed to be true, that she herself was no immediate danger. She would only be in trouble if she had contact with Ned or Monkey.

In Allouette, they parked in front of the Mocha Moose. The coffee shop closed at two every afternoon, but Sarah was waiting and she opened up for Beulah. "*Boozhoo,*" she said in greeting.

"Thank you," Beulah replied, almost in tears. "Thank you, Sarah."

Cork stood in the doorway. "If you have any concerns at all, call me. I mean immediately, Sarah."

"I've got this, Cork." Sarah gestured toward the outside world. "Go do whatever you have to do."

He left the two women, knowing they would go to the living area above the coffee shop, which Sarah had occupied alone ever since her husband was murdered. This thought caused Cork's mind to leap back to the memory of his first wife, Jo, whose death had been caused by the same men who'd killed George LeDuc. For a moment, everything inside him tensed, and he was suddenly uncertain in his belief that Sarah and Beulah weren't in any real danger. How could he know that for sure?

On the other side of Manomin Street, the main route through Allouette, was the little gallery where Harmon Goodsky showed his photographs and those of other Native artists. Cork crossed the street and entered the gallery. A small bell above the door rang, but no one came forward immediately. Then a young man stepped from behind the curtains across a doorway that led to the back area of the gallery.

"*Anin*, Winston," Cork said in greeting.

Winston Goodsky, Harmon's grandson, was fourteen years old, willowy in the way of youths. He was a shy boy, one who didn't often lift his gaze from the floor. In his hand, he carried a framed photograph.

"*Anin*, Mr. O'Connor," the boy replied, studying the wood planks at Cork's feet.

"Is your granddad around?"

"In back. In the darkroom."

Goodsky was a photographer of the old school. He still used film in all his work.

"What do you have there?" Cork asked, indicating the photograph the boy held.

"Nothing." The boy hid the framed photo behind his back.

"Nothing?" Goodsky limped in from the back room. Although he towered over his grandson, he was still bent, resembling an old tree about to fall.

Like many Native children, Winston was being raised by a relative, not his parents. His father was in prison, his mother long dead from a drug overdose. Harmon Goodsky was his legal guardian. Cork knew that with the cancer eating him up inside, Goodsky worried about what would happen to Winston when he was gone. There were other relatives, but Social Services was bound to step in, and who knew what might be the final determination and in whose hands Winston might end up. If it was foster care, then Cork knew Goodsky had every right to be gravely concerned.

"Show him your work, Winston."

Without lifting his eyes, the boy offered up the photograph, a lovely shot of a single aspen leaf fallen on the ground. The leaf was gold-orange, the color of a ripe peach, cut evenly by deep veins, and framed dramatically by the dark soil beneath it. Cork had seen this leaf a million times across decades of autumns, but the photograph made him realize that he'd never taken the time to look closely, to appreciate fully the beauty in that simple image.

"I try to get him to use a good thirty-five-millimeter, like my Nikon, but he's all into digital," Goodsky said.

"It's a great picture, Winston." Cork handed it back.

"And we're going to put it up." Goodsky took the photograph from his grandson's hand, walked to an emptied place on the wall, and hung it. "There, right next to some of my best work."

"It's not as good as yours," the boy said quietly.

"It's promising," his grandfather said. "And it'll sell, mark my words. Something you need, Cork?"

Cork glanced at Winston. "Could we talk in private?"

"How about you start us some dinner?" Goodsky said to his grandson. "There's leftover meat loaf and some scalloped potatoes that can be heated up. Maybe a can of peas along with it."

The boy disappeared through the curtains. Cork heard his steps as he climbed the stairway to the second floor, where he and his grandfather lived.

"So, what's up?" Goodsky asked.

"Some trouble. Beulah Love is staying across the street with Sarah. Somebody's been following her and she's scared."

Goodsky scowled. "Following her? Who?"

"Don't know that yet."

"Why would anyone follow Beulah? You're sure she's not imagining things?"

"I think it has something to do with Ned and Monkey, some people who are trying to track them down."

"Why would anyone be after Ned and Monkey?"

"Again, I'm not sure. But I think Beulah isn't imagining things."

"What do you want from me?"

"Keep an eye on Sarah's place. If you see anything that seems odd, strangers hanging around maybe, give me a call. Will you do that?"

"That's it? Why don't I just go over and take care of them myself?"

Before the cancer began chewing him alive, Goodsky could have handled almost anyone, even a couple of anyones. Cork wasn't sure what Goodsky was or wasn't capable of now.

"Think of me as backup, Harmon. Give me a call and wait. We'll handle it together. Okay?"

"Sure," Goodsky said.

But Cork wasn't at all certain he meant it. "Before you do anything rash and get yourself into trouble, think about Winston."

Goodsky glanced up, where the sound of his grandson's footsteps moved across the floorboards. "Yeah," he agreed soberly.

From the gallery, Cork walked two blocks to the tribal clinic, where he found that Rainy had already left for the day. A few minutes later, as he stood on Manomin Street, which was empty, he remembered the dream Waaboo had related to him that morning, his nightmare about a monster with lots of heads. Which was precisely the way Bo Thorson had described the government, a many-headed Hydra. He considered all the elements at large in Tamarack County, all the agencies named and unnamed, and he wondered if Waaboo, like Stephen, saw things that others could not.

CHAPTER 21

Cork spent over an hour knocking on doors in Allouette, asking friends and relatives of Sue and Phil Hukari if they'd seen the couple that day. He'd spread the word about the shooting of Noggin. Most had already heard about Fanny Blessing. Because he had no answers, only questions, he worked at keeping things calm—his demeanor, his approach, his vague explanations. He decided to say nothing yet about Ned or Monkey Love, or about Cyrus staring dead-eyed up at him from the bottom of Little Bass Lake. For the moment, simpler was better and probably scary enough.

He headed out of Allouette after the sun had set but while the sky was still red, his mind hard at work, trying to find a thread that, if he pulled it, might help unravel the knot of troubling occurrences since the senator's plane went down. He wasn't focused on his own current situation, and the vehicle in his rearview mirror, when he finally became aware of it, was already closing on him.

Because it was dusk, he'd turned on the headlights of Stephen's Jeep. The vehicle fast approaching from behind was running without lights. Cork hit the accelerator, but the Jeep was old and hadn't been made for speed. The SUV—he could see that it was big and black, with tinted windows—continued to gain. A couple of hundred yards ahead of him glowed the taillights of a slower-moving vehicle. Although he knew he might be paranoid—not without good reason—he thought he was about to be put in a squeeze play.

He'd driven that road a thousand times and knew every twist and turn. His mind raced, visualizing what was ahead. The red embers of the taillights in front of him disappeared around the first curve of an *S* in the road. Cork flicked off his headlights and put the accelerator to the floor. He careened around the curve, just in time to see the taillights ahead of him move into the second curl of the *S*. For the next ten seconds, because of the thick woods along the first curve, he would be invisible to the SUV behind him. He hit the brakes and swung onto the gravel access to Wolf Point on Iron Lake. There were no signs for the turnoff. If you didn't know the road, you'd never see it coming. He shot up the first hundred yards, then slowed down. Dark was gathering and speed was a risk. Another hundred yards and he came abreast of the ruins of an old bait shop on a small inlet. He pulled off the road opposite the dilapidated shack, maneuvered the Jeep deep into the trees, and killed the engine. The descending dark was silent all around him, and he waited.

A few minutes later they came, two vehicles moving slowly, tires growling over the gravel, headlights stark and glaring. They approached the old bait shop, shone spotlights on the gray, flaking wood, the glassless windows, the sagging porch. They moved on toward the end of the point, another quarter of a mile west.

Cork considered hightailing it. He could probably be back on asphalt before they were able to swing around in quick pursuit. But he wasn't sure he could outrun them in the old Jeep. He continued to sit and wait.

They returned, their spotlights probing the woods with long white fingers as they crept along. The lights played across the Jeep.

Cork held his breath, hoping the scratched, dull green paint and the dried mud and dust that coated it would camouflage the old heap. The vehicles moved on.

His cell phone rang, and it made him jump.

"Where are you, Cork?" Daniel said on the other end.

"Hiding at the moment."

"Where? Who from?"

"Out on Wolf Point. And I don't know who from. Where are you?"

"At Uncle Henry's. We're all here."

"Rainy, too?"

"Yes."

"I'll come as soon as I can."

"Do you need help?"

By the time Daniel or anyone else reached him, Cork knew it would be too late. "I've got this."

After ten minutes, he eased the Jeep back onto the gravel access and drove to the main road. Both directions, the asphalt tunneled into the empty murk of descending night. He eased back onto the road.

He'd gone less than a mile when the SUV pulled out of the woods ahead and blocked his way. He slammed on the brakes, planning a desperate U-turn, but behind him, the second vehicle cut off any escape. He never carried a firearm, though this was one of those times he wished he did. There was nothing for him to do but sit and see how this played out.

Two men exited the SUV, both dressed in the kind of military fatigues worn by the searchers in the aspens on Desolation Mountain. They walked toward Cork, blinking into the glare from the Jeep's headlights. One was tall, older, craggy, with a silver crew cut, the other much younger, female, with a face set in an expression of iron grimness and a rifle in her hands. Cork lowered his window.

"I warned you already, O'Connor," the craggy one said while

the headlights still blinded him. Then he saw who was behind the wheel. "Who the hell are you?"

"Not the O'Connor you think, Gerard."

"All right, out of the Jeep."

"Not until I see some identification."

Gerard squinted, his face pinched and impatient. "Craig," he said to the woman with him. "Show this man some ID."

The grim blonde in camo lifted the rifle she carried and aimed it at Cork.

"Is that ID enough?" Gerard asked.

"You'd really shoot me?"

"You have three seconds to find out."

Cork opened the door and stepped from the Jeep.

"Who are you?" Gerard asked again.

"Cork O'Connor. You spoke to my son this morning."

Gerard looked past him at Stephen's Jeep. "What were you doing at Olson Field this afternoon?"

"Chalk it up to curiosity. A lot going on around here."

"What's your interest in Beulah Love?"

"I'm interested in her safety. And I'd like to know what's become of her brother and nephew. And while I'm at it, I'd like to know the same about Phil and Sue Hukari. I don't suppose you could enlighten me?"

Gerard studied him. "You were at the site where Senator McCarthy's plane went down. You and your son both. You were a part of the early search."

"Others were there earlier."

"You were with the Indians going over the woods."

"I was one of the Indians going over the woods."

"You're not Indian."

"Because I'm not wearing a headdress and feathers? *Anishinaabe indaaw.*"

The man's eyes were steely, as if he believed Cork was taunting him.

"In the language of my people, that means 'I am Anishinaabe.'"

Gerard made a sound in his throat, a dismissive grunt.

"What is it that everyone is looking for in Tamarack County, Gerard? What is it that you all believe one of us has taken? The black box?"

"There is no black box."

"Then tell me what it is."

"The only thing I'm going to tell you is this: Keep out of our way. I have the power and the authority to see that you're put somewhere you won't like."

"Authority granted by whom?"

"Are you a patriot, O'Connor?"

"I'm an American citizen and proud of that."

"Proud of being a Redskin, too, I suppose," Craig said.

Gerard's head swung around and he snapped, "That's enough, Lieutenant." He looked at Cork again. "Are you a hunter? Of course you are. Every man up here is a hunter. You're after what? Deer? Bear? Grouse? Pretty easy to know what you're shooting at. Me, I'm a hunter of the enemies of our democracy. They are many, O'Connor, and they often look just like you and me. Separating the good guys from the bad isn't such an easy job." He paused, and Cork thought he might go on with his lecture. Instead he said simply, "You're free to go." He signaled the black SUV, and it backed onto the shoulder, clearing the road.

Cork grabbed the Jeep's door handle, but before he got in, he said, "To a man who's really hunting the truth, guys up here like me could be a big help."

"Good night, O'Connor. And a last warning, to you and your son and your friends. Stay out of our way."

As he passed the SUV, Cork tried to get a look at the license plate, but the darkness made this impossible. He kept an eye on the rearview mirror, uncertain if Gerard's dismissal was for real. He couldn't read the man. Which served to drive home Gerard's point about knowing the good guys from the bad. In Tamarack County, that was becoming next to impossible.

CHAPTER 22

Trixie had settled herself comfortably in a corner of Henry Meloux's cabin, which was the spot all of Henry's dogs had claimed for themselves over the years. Henry's last dog, an old Irish setter named Ember, had died quietly a few weeks earlier, and the Mide had decided that was enough. He joked that the next thing he would deliver into Mother Earth's waiting arms was his own body.

"*Mishomis*," Waaboo said, addressing the old man respectfully, using the Ojibwe word for grandfather. "Baa-baa says that you were a warrior. Did you ever fight white people?"

The child sat at the table in Henry's cabin, along with Stephen and the old man. Jenny and Rainy and Leah Duling were absent at the moment, preparing Leah's cabin to shelter this sudden influx of visitors. Stephen smiled at the innocence of his nephew's question.

"Fight them how?" the old man asked. Henry carved on a stick, his old hands working skillfully, shaking not at all.

"You know. Shoot them with arrows." The boy pointed toward a bow that hung on the wall.

"I never used it to kill anything that walks on two legs," the old man told him.

"Did you use that?" This time the boy pointed toward an old Winchester mounted near the bow.

"Not that either. When I have found it necessary to fight white people, I have used this." The old man pointed at his head. "It has always served me better than any weapon."

"My dad uses a gun."

"He carries a gun," Stephen clarified. "He's never had to use it against anyone, Waaboo."

"What if someone wanted to hurt him? Or Mommy? Or you?"

"I hope that's a bridge he never has to cross."

It was a phrase Waaboo clearly didn't understand and he looked at his uncle with confusion.

"I have something for you, Waaboozoons." Meloux handed the boy the stick he'd been carving.

"A whistle," Waaboo said with delight. "*Migwech, Mishomis.*"

"Not a whistle. A flute."

"What's the difference?"

"A whistle makes noise. A flute makes music."

Waaboo put the little instrument to his mouth and blew, his fingers dancing over the holes, which made Stephen smile. It wasn't music, but neither was it just noise.

"Why don't you show the flute to your mom?" he suggested.

Waaboo was out the door and running through the dark toward Leah's cabin. Stephen shut the door behind him.

"Before the night is out, you might be sorry you gave him that gift, Henry."

The air smelled of the stew simmering on the stove in the middle of the cabin. Leah had prepared enough for them all, if they ate moderately. Stephen wasn't comfortable barging in this way.

"*Migwech,* Henry," he said, his heart full of gratitude. "For taking us in."

"We will fast tonight, you and me," the old man told him. "Tomorrow, we will sweat."

The door opened, and Daniel stepped in with an armload of split firewood. Because of the dark, he wore a headlamp. He restocked the wood box near the stove and turned off the lamp. "I just spoke with Cork."

"Where is he?" Stephen asked.

"Hiding on Wolf Point."

Stephen went rigid. "Who from?"

"He doesn't know."

"We need to go." Stephen was up and moving toward the door.

"He said he could handle it."

"I'm going." Stephen reached for the latch.

"Patience, Stephen O'Connor," Henry said at his back.

"My father's in trouble."

"Your father is hiding. That is one way to avoid trouble."

"What if they find him?"

"He has said he can handle it. Do you trust him or not?"

Stephen stood with his hand on the door latch, torn.

"Wolf Point is far away. Whatever happens there, it will happen long before you arrive."

Stephen lowered his hand. The door opened, and the others came in from the dark. Rainy looked from Stephen to Daniel and finally to her great-uncle Henry. "What's wrong?"

Daniel explained.

"I should go," Stephen told her.

She replied calmly, "Cork said he could handle it."

"What if he's wrong?" Stephen reached again for the door latch.

"If you're bound and determined, we'll go together," Daniel said. "Henry, that old Winchester on the wall, is it in working order?"

"It will do what a rifle does."

"Aunt Rainy?" Daniel said.

She nodded. "I know how to use it, if it comes to that."

Jenny put her hand on Daniel's cheek. "Be careful. Dad wouldn't want you to do anything that will get you hurt. I don't want that either." She hugged him, then Stephen. "Take care of each other."

They moved quickly down the path through the forest, away from Crow Point. Trixie trotted ahead. It was little Waaboo who'd insisted the dog go with them.

"He smells monsters," the boy had assured them.

"Monsters, maybe," Meloux had said. "But also other things a man might not sense. A dog is always good protection on a hunt."

And so the old dog was at their side.

The sky was filled with stars, the moon on the rise but not high enough yet to illuminate the landscape. Daniel's headlamp lit the way. Stephen had always felt a comfort in these woods, but now they seemed to hold only menace. Anything might come at them from the dark, and he was glad to have Trixie along.

He had always wanted to be Mide, like Henry, like Rainy. A healer. A person who understood *ninoododawdiwin,* which was harmony, who lived in the way of *bimaadiziwin,* which was the good life. But since he'd first had the vision of him and the boy and the falling eagle, he'd felt unbalanced, lost. Maybe even unworthy, because although he could usually see the right path with his mind, he hadn't always been able to follow it. Like right now. His father said he could handle the situation on Wolf Point. Henry had counseled patience. And yet there he was, rushing headlong toward a situation he didn't fully understand, dragging Daniel with him.

"You didn't have to come."

"Right back at you," Daniel replied.

"If it was you hiding on Wolf Point, I'd be coming to help."

"Not if I thought I could handle it."

"Why didn't you let me go alone, then?"

"Your dad, when he says he can handle something, knows what he's talking about. You're a good man, Stephen, but you've still got a lot to learn."

"Just because I've never worn a badge?"

Daniel stopped and turned to him. The glare of the headlamp was blinding for a moment, and Stephen lifted his hand to block the light.

"You're not your father and you're not me and you never will be. You aren't *ogichidaa*. You aren't a warrior. You need to be okay with that. You have something Cork and I will never have, and it makes you a kind of man Cork and I will never be. You are *Mide*. Like Uncle Henry."

"He was a warrior once."

"Don't try to be Uncle Henry either."

Daniel continued down the dark path, where Trixie had paused, waiting for them. Stephen followed, twisted inside. But Daniel wasn't the target of his anger. It was Stephen himself. If he'd understood the vision in time, he might have been able to do something to prevent all this upheaval. If he'd understood his earlier visions, maybe his mother would still be alive. Maybe he wouldn't have let a madman put a bullet in his back. Maybe, if he was a little less who he was and a little more like his father and Daniel and even Henry, everything would be different.

Just as they reached the road and the place near the double-trunk birch where they'd parked their vehicles, Daniel's phone rang.

"It's your father." Daniel answered the call. "I'm here, Cork." He listened. "Stephen and I have left Crow Point. Do you want us to meet you somewhere?" He studied the stars. "All right. We're on our way."

He put the phone in his shirt pocket. "Your dad's fine. He wants us to meet him at the house. He's going to try to get Bo Thorson there, too. A little strategizing."

Stephen drove his father's Expedition. Trixie lay on the backseat, tired from the long walk. Daniel led the way, with Stephen following the red eyes of the pickup's taillights. The road to Aurora was a familiar one, but Stephen found himself scanning the dark on either side, wondering what great evil might, even at that moment, be watching him.

CHAPTER 23

Bo Thorson had been in love, deeply in love, only once in his life. She had been married. More than that, her husband had been the president of the United States. When he saved her life, he understood—they both understood—that they were bound in a deeper way than duty would allow. For both of them, duty dictated separate paths. Bo had found that the heart, once pierced, never fully heals. Sometimes when he was alone on surveillance, as he was now, he imagined a different life, a different duty, a different path. For himself and for her.

He was on a small island in Iron Lake, a hundred yards offshore. The sky was a black plate sugared with stars, the moon still below the treetops. He had a powerful set of ATN night-vision binoculars to his eyes, watching the lodge where Gerard had set up the headquarters for his operation. Much earlier, he'd placed a listening device the size of a postage stamp on the window glass. Gerard wasn't a bad strategist when he believed he was on the offensive, and in Tamarack County, he'd pretty much been bullying his way around. Which meant he probably wasn't watching his back as he should.

The big room with its maps and charts was unoccupied. Gerard had a man posted for security, a young guy who circled the lodge every few minutes on a regular schedule. Rookie mistake, one that had allowed Bo the brief interval he'd needed for placing the bug on the window.

He hadn't figured the truth of Gerard's involvement yet. Nor had he figured exactly who the other players might be. One thing was certain: Gerard believed the crash of Senator McCarthy's plane wasn't the result of pilot error. Who caused it and how were probably what Gerard's presence was all about. He'd brought Bo in, he'd said, to help identify the other interests in this affair. But Bo knew that he'd been told only half-truths, Gerard's modus operandi. Bo, for his part, had responded in kind.

In the period of waiting for something to develop at the lodge, Bo considered the past, the path of his life. He had no real family. He had cultivated many allies but few true friends. He lived alone in a condo high in a building in downtown St. Paul with a view of the Mississippi River, but he was seldom in residence there. More often, he was on a job that took him far from Minnesota.

He considered Cork O'Connor, a man who had built a life in one place and invested his heart in the people there. It was enticing, that comfortable, intimate existence, isolated from the world. Bo tried to imagine what it might have been like for him, had he made other choices. But that wasn't who he was, or who he was ever likely to be. The kind of life Cork led, if it was threatened, became a dangerous entanglement. Once your heart was involved in life-and-death choices, you were vulnerable. Your heart got in the way of your head, clouded your judgment. It was a lesson Bo had learned the hard way. He liked Cork, liked that part of the family he'd met, but he kept the door shut on his heart. In the end, he needed to be prepared to sacrifice Cork. To sacrifice them all, if necessary.

His cell phone vibrated. He checked caller ID. It was O'Connor.

"We need to talk, figure a few things out. Can you meet me?"

"Where?"

"At my house on Gooseberry Lane."

Cork gave directions, although Bo knew the address. When the call ended, he placed the receiver-recorder, which was tuned to the bug on the window, at the base of a pine tree and covered it with needles. He returned to the inflatable kayak he'd come in and paddled a quarter mile to an empty point where he'd parked. He deflated the kayak and stored it in the back of the Jeep. In another ten minutes, he was turning onto Gooseberry Lane.

Before knocking on the door, he stood in the front yard a few minutes, assessing the scene. It was a nice two-story house, with a lovely porch where a swing hung, the kind of house that Bo, when he was a kid living in ratty one-bedroom apartments with his drunken mother, had dreamed of having. But there was no resentment in him. No envy either. A man's life was what it was.

Cork greeted him when he knocked. They went to the kitchen, where Stephen was sitting at the table, along with Daniel English. In the middle of the table sat a cookie jar shaped like Ernie from *Sesame Street*. Stephen munched on a chocolate chip cookie. English sipped from a cup of coffee. To Bo, it felt more like a family council than a war council.

"Have a seat," Cork said. "Can I get you something?"

"Nothing, thanks."

"Where is everybody?" Bo asked, because it was evident that the house was empty.

"We thought it best to move them someplace safe, so they can't be used as leverage against Daniel," Cork explained.

"A good idea," Bo agreed. "Where are they?"

"Safe," Cork said.

Bo held back a smile. Cork was more careful than he'd imagined.

"I just came from a meeting with Gerard," Cork told him. "The man who questioned Stephen this morning."

Bo let nothing show on his face. "How did that come about?"

Cork explained the encounter, then held out a small transmitter. "I found it under the dash of the Jeep after they let me go. Gerard's people must have put it there when they questioned Stephen this morning."

"This Gerard," Bo said. "Think he's in charge of whatever's going on?"

"Here, anyway. Who knows who's pulling the strings and from where?"

"What strings, do you think?"

Cork eyed him frankly. "I thought you might have a better idea than we do. These people who hired you, they didn't give you any information to go on?"

"Just their concerns."

"Family?"

"I can't say, you know that."

"People on the rez, friends of mine, are missing. At this point, they may even be dead. Bo, this has gone way beyond professional courtesies."

"All right." Bo reached into Ernie's head and pulled out a chocolate chip cookie, clearly homemade. He couldn't remember the last time he'd had a homemade cookie of any kind. He took a bite and chewed while he considered what to tell them. "NTSB will continue to put out the story of pilot error. It's the safest explanation for the general public. But as this Gerard hinted to Stephen, there may be other forces involved."

"Terrorists," Stephen offered. "That's pretty much what Gerard said."

"Why would terrorists want to take down Senator McCarthy's plane?" English asked.

"Don't let Gerard or anyone like him fool you," Bo said. "This terrorist thing may be just one of the cover stories."

"You have a better idea?" Cork said.

Bo did have an idea, though not as solid as Cork might be hoping. "Senator McCarthy sits on the Foreign Relations Committee. She's the staunchest opponent of the proposed Manila Accord, which comes up for debate in the Senate in a couple of weeks. If it's passed, it not only makes trade with Southeast Asia easier but also provides for the sale of significant military hardware, much of it to regimes with horrible human rights records. One of the senator's main concerns was the arms part of the accord. She was adamant that we shouldn't try to buy friends with bullets or ignore atrocities because it's convenient for our economic and political interests. One of the inside pieces of information I was given by those who hired me is this: Senator McCarthy had been briefed on threats to her life. It's possible some of those threats came from one of the nations that would benefit from the accord."

"I haven't heard anything about that on the news coverage," Cork said.

"They're probably trying to keep a lid on that."

"Who's they?"

"NSA is the first agency that comes to mind, although I can't say for sure."

"Gerard is NSA?"

"Your guess is as good as mine." The first real lie Bo had told them. "But it would make sense that the government wouldn't want the possibility floated out there that a country we're going to call an ally has assassinated a U.S. senator. That would put an end to any hope of Senate approval."

"You're really saying it might have been agents from the Philippines or Thailand or Indonesia?" Cork said.

"You asked what I thought was really going on. That's my best shot at the moment. If you have a better idea, let's hear it."

The others were sitting back in their chairs. It was as if news of this magnitude had knocked the wind out of them. Geopolitical conflicts intruding on their quiet lives in such a huge and unexpected way. *Foreign agents?* their faces said. *Really?*

"However," Bo went on, offering a nugget of truth, "there are so many interests affected by the Manila Accord that God only knows who might actually be at work here. It doesn't matter who that is, it's in the government's best interest to continue the drumbeat of their story of pilot error. They understand that if you repeat a lie often enough, eventually the public is going to accept it as truth."

"What about the media?" English tossed in. "Newspapers, television. If they got wind of foreign involvement, they'd scream to high heaven."

"Maybe."

"I'd be happy to repeat publicly what Gerard said to me," Stephen said.

"And what, exactly, did Gerard tell you? Did he actually say anything about terrorists?"

"Alex Quaker paid a visit to our sheriff today," Cork said. "The number two man in the FBI's National Security Branch. They oversee the Bureau's Counterterrorism Division."

Bo offered a shrug. "Easily explained. In this day and age, with an accident that kills someone of Senator McCarthy's stature, it's important to eliminate terrorism as a possibility. And they will, mark my words. As long as this is in the news, pilot error will be the constant refrain."

"How do you sort any of this out?" Stephen sounded overwhelmed.

"Exactly." Bo looked to Cork. "Any more word on the reservation about the folks who've disappeared?"

"Nothing."

"That's a place to keep poking."

"We will. What about you?"

"I have a resource I haven't tapped yet but I think it's time."

They waited for him to explain further.

"Sorry," he told them. "Confidential." It was getting late. It had been a long day. Bo could feel the weariness in them all. "Let's call it for tonight and get some rest. It's hard to think clearly when you're tired."

"We're going to do a sweat tomorrow," Stephen said.

"A sweat? You mean like in a sweat lodge?"

"You might find it interesting."

"Is that an invitation to join you?"

"If you'd like."

"Think I'll pass."

Stephen said, "It clears your mind and your spirit. It might help with your thinking."

"My thinking is fine, thanks. But let me know if it helps with yours." Bo stood. "Thanks for the cookie."

"Where are you staying?" English asked.

"The cabin of a friend."

"We know this friend?"

"Confidential. If that sweat clears your thinking, Stephen, and we need to talk, let me know. And remember, Cork, just because you found the transmitter and removed it, that doesn't mean you're not still being tracked somehow, so be careful. Good night, gentlemen."

He left them at the kitchen table and returned to the night. He drove around the block, parked, and walked back to Gooseberry Lane. If he'd known about the transmitter, about Gerard's interest in the O'Connors, he wouldn't have agreed to meet with them. He studied the street. There were only a couple of vehicles parked along the curb. The one that interested him, a black pickup, was half a block from the O'Connors' house, out of the glow of any streetlamp.

Gerard's people? Whoever they were, if they didn't know before that he was working with O'Connor, they knew it now.

CHAPTER 24

He watches the boy on the steep rise above him. He is that boy and he is not.

The vision played out as it always had: the eagle appearing; the boy shooting it from the sky; the egg and the eagle falling; something huge looming at Stephen's back, so monstrous that he can't look. He and the boy screaming bloody murder.

He woke in the quiet of night, rose from his bed, and walked to the window. Bright moonlight illuminated the landscape, silvering the front yard, making the empty street the color of winter ice.

It wasn't over. He understood this was what the vision was trying to tell him. It wasn't over. Maybe there was still a chance to . . . to what? He lay his forehead against the cool glass of the windowpane. *There must be a way to know*, he thought. *Maybe the sweat.*

He was too restless to go back to bed and stepped into the hallway. The house stood silent all around him, his father and Daniel asleep. He waited for Trixie to come trotting from somewhere. She may have been old, but Trixie still heard everything. When she didn't show, Stephen moved to the top of the stairs. Moon glow through the front door window lit the bottom landing in a ghostly way. He expected to see the dog there, waiting for him to come down, but the landing was empty. He descended, telling himself she was just deep in the slumber of an aged hound. Which was his head talking to him. His gut told him something different, reminding him of the fate of Cyrus and Noggin.

He stood on the carpet of the living room and called, "Trixie," in a hushed voice. "Come here, girl."

He crossed to the kitchen. During the day, Trixie's usual resting place was the corner in the kitchen nearest her food dish. The dog wasn't there. He turned back and stepped on shattered glass. It didn't cut him, but it made him stop dead in his tracks. He saw that one of the panes in the mullioned window had been broken. He walked carefully to the door and tried the knob. It was no longer locked, and he understood that someone who didn't belong there was inside the house.

He listened carefully but heard only his own soft, fast breathing. Gingerly, he stepped around the broken glass and into the dining room. A long, translucent drape was drawn over the patio doors, and against the sheer fabric, the moon cast two shadows, human in shape but exaggerated into things monstrously huge. For a moment, Stephen was unable to move. It wasn't just uncertainty that paralyzed him. It was also fear. The kind of fear that, in his nightmare, kept him from turning to look at the monster at his back. The shadows moved across the drape and disappeared. Stephen forced himself to the patio doors. Hesitated another long moment, and finally pulled the drape aside. The silver eye of the moon stared down at him. The patio was empty.

He crept through the first floor of the house, checking it room by room. He quietly mounted the stairs to his father's bedroom. His father's bed was empty. The squeal of the screen door hinge and the click of the front door handle as it was turned brought him to the top of the stairs, where he caught a glimpse below of someone stealing into the living room. He darted to his bedroom closet, grabbed the Louisville Slugger his father had given him on his twelfth birthday, gripped it with determination, and descended to the first floor. Whoever it was in the house now had moved into the dark of the kitchen. Stephen heard a drawer opened, wood scraping softly along wood. He clutched the bat as he had when he'd played Little League and had bent over the plate, waiting for a pitch. He eased into the kitchen doorway.

"You heard him, too," his father said.

Trixie came trotting, tail wagging, and Stephen lowered the bat. "Where were you?"

"Outside." It was Daniel who answered. Stephen saw him then, near the window above the sink, peering out into the dark.

"Both of you?" Stephen wondered why he hadn't been included.

"Trixie was sleeping in my room," his father said, rummaging in the drawer. "She woke me up with a woof. Daniel was already awake."

"Couldn't sleep," Daniel explained. "Worried about Jenny and Waaboo."

His father closed the drawer, flashlight in his hand. "We both came down to check on things. Someone tried to break in through the back door. We spooked him. He's gone now."

"You saw him?"

His father shook his head. "Got a glimpse of him, but he ran. We followed him to the street, saw a truck down the block pull away. Probably him."

"Who do you think it was?"

"No idea."

Stephen looked at Daniel. "Someone coming for you?"

"Maybe."

"I think that's all the excitement we'll see," Cork said. "I'm going to sweep up that broken glass and hang out down here tonight with Trixie. You two try to get some sleep."

But Stephen lay in his bed, staring up at the ceiling, searching for answers that, like sleep that night, continued to elude him. Along with everything else that troubled him, he wondered why his father and Daniel had gone after the mysterious visitor without him. Did they think he couldn't handle a violent confrontation, if it came to that? In the long hours of dark, he was tortured with doubt, asking himself, *What kind of man do they think I am?* He searched his heart and wondered, *What kind of man am I?*

In his cabin, Bo listened to the conversations the transmitter had picked up in the little war room Gerard had established at the abandoned lodge. There was nothing of substance, mostly Gerard talking with subordinates about the search on Desolation Mountain. They referred to the object of their search in code: bear tracks. As in "We didn't find the bear tracks, sir." And, "Maybe there aren't any bear tracks on the mountain. Maybe the bear tracks are somewhere else." They decided to abandon the search on the mountain and concentrate on something they called the "beach." As in, "Let's hit the beach and see if we can find any evidence of waves."

Bo had himself been a part of covert operations before and knew that this kind of veiled reference was meat and potatoes in any black-ops conversation. Part of the game.

It was late when he finally laid himself out in his bunk. He wasn't sure where the long day had gotten him. Things had only become more complicated. The shot dogs, the missing people on the reservation. Cork O'Connor and his family. They rattled around in his thinking like gravel in a tin can. He needed sleep, but no sooner had his head hit the pillow than his cell phone rang. Not his personal cell phone. One of his burner phones. It was her.

"I just wanted to make sure they haven't killed you yet," she said.

He smiled at the sound of her voice. "I don't kill easy. You know that."

"Doesn't mean I don't worry. Are you all right?"

He rose from his bunk, left the cabin, and stood on the deck in the cool night air. The moon was high overhead, the lake water a mirror.

"Confused, but okay," he told her. "Do you have something for me?"

"Nothing specific. Directives have come down to clamp a lid on any hint of a terrorist attack. A black eye for an administration that campaigned on keeping America safe. On our end, we're sifting through all the threats Olympia received, looking for something specific. Nothing concrete so far. She was on the front line in so many causes. She thought of the threats as proof that she was being heard and insisted they didn't scare her."

She was quiet. He could hear her breathing, soft. Like wind in tall grass.

"Any help from the FBI?" he asked.

"They're not very forthcoming, all the way up the ladder. We're tapping every resource on the inside that we can, but we don't have the leverage we used to. And you've probably heard that the governor's going to be in Aurora tomorrow night for the town meeting about the mine, the meeting Olympia was supposed to attend. It would be good for you to be there, Bo. Take stock of the audience. Maybe someone will stand out."

"Like who?"

"The anti-McCarthy zealots. Someone so rabid they might actually have been motivated to assassinate her."

"In my experience, those people don't tend to be particularly sophisticated in their methods."

"Unless they had help from those who have the wherewithal to be sophisticated or the power to cover up a crude killing."

"Any suggestions in that regard?"

"That's what we're looking to you for." He heard her sigh. "I wish you had someone watching your back up there."

"I've got help, of a sort. A guy who used to be sheriff here. Name's O'Connor."

"Does he know how deep you're in this?"

"That wouldn't be healthy for either of us. As far as he knows, I'm working for an unnamed client."

"The truth," she said. "At least part of it. Tell me about Gerard."

"I'm still not sure who brought him in. Someone's after something that came down with the plane. Maybe the flight recorder, maybe something else. People involved in the early search of the crash site have gone missing. Could be someone thinks they snatched whatever's so important. Gerard might be behind the disappearances, I don't know yet."

"If Gerard gets the recorder, we may never know the truth."

"Then I'll have to find it before he does."

Something jumped in the water, shattering the mirrored surface. Bo watched the dark rings spread out, ripples extending far beyond the point of disturbance.

"You be safe," she said.

"I'll do my best."

The call ended without goodbyes. Bo turned off the burner phone for good. He had many others and she had all their numbers. Only one call per phone, he'd told her, just to be safe. Then he stood a long while, waiting for the lake water to return to glass.

CHAPTER 25

When Stephen, Daniel, and Trixie reached Crow Point early the next morning, the fire had already been prepared and the Grandfathers, the rocks to be used in the sweat that day, were heating. The lodge was on the shore of Iron Lake and surrounded by birch trees. It hadn't always been in its current location. Two years earlier, it was on the other side of Crow Point. In that location, while sweating alone in winter, Stephen had seen the vision of the man who would put a bullet into his back. That shooting had taken place at the sweat lodge not long thereafter.

Following that brutal violation of a sacred place, Henry Meloux had ordered a new sweat lodge built far from the other. Stephen hadn't helped in that construction. He'd had his hands full struggling to walk again. But his injury didn't keep him from participating in sweats, and he was certain that the cleansing rituals had helped his body and his spirit heal.

Trixie trotted ahead, and Waaboo raced to greet her. Then the boy ran to Daniel, who bent, wrapped his son in his arms, and lifted him.

"I helped make the fire," Waaboo told him proudly.

Which was a significant honor, particularly for one so young.

Daniel carried Waaboo piggyback and they continued across the meadow to Henry Meloux's cabin, where the others were waiting. Rainy looked troubled.

"Where's Cork?" she asked.

"Trying to convince Bo Thorson to come out here," Stephen told her. "He thinks Bo might benefit from taking part in the sweat."

"Ah," Rainy said, but looked unconvinced. "An interesting speculation."

"Everything okay here last night?" Daniel asked Jenny.

"Blessedly quiet."

"Where are Henry and Leah?"

"Walking," Rainy said. "They walk together every morning."

"Is he teaching her about the medicine plants?" Stephen asked.

Although he hadn't yet begun his formal preparation to become a Mide, a member of the Grand Medicine Society, Stephen already knew a good deal about the medicines Henry and Rainy used in their healing work.

Rainy smiled. "That's what he says. I think he just likes her company."

Henry Meloux was more than a hundred years old, Leah nearly thirty years his junior. They lived in separate cabins but had joined their lives on Crow Point in a way that someone on the outside might think strange. At twenty, Stephen didn't fully understand the arrangement himself. Was it love? Just companionship? He had never asked Henry to explain what connected them. One day he might broach the subject with the old man, but this was not that day.

"Everything quiet on Gooseberry Lane?" Jenny asked.

Stephen and Daniel exchanged a look.

"What?"

"Waaboo," Daniel said. "Why don't you take Trixie outside to play?"

"Sweats have many purposes," Cork explained to Bo as they traveled north along the shoreline of Iron Lake. "Healing. Cleansing. Visioning. Seeking."

"If I were a religious kind of guy," Bo replied, "I'd say it sounds like praying."

"Prayer is a part of it. It can be about asking. It can be about gratitude. It can be about simply connecting with the sacred spirit that resides in all things, the great spirit that weaves all life together."

Bo studied the lake, which, under the morning sun, shot blinding arrows of light. God was an abstract to him, something he'd discussed only as he might discuss the philosophy of Kierkegaard. He found it almost quaint, the way Cork talked about this belief in spirit.

"So the sweat today, what's that about?"

"Stephen believes he might be given a better understanding of the vision that comes to him."

"'Given,'" Bo said. "'Comes to him.' Cork, I've got to tell you, this is all a little woo-woo for me."

"I understand. I've lived all my life seeing things I can't explain in a rational way. I just ask that you keep an open mind."

They parked along the gravel roadside, behind Daniel English's truck. English and Stephen O'Connor had come out much earlier, Bo knew, probably about the time Cork called to convince him to join them in this Indian ritual. He'd agreed, but not for the reason Cork believed. What Bo wanted to know was the location of the family who might be used as pawns in the game that was afoot in Tamarack County.

"We walk the rest of the way," Cork said.

"How far?"

"A couple of miles."

"I don't do much hiking in the woods. I'm a city kind of guy."

Cork laughed. "You look pretty North Country right now."

The morning was cool, high forties, the air fresh and filled with the scent of pine. The sky was blue and cloudless. Cork talked little as they hiked the trail, and Bo found this to his liking. Although he wasn't an outdoorsman, on such a morning, he couldn't help but believe that any conversation would be a disruption of a quiet that felt, he had to admit, a little sacred.

They came to a stream whose water was red-hued.

"Nibi-Miskwi," Cork said as he danced across rocks to the other side. "That's the Ojibwe name for this stream."

"What's it mean?"

"Blood Water."

"Why the red color?"

"A couple of factors. The iron in all the soil up here, and also tannin from the bog seepage that feeds the stream."

"Nibi-Miskwi. It has a poetic ring."

"It's a beautiful language, Ojibwemowin."

"You speak it well?"

"Not at all," Cork told him. "When I was a kid, it was spoken mostly by elders, but that's changed. More and more children learn to speak it now. We have programs for that. Waaboo's becoming pretty fluent." Cork turned from the red water of the stream. "Still a distance to go before we hit Crow Point." He continued down the path, and the conversation was at an end.

They broke from the trees onto a meadow that began wide but narrowed to the south. The meadow was outlined in birch and aspen trees, and beyond the trees was the silver-blue glitter of Iron Lake. Two cabins stood at the far end of the point. A little to the west rose two outcrops of high rock. Among the trees along the shoreline north of the outcrops was a squat structure with a fire in front sending up white smoke. Several figures were gathered around the fire.

"The sweat lodge," Cork told him. "We'll head over in a bit. First I want you to meet Henry."

They crossed the meadow. The cabin door opened before they arrived, and an old woman stepped out, dressed in jeans and a green turtleneck sweater.

"*Anin*, Cork," she said. "*Aaniish naa ezhiyaayin?*"

"*Nminoyaa gwa*, Leah. This is my friend Bo Thorson."

"Welcome," Leah said with a polite smile. "Won't you come in?"

Inside the cabin was the oldest man Bo had ever seen. His hair was white and long, his face a wrinkled sheeting of flesh. He sat with a boy who was blowing notes on a little handmade flute. The music stopped and the old man and the boy looked up.

"*Anin*, Baa-baa," the boy said to Cork. To Bo he said, "*Boozhoo.*"

"Henry, Waaboo, I'd like you to meet Bo Thorson."

The old man rose. He'd seemed bent when he was listening to the boy play the flute. Now his back was straight and his shoulders squared, and Bo saw that the old man was as tall as he.

The old man studied him, eyes dark and penetrating, and Bo felt uncomfortable under their gaze, as if he was being probed. With surprising strength, the old man finally shook the hand Bo had offered.

"You are not what I expected," the old man said.

"Someone taller?" Bo replied with an amiable smile.

"Someone truer." The old man didn't smile nor did he release Bo's hand.

DESOLATION MOUNTAIN   153

In his time as an agent of the U.S. Secret Service, and as an operative for hire since, Bo Thorson had met many people of high rank—presidents and premiers and CEOs and holders of extraordinary wealth. Standing in that simple cabin in the middle of nowhere, his hand in the grip of the oldest man he had ever seen, Bo realized that he was in the presence of someone whose power was of a remarkably different kind.

CHAPTER 26

Like most white people, Bo had lived with two different images of American Indians. One, perpetuated by Saturday matinee Westerns, was all war whoops and feathered bonnets. The other was of a population beset with a weakness for alcohol, a tendency toward violence, incapable of rising out of poverty, and leading an existence generally bereft of moral grounding; when you were in the proximity of someone clearly Indian, you took stock of your merchandise and you watched your back. His time in Tamarack County had begun to change his thinking.

He sat among the birch trees near the sweat lodge, talking with Daniel English; his wife, Jenny O'Connor; and Leah Duling. Rainy and Waaboo had moved to the lakeshore not far away, Rainy helping the little boy work out some tunes on his flute. From inside the sweat lodge came the sound of low chanting. Bo had opted not to join the two O'Connor men and Meloux in their sweat, hoping he might learn a good deal from conversation with the others that could prove useful to him in getting to the bottom of what was going on.

"She was a great senator," Jenny was saying. "It was like she spoke my thoughts. Cut the defense budget and shift the spending to education, public assistance programs, infrastructure. Keep our wilderness areas wild and safe. Open our arms to the refugees from all the damn wars. Put teeth in all the laws that guarantee civil rights. You ask me, she would have made an ideal presidential candidate in the next election. I'd have voted for her."

"You sound just like her," Bo said with a smile. "But all those ideals put her at odds with lots of powerful people."

"You can't change the world without ruffling feathers," Jenny replied.

"The town meeting that brought her up here was going to be about granting permits for this new mining operation. I know she wasn't in favor of it," Bo said. "But as I understand it, the mine would bring lots of jobs back to the Iron Range."

English stepped in. "The iron mines devastated this area last century, but with time the land has recovered. When rain falls on the tailings from an iron mine, the result is simply rust. This new operation would involve sulfide mining. Do you know what happens when rain falls on tailings from a sulfide mine, Bo? It creates sulfuric acid. Do you have any idea what that would do to the ecosystem here? Or everything downstream of this watershed?"

"The mining company's given assurance that wouldn't happen. I understand there would be lots of checks in place."

"Assurance," English scoffed. "Do you know anything about the Mount Polley Mine in B.C.?"

"Never heard of it."

"A few years ago, a tailings pond, basically a huge reservoir of poison, was breached, releasing over a billion gallons of tainted water into the streams up there. It was an eco-disaster of extraordinary proportion. The mining companies all said this was an incredibly rare occurrence. But the same thing happened in Colorado the following year. And it's happened in hundreds of other places around the world. Mining is about momentary profit. Have you heard of seven-generational thinking?"

"If I'm correct, it's the question of how what we do today will impact the world seven generations from now."

"Exactly. This mine flies in the face of every reasonable consideration of the future."

"Except economic."

"Any gain is only in the short term. If the land and water are poisoned, the long-term effects could be devastating in every way, including economically."

"Well," Bo said, "you've got me convinced."

"I wish our governor was as easily convinced," Jenny said. "He's thrown his support behind the project."

"And if he wrangles an appointment to complete Olympia McCarthy's term, he'll do a lot of damage on a national scale," English added.

"You don't like our governor?" Bo said.

"He owes a lot of favors to big business."

The blanket over the door of the sweat lodge was lifted from the inside and Cork O'Connor crawled out. The old man followed next, and Cork helped him stand. Young Stephen O'Connor was the last to emerge. All of them dripped from head to toe, their hair flat and clinging to their faces, the boxer shorts they wore drenched.

Leah dipped a ladle into a wooden bucket of cold water, and one by one the men refreshed themselves.

"That's it?" Bo asked.

"That's only the first door," English said. "The first round of their sweat."

The old man already looked exhausted.

"Are you okay, Henry?" Leah asked.

The old man sat on a blanket that had been laid on the ground. "A few minutes and I will be fine."

"You two doing okay?" Jenny asked of her father and brother.

"We're good," Cork replied. But Bo could see that both he and his son were looking at the old man with deep concern. "Henry," Cork began.

The old man lifted a hand to stop whatever was about to be said. "I have a heart that is strong and willing and a spirit that whispers 'More.' A few minutes, and I will be ready."

Cork had laid his clothes in a pile near the lodge. Somewhere among all that clothing, a cell phone rang. Cork dug in the pocket of his folded pants.

At the same time, Bo's cell phone vibrated. He stepped away from the others to take the call.

"Where the hell are you?" Gerard demanded. "Why haven't you checked in?"

"Nothing more to report at the moment," Bo said quietly.

"Well, here's something for you. They found the truck that belongs to the missing couple. The Hukaris."

"Where?"

"Some back road out there on the reservation. The truck was pretty well destroyed by fire. No sign of the couple."

"Not the work of your people, I take it."

"If that was meant as a joke, it's not funny. Where are you?"

"You remember the O'Connors, father and son?"

"What about them?"

"They've become my eyes and ears on the reservation. I'll explain later." Bo ended the call abruptly.

When he returned, he found Cork dressing. Rainy and Waaboo had joined the others.

"That was Sheriff Dross on the phone," Cork told Bo. "They've found the Hukaris' truck. Or what's left of it."

"Where?" Bo asked.

"On the rez. It's a burned-out hulk."

English said in a dead voice, "And no sign of Phil or Sue."

"Another thing," Cork said. "The blood we scraped off the dock at the Loves' cabin? It's the same type as Monkey's blood."

"What about the sweat, Dad?"

"The sweat's over for me, Stephen," his father replied. "You have to make your own decision."

The kid looked unhappily toward Meloux. "If I stay, I won't be able to focus, Henry. I'll be thinking about the Hukaris. I'm not sure the sweat would do me any good."

The old man sat on the blanket with his thin legs crossed, his knee bones like doorknobs. When he'd emerged from the lodge, he'd looked done for. But he seemed fine now, recovering quickly from what Bo imagined must be the ordeal of a sweat. More and more this man they called a Mide surprised him.

Meloux gave young O'Connor a wistful look. "An ending for you does not mean an ending for me."

"You're going on with the sweat?" Concern was all over Stephen's face. Except for the old man, they all looked concerned.

"Your path is your path and mine is mine. What I am waiting for has not yet been given. I will wait some more and while I wait I will sweat."

Stephen held himself very still, eyeing the old man, clearly torn.

The choice had been his and he'd made it, but Stephen was angry that the sweat had come to an early end for him. Although he understood that a sweat was about opening to whatever was given, which didn't necessarily mean answers, he'd been hoping the burden of his vision might be lifted somehow.

Now, as he rode with his father and Bo Thorson toward Aurora, he was having real trouble with acceptance. He felt more stuck than ever, as if he were still hammering at a door that wouldn't open for him. Which wasn't, he knew, the way of a Mide. Or the kind of Mide he would like to become someday. The kind of Mide that was Henry Meloux.

Cork and Bo talked up front, discussing the visitor to O'Connor's house the night before.

"Probably the same people who were after the Loves and the Hukaris and Tom Blessing," Bo speculated.

"And who would that be?"

"That's the question, isn't it? I'll do some checking on my end. What about you?"

"I'm going to talk to our sheriff, bring her up to speed on everything."

"Everything?" Bo asked.

"Within reason," Cork said.

They dropped Bo at the house on Gooseberry Lane, where he'd parked his Jeep. Then they headed to Sam's Place.

"Wait here," Cork told Stephen.

He went into the Quonset hut, and a few minutes later, Stephen saw him post a handwritten sign in the serving window that read: CLOSED UNTIL FURTHER NOTICE.

When they walked into her office, Marsha Dross was talking with David Foster, one of her deputies. She put up a finger, signaling them to wait.

"I'm authorizing overtime for every officer, Dave. They're to be in the conference room in an hour. And get hold of Azevedo. His vacation's over. I want him back here. Pronto."

As Foster headed out the door past Stephen and Cork, he lifted his eyebrows in a way that signaled, *Be careful.*

Dross crossed her arms and glared at Cork. "What do you know that I don't?"

"Why do you say that?"

"Sit down." She waited for Stephen and his father to take the two empty chairs. "You know the Iron Lake Reservation and the people out there a lot better than any of us. They whisper things to you that they would never tell me or any of my officers. What I see is that everything that's happened in this last awful week has happened on the reservation. So, tell me what's going on out there that I don't know about."

"For starters," Cork said in a calm voice, "it's not just on the rez, Marsha. Someone tried to break into our house last night."

"Who?"

"No idea. But I'm guessing they're the same people who are responsible for the disappearances on the rez."

"Everyone's okay?"

"We moved Jenny and Waaboo out of harm's way. It's clear that everyone who's been targeted so far was at the scene of Senator McCarthy's plane crash very early, which includes Daniel. We want Jenny and Waaboo safe."

"So they can't be used as leverage?"

"Exactly. That may have been the plan with Fanny Blessing, to use her to get to Tom, except something went wrong. Grabbing Sue gives these people leverage with Phil. Ned Love's sister, Beulah, has been followed, too."

"Where is she?"

"Staying with Sarah LeDuc. I've got Harmon Goodsky keeping an eye on them both."

"What's it all about?"

Cork took a deep breath. "My best guess is that they're trying to find the black box and they believe someone who was at the crash site early picked it up."

"First of all, the official word is that there wasn't a black box. And if there was, why would NTSB lie about it?"

"I'm just guessing here, but maybe the black box would show something they don't want made public."

"That the cause of the crash wasn't pilot error? Hence, the presence of the FBI's number two man from the National Security Branch. But Monkey Love, Fanny Blessing, the Hukaris? That doesn't strike me as the work of the FBI."

"There are other actors involved, but at this point, I've got no idea who they are."

"I called BCA, asked them to come in on this." She was speaking of Minnesota's Bureau of Criminal Apprehension. "I got a song and dance about how they don't have any agents to spare at the moment."

"That's a new one."

"Know what I think? I think the governor's office delivered some kind of directive."

"You'll sound like a conspiracy crackpot if you say that publicly."

"Then I won't say it publicly. But I'm going to get to the bottom of what's going on in this county if it takes every officer I have working twenty-four seven."

"They might not like that."

"My guys?"

"Them, too. But I was thinking about whoever's behind whatever's going on."

"Cork, I need a promise from you. I need to believe you won't keep anything from me that might help in this."

"You've got my word. Can I expect the same?"

"Deal. Oh, and one more thing. The preliminary autopsy finding on Fanny Blessing doesn't show anything unusual. Looks like the cause of death will officially be listed as cardiac arrest. Reasonable, considering the state of her health."

"The timing is interesting, though, don't you think?"

"Is it possible for someone to be scared to death?" Stephen asked.

"I suppose someone whose physical condition is already precarious," the sheriff said, nodding as if she thought the idea had merit. "If anything changes officially, I'll let you know."

Outside the building, Stephen stopped and gave his father a long look.

"What?" Cork asked.

"You promised Marsha that you would tell her everything."

"I did."

Stephen cocked his head. "You never mentioned Bo."

CHAPTER 27

Bo pulled up beside the black SUV. Inside the cabin, Gerard was waiting for him, drinking a Leinenkugel's pulled from the refrigerator.

"I see you didn't stand on ceremony. Just made yourself right at home."

"You know your Robert Service, Thorson? 'Politeness is a platitude in this fair land of gallant foemen.' It's a poem about the cost of chivalry." He sipped his beer. "Here I am tracking you down again. What's this about you and the O'Connors?"

Bo tried to read him. He'd thought the truck that had staked out Gooseberry Lane the night before was Gerard's doing, but maybe not. Maybe Gerard really was as clueless as he seemed.

"I worked with O'Connor years ago when I was Secret Service. He's part Ojibwe, knows the territory. I'm getting good intel from him."

"Yeah? So tell me about the Hukaris."

"The husband was one of the Indians first on the scene of the crash."

"And if someone were looking for the black box, they might think he grabbed it?"

Bo headed to the kitchen area and began to put together a pot of coffee. "That burned-out truck, your handiwork?"

"I wondered if maybe it was yours."

"I don't operate that way. But I wouldn't put it past you. By the way, O'Connor found the transmitter you put under the dash of his son's car. He left it in place, but I doubt they'll be using the Jeep in any way that would be useful to track now. What were you thinking when you bugged the kid?"

"After we caught him up on the mountain and questioned him, it was clear all he was giving me was lies."

"And you thought a twenty-year-old kid might be involved in some grand terrorist plot?"

"Kids younger than him blow themselves up in the name of all kinds of harebrained causes."

"And what kind of harebrained cause do you think he might represent?"

"I was hoping you could tell me. You're the one with an inside line to the Indians around here now."

Bo turned to Gerard as the coffee began to drip. "Someone tried to break into the O'Connors' house last night. Your people?"

Gerard lowered his beer. "Not mine."

Bo opened a cupboard door, took a mug off the shelf. "Your guys up on the mountain, have they found anything yet?"

"Nothing. And nothing in the woods where the tail section broke off or in that muck where the plane crashed or anywhere around it either. Someone grabbed that black box."

"Someone afraid what the flight recorder might say about the true nature of the crash?"

"Maybe."

"Kind of flies in the face of most terrorist agendas, don't you think? A real terrorist would want the cause front and center, blasted all over the headlines. On the other hand, I suppose if someone on the inside were responsible, they wouldn't be eager for things to come to light. So, if the senator was murdered and it wasn't done by terrorists, the question is, who wanted her dead? And also, who has the power to misshape an investigation?"

"Any theories yet?"

Bo removed the pot from the coffeemaker and poured himself what had brewed so far. "The NTSB continues to deliver the same line of pilot error bullshit. The FBI is doing nothing but obfuscating. The BCA here in Minnesota hasn't been brought in, so I'm guessing somebody is sitting on them. Whoever is doing the strong-arming, they've got a lot of clout. And a lot to lose if the truth ever comes out. The assassination of a U.S. senator." Bo blew across the surface of his coffee to cool it and eyed Gerard over the rim of his mug. "You have the clout to misshape this investigation, if you had a mind to. You're looking for the flight recorder, and I still don't know at whose behest."

"Is that important?"

"Only if I find the truth and it gets me killed. Will it?"

"Know the truth and the truth will set you free. Isn't that how it goes?"

"It's not just about the black box, am I right? Did something else come down with that plane?"

Gerard's look was appropriately stony. "What do you mean?"

"Why search the mountain? The flight recorder would have been with the tail section in the woods next to the bog."

"As it came down, the plane clipped trees up on that mountainside. Seemed appropriate to include the area in our search."

"That explanation might read well in the newspapers."

"I'm not one of the bad guys, Thorson. Save your questioning for them." Gerard set his beer, still half full, on the table and started for the door. "I want to hear from you tonight. Don't make me come looking."

Bo waited until Gerard had driven away, then from a case in the bedroom closet, took a radio frequency detector wand and swept each room, searching for bugs. The cabin seemed clean. He stepped outside and ran the wand over his Jeep. Also clean. None of which surprised him. Gerard would have anticipated this move. If Bo were being surveilled, it was in a far more sophisticated way.

He drank his coffee and listened again to the recorded conversations from Gerard's war room. He considered what they might have been referring to when they talked about the "bear tracks" on Desolation Mountain and what they might have meant when they discussed moving their search to the "beach" to look for "waves."

Bear tracks. Evidence left behind that would identify the presence of something on the mountain? If so, the presence of what?

The beach. Waves. A veiled reference to . . . to what? You could see tracks. But waves, not necessarily. Unless they were talking about water, which seemed unlikely, waves couldn't be seen. So airwaves? Radio waves? How would they show themselves on the beach? Electronic detection of some kind?

Bo would have loved to be able to hear what had gone on in the war room since he'd last checked the recorder on the island, but that would have to wait until the cover of dark.

CHAPTER 28

"I made Bo a promise," Cork tried to explain. "He needs to stay off the radar."

They were heading toward home to grab some lunch. Stephen sat stiff on the passenger side, looking disappointed in his father.

"Professional courtesy, one PI to another?" he said.

"That's part of it."

"Marsha's a friend. Seems to me friendship would supersede professional courtesy."

"There are forces at work here that are still very much in the dark, Stephen. With Bo out there in that dark with them, rooting them out, we might have some advantage."

"If Bo can be trusted."

"You don't trust him?"

"I don't know him. How well do you?"

"I worked with him several times. Important work."

"When he was with the Secret Service. That was a long time ago. Is he the same man now he was then?"

"I get the same feel from him now that I got then. A man I can trust."

"He asked you for a promise that made you lie to a friend. I can't remember you doing that before."

"It wasn't a lie exactly."

"If you say so." Stephen looked away, out his window.

"Two things to think about," Cork said. "One, it's clear that Bo knows more than he's telling us, but that doesn't mean he can't be trusted. My guess is that he's made promises he's trying to keep. That's something I understand. Two, Bo risked his life in the line of duty. He put himself between the First Lady and a bullet. That takes a special kind of person."

"You're telling me he's *ogichidaa*, like you, both of you standing between evil and the people you care about. I get that. All I'm saying is that people can change, Dad. Even the best."

Before Cork could argue the point further, his cell phone rang. He pulled to the side of the street. The call was from Daniel English.

"Tom Blessing's gone, Cork."

"Gone?"

"As in missing. He was supposed to meet with the folks at the funeral home this morning to discuss his mother's burial. He never showed. I asked around Allouette. Nobody's seen him since yesterday. I went out to his place. His truck's gone."

"How'd you find out about the funeral home meeting?"

"I was at the tribal building, checking in with Kingbird. We've had more reports of those poachers. While I was there, the funeral home called Tom's office, got no answer, then they called Kingbird wondering if he or anybody else had seen Tom. Considering that his mother died yesterday, he ought to be surrounded by relatives, but like I said, no one's seen him. You add in the missed meeting with the funeral home and what's gone on with Phil and Sue and the Loves, and it seems pretty worrisome."

"Where are you now?"

"Still at the Blessings'."

"Wait there. I'm coming. And, Daniel, you have your sidearm with you, right?"

"You better believe it."

"Who's gone?" Stephen asked when the call ended.

"Tom Blessing."

"Just like the others?"

"That's how it looks."

"What do we do?"

Cork punched in Bo Thorson's number on his cell phone. The call went immediately to voice mail. "Bo, it's Cork O'Connor. Tom Blessing's gone missing. Give me a call when you get this message."

"What do we do?" Stephen asked again.

But Cork was punching in the sheriff's number now. When Dross picked up, he explained the situation, then said, "Stephen and I are heading out to the rez, Marsha. I'll let you know what we find."

He started to punch in Rainy's cell phone number, but Stephen said, "I'm not going with you."

"No?" Then it dawned on him that his son was a college student. "Classes this afternoon?"

Stephen rolled his eyes. "While all this is going on? School can wait. No, you and Daniel don't need me."

"What are you going to do?"

"Head back to Crow Point, finish my sweat."

Cork gave a nod. "All right." He called Rainy and filled her in. "How's Henry?"

"Recovering. The sweat was hard on him."

"Anything good come from his ordeal?"

"He's oddly quiet. It's good Stephen's coming back. Maybe Uncle Henry will talk to him. You take care of yourself."

Cork drove to Gooseberry Lane, spent a couple of minutes removing the tracking device from Stephen's Jeep, and put it in the garage. "We don't want anyone knowing where you're going. Make sure you're not followed, okay?" He reached out his hand to his son. "I hope the sweat gives you what you need."

Stephen's grip was less than firm. "I wish I knew exactly what that was."

Cork watched his son drive away. Among all the weights that had settled on Cork's shoulders lately, one of the heaviest was his concern for Stephen, who seemed so lost. Or maybe not lost but searching desperately for deeper truths. In that search, Cork, who was one kind of man, didn't know how to help his son, who was another. Or maybe Stephen already understood the world in a way that would forever elude his father. So Cork wondered, as he stared at the rearview mirror watching Stephen grow distant in the Jeep, which of them was nearer the important truths. Who was it who was really lost?

His cell phone rang. He figured it was Bo returning his call. It wasn't.

The voice on the other end, electronically altered, said, "What's on the black box will make headlines. You want the black box?"

"Who is this?"

"Do you want the black box?"

"I want the box."

"It will cost you ten thousand."

"What about my friends?"

"First the black box. Then we'll talk about your friends."

"I want to know they're all right."

"Okay, for another ten grand you get them, too."

"Are they all right?"

"They're in one piece."

"How do I know that?"

"Get the money and you'll have proof."

"How do we do this?"

"There's a town meeting tonight. Go to it."

"Then what?"

"You'll be contacted there. I want the money in small bills and in a backpack, the kind a kid might use to carry his schoolbooks. Got it?"

"Yeah, I got it."

"One more thing. No cops. Bring in cops and you'll never see that black box or your friends again."

The call ended and Cork stood for a moment, a little stunned. Then his cell phone rang again. It was Bo this time, finally calling back. Cork explained the two situations: the extortion demand and Blessing's disappearance.

"The money's no problem," Bo said. "Let me handle that. Stupid question, I know, but did you happen to recognize the caller's number?"

"A six-one-two area code. The Twin Cities."

"I'd lay odds it's from a burner phone, but give it to me and I'll have it checked. Where are you now?"

"I'm about to head out to Blessing's place."

"Where is it?"

Cork gave him directions.

"I'll arrange for the ransom money, then meet you there."

Although he'd swept the cabin to be sure there were no bugs, Bo stepped onto the deck to make the call. He stood in the warm autumn sunlight, with gold-leafed birches all around him.

"Twenty thousand?" she said. "That's it? They could have asked for ten times that amount." She was quiet. Then, "O'Connor got the call. Or claimed he did. But he was one of the men searching the woods where the tail section came down. Bo, is it possible he's not the man you think he is?"

"He's the man I think he is, all right. But maybe some of the others aren't."

Bo considered the disappeared Ned and Monkey Love, the vanished Hukaris, Tom Blessing, Daniel English. He'd never met the Loves, so had no idea about them. Ditto the Hukaris. Blessing? He'd seemed a man truly distraught about his mother's death, but that didn't mean he wasn't capable of trying to extort money from wealthy people. English? A family man. Would he jeopardize his family for a mere twenty grand?

"I'll relay this to Olympia's father. We'll get the money to you this afternoon."

"No cops. O'Connor said the guy was clear about it."

"And we'll go with that?"

"For now. One more thing. Could you check the number the call came from? It's probably a burner phone, but let's be sure."

After he'd given her the number, a wind rose, rustling the leaves and branches of the birch trees, a sound like whispering.

"Does he know?" Bo asked. Even though he was sure the phone wasn't bugged, he still used no names. "Does he know about you and me, about all of this?"

"We've kept him in the dark. Plausible deniability. When the money's on its way, I'll let you know. And, Bo?"

"I'm here."

"Thank you. For everything."

"Yeah."

She was gone. No goodbye. He slipped the cell phone into his pocket, listened to the whisper of the golden trees, watched a small sailboat far out drift across the ruffling blue of the lake, and he thought: *Some people lead simple lives. Lucky them.*

Daniel was waiting beside his truck when Cork pulled up. "I checked the house. Nothing apparent. Where's Stephen?"

"He went back to Crow Point to finish his sweat. There's another complication." Cork told Daniel about the ransom call.

"This just gets weirder and weirder. You can get the money?"

"Bo said he'd take care of that. He's on his way here now. I'm going inside to have a look for myself."

He moved through the Blessings' house room by room. Like Daniel before him, Cork found nothing helpful.

When Bo arrived, Cork and Daniel met him in the yard. "Just like the others, Tom's vanished into thin air," Cork said.

"Think we'll find his truck burned out somewhere?" Bo asked.

"At this point, I don't know what to expect. You arranged for the money?"

"It'll be here this afternoon."

"Coming from Jerome Hill, the senator's father? He's your client, right?"

Bo gave him a stony look and said, "How do you figure?"

"Our former First Lady, Kate Dixon, has been with the senator's family since the crash, offering comfort, the media say. You saved Kate Dixon's life. Now you're a hotshot private security operative. If the senator's family wanted Olympia McCarthy's death investigated outside official channels, who would she counsel them to use? And pulling together twenty thousand dollars on the spur of the moment is nothing for someone like Jerome Hill. Tell me I'm wrong."

Bo hesitated, then said, "How long have you suspected?"

"A while."

"This stays between us." He glanced at Daniel, who gave a nod of agreement.

Cork said, "Jerome Hill is a very wealthy man. I imagine he'd be willing to pay ten times twenty thousand for the flight recorder."

"What does that tell you?" Bo said.

"My first guess is that it's someone who thinks twenty grand is a lot. There are plenty of folks on the Iron Range who've been strapped for cash for years. Twenty grand might seem like a pretty big windfall."

"A lot of risk."

"Risk and the Iron Range go hand in hand."

"It's somebody who knows you, Cork, knows you're involved in all this. If they know what's on that flight recorder, it's probably somebody who understands how to read that information. So someone savvy with electronics. Sound like anyone you know?"

Cork and Daniel exchanged a glance.

"Tom Blessing," Cork told him.

"Fill me in."

"Tom was always a smart kid," Cork said. "When I broke up the Red Boyz—that was the gang he was part of on the reservation—he began taking coursework at the community college. Computer technology, programming, electronics. He's the tech wizard for our tribal offices, teaches classes at the community center in Allouette to folks who want to learn more about computers, or any new electronic technology, for that matter. Cell phones, tablets, computers, you name it."

"Another thing," Daniel said. "Tom's been taking flying lessons from Cal Blaine out at the airport. I don't know how that fits in, but I'm guessing it adds to everything he might know about the senator's plane."

Cork scanned the wild landscape that surrounded the Blessings' house—the wide marsh with tamaracks along the edge, the rugged, pine-covered hills. It had been an isolated world once, but no longer. The digital age.

"Tom Blessing?" he said quietly. "It doesn't feel right."

"Easy enough to find out," Daniel said. "Somebody waits here to see if he comes back."

"Could be a long wait," Bo said. "Maybe a waste of manpower."

"Better idea?" Daniel asked.

"Not at the moment. You volunteering?"

"I'll take the first shift anyway."

Cork gestured toward Daniel's sidearm. "Keep that thing handy."

Daniel gave him a two-fingered salute and headed into the house.

"Feels clunky," Cork said. "The paltry amount, me as the go-between."

"If you've never been involved in extortion before, clunky's probably the norm," Bo replied. "If it's a ruse, I can't think of any reason why. We don't have a solid handle on anything, so there's no real investigation to sidetrack."

"You said you had some contacts to check with about our visitor last night. Anything there?"

"Didn't pan out," Bo said. "Sorry."

"You still have anybody inside Secret Service who could check something for you?"

"I still had a lot of friends there when I left."

"If I gave you some government license plate numbers, think you could track down who they belong to?"

"I could give it a try."

Cork tore the sheet from the notepad on which he'd written the plate numbers of the vehicles he'd spotted coming and going from the airport hangar where the crash investigation continued.

"No agency prefix code," Bo noted. "These people want to

remain anonymous. I can't guarantee anything, but I'll give it a shot. So what next?"

"I'm going to track down Cal Blaine, find out about Tom Blessing and his flight lessons."

"So, the regional airport?"

"That's right. Maybe you should come along. That way we're together if instructions for the exchange come."

"All right," Bo agreed.

As he prepared to leave, Cork took a last look at the little house isolated in the great woods. Daniel could take care of himself, but with no idea of what was going on in Tamarack County, Cork was still deeply concerned. The last thing he wanted was for his daughter's husband to join the missing.

CHAPTER 29

The guards in front of the large hangar that was being used to store and sort the pieces of the wreckage made no attempt to interfere with Bo and Cork as they parked in front of a small office a hundred yards away. A sign above the office door read: NORTH COUNTRY AIR ACADEMY.

"Delusions of grandeur," Cork said, pointing toward the sign. "It's just Cal, a one-man operation."

Scrawled on a sheet of paper taped to the office door were the words *Flight Lesson. Back 2:30 P.M.* Cork peered through the glass on the door. "Empty." He checked his watch. "Half an hour to kill. There's a little food place across the road. I haven't had any lunch. You hungry?"

"Come to think of it," Bo said.

At the roadhouse, they ordered burgers and fries and sat on the patio, eating and watching vehicles come and go. Cork was right. Almost all the plates were government issue.

"Must feel like a violation," Bo said.

"The quiet is one of the things I've always loved about where I live."

"Busy in the summer, I imagine."

"Not this way."

"I grew up in the city, but when I was a teenager, I spent time on a farm near Blue Earth. I understand about the quiet. You're a lucky man, Cork."

"Because of the quiet?"

"And the family. And that you have a place you call home."

"You don't?"

"Never have."

"Ever thought of settling down?"

"Lone wolf."

"The strength of the wolf is the pack."

"Is that an Indian saying?"

"Rudyard Kipling, actually. *The Jungle Book.* One of my grandson's favorite movies."

Bo wondered what it would be like to have children and grandchildren, a thread of responsibility that ran through generations. He figured he had enough trouble just worrying about himself.

His cell phone rang. The new burner phone he was carrying.

"I've got to take this." He moved away from Cork.

"The money is on its way," she said. "Olympia's brother is bringing it up by helicopter. He'll call you when he arrives. Any more ransom instructions?"

"Nothing so far. Were your people able to trace the number?"

"Not yet. Like you said, probably a burner phone."

"I might have something for you on this end. One of the Indians who was first on the crash scene is an electronics whiz. He was also a gang member in his younger days. He's gone missing. There's a chance he's behind the extortion. It's possible he grabbed the flight recorder. If so, he may very well know what's on it."

"Name?"

"Tom Blessing. His mother died yesterday, questionable circumstances."

Nothing from her end for a moment. "I worry about you."

"That's something."

And she was gone.

Bo relayed to Cork that the ransom money was coming.

"I keep wondering why the town meeting," Cork said. "It seems way too public."

"Like you said, this feels clunky. Strikes me as someone who's never been involved in this kind of thing before. Would that fit Blessing?"

"Yeah, and me, too. How about you? Ever been in the middle of something like this before?"

"A couple years ago, I was asked to be the go-between in a kidnap ransom that involved the son of an Argentine diplomat."

"How'd that go?"

"Not well. I made the drop. We got the info to locate the boy. Turned out what we paid for was his body."

"Did you find out who was behind it?"

"We knew who was behind it, just couldn't touch them."

"Must have left a sour taste."

Bo heard the sound of a small plane and scanned the sky. "Officially we couldn't touch them. Unofficially? That was another thing. There was payback. But in the end, the taste was still bitter."

Under the cloud of that memory, Bo watched the plane descend and approach the airport runway.

"That'll be Cal," Cork said. Then his cell phone rang. "Yeah, Harmon," he answered. He listened, looked concerned. "I can't be there for a while. Stephen's out on Crow Point. Okay if I send him?" He listened some more. "I'll tell him to make it fast." He ended the call. "Harmon Goodsky, from Allouette."

"The one surveilling Sarah LeDuc and Beulah Love?"

"That's him. He says a couple of strangers have been cruising through Allouette with a particular interest in the Mocha Moose. He took some shots."

"Fired at them?"

"No, photos."

"Have they tried anything with Beulah?"

"Just keeping an eye on the place, sounds like."

"Stephen can handle this?" Bo liked the kid, but he wasn't sure how he might deal with a situation that could easily go south.

"I think he needs to understand that he can." And Cork made the call to his son.

Bo and Cork were waiting at the office when Cal Blaine returned. He was bald, a little heavy, wearing a red flannel shirt. A kid was with him, maybe nineteen. They shook hands; the kid got into one of the vehicles parked in front of the office and drove away.

"Hey there, Cork," Blaine said. "Decided to take up flying?"

"Not me, Cal. Just wanted to ask you a few questions, if I could."

"Sure. Come on in."

Blaine unlocked the office door, and the men followed him inside. It was simply furnished: a gray metal desk, three roller chairs, two file cabinets, a bulletin board with lots of papers tacked to it, a radio set.

"Have a seat." Blaine took the one behind his desk. "Didn't catch the name, stranger."

"Just call me Bo."

"Good enough." He looked to Cork. "So, ask away."

"I understand you've been giving Tom Blessing flight lessons."

"Yeah, he's working on getting his private pilot's license. Say, I heard about his mom. Too bad."

"Did he say anything about why he wanted to fly?"

"Why does anyone want to fly?" Blaine opened his arms. "Freedom."

"Would the instructions you give him or the manuals he reads tell him about the safety equipment that planes are required to carry?"

"Of course."

"Did he ask you questions in that regard?"

"Nothing special, at least that I recall. Why? What's this about?"

"Tom's gone missing. I'm trying to find him. Anything I can learn might help."

"You think he, what, flew away?"

"You never know. And with all this going on." Cork eyed the hangar visible beyond the window, where the NTSB was at work.

"I know. Terrible, terrible."

Bo asked, "Were you out here the day Senator McCarthy's plane went down?"

"I'm always out here."

"Anything unusual about that day?"

"Matter of fact, yeah."

"What exactly?" Cork said.

"The runway lights never came on."

"What do you mean?"

"We're a small airport, no control tower. Planes that want to land have to click the runway lights on."

"Click?"

"The pilot turns to the local frequency and keys the mic. Three clicks for low intensity, five for medium, seven for high. There were low clouds that day, so the runway might have been tough to spot without the lights. Any good pilot would have clicked them on."

"But the pilot in Senator McCarthy's plane didn't?"

"That's right."

"When would the pilot have clicked the lights?" Bo asked.

"On the approach, about seven miles out. A lot of pilots use Desolation Mountain as a visual cue."

"Why wouldn't the pilot have turned on the lights?"

Blaine shrugged. "From what I understand, he knew our airport. So, either an oversight or a misjudgment. Or equipment failure, I suppose."

"Equipment failure?"

"There was lightning in the area that day. Maybe a lightning strike to the plane knocked out the electronics."

"Does that happen a lot?"

"Pretty rare, but it does happen, mostly with small aircraft. As I understand it, after the Duluth control tower gave them their approach heading, there was no more communication from the plane, which wouldn't be unusual unless they sent out a distress call."

"Wouldn't the pilot have done that if they were going down?" Cork asked.

"If he had time and didn't panic."

"And if the radio worked," Bo added.

Blaine sat back. "Too bad there wasn't a flight recorder aboard. Would have answered a lot of questions."

"Yeah," Bo said. "Too bad."

"Did you tell anybody this?" Cork asked.

"Talked to an FBI agent," Blaine said. "He told me it probably wasn't important. Haven't heard anything since. Nobody's followed up."

"Do me a favor, Cal. You hear from Tom Blessing, will you let me know?"

"You got it."

As they walked to their vehicles, Cork said, "I hope the twenty thousand buys us some answers tonight."

Bo made no reply, but he couldn't help seeing in his mind's eye the image of the Argentine boy, his body curled in the trunk of an abandoned Saab and, except for his wrists and ankles bound tightly with white cord and the red gash across his throat, looking as though he might have been sleeping.

CHAPTER 30

Once again, Stephen's attempt at a sweat had been thwarted. The call had come just as he was preparing to enter the lodge. His father had called Rainy, who'd handed Stephen her cell phone. When he'd heard his father's request, what could he say?

Henry Meloux was there, recovered from his own sweat. On his arrival at Crow Point, Stephen had asked the old Mide if the sweat had given him the answers he was hoping for.

"I did not ask for answers," Henry had said. "I asked for understanding."

"Do you understand?" Stephen had asked.

"I understand that an old man's body is not so weak as you might expect." The Mide had grinned. "And I understand that all things come in their time. That includes answers."

Although Henry had seemed satisfied, Stephen found this not helpful at all.

He was on his way to Allouette now, driving the ATV side-by-side Leah Duling kept at her cabin and used when she wanted to go into town. In the winter, she drove a snowmobile. These were new additions to Crow Point, ones that Leah had insisted on when she took up residence there to see to Henry's needs. It was a full five miles into Allouette. For most of his life, Henry had walked to the little rez town, or the farther distance to Aurora, with no problem. The old man seemed just fine letting Leah drive the noisy machines. Stephen suspected it had more to do with Leah's weaknesses at seventy-plus years of age than Henry's at over a hundred.

All things come in their time. A variation on Henry's usual mantra: Patience. So what had the sweat delivered to Henry that he didn't already know?

Then Stephen thought about Rainy, who was also a Mide, and who'd told him many times that one of the things a healer knows is that human beings already have within them an understanding of how to heal themselves. Often, all a Mide did was help guide them to this understanding. A sweat was like that, Stephen decided, and he wondered, *So what do I already know that I need to understand?*

When he reached Allouette, he was still in the dark.

He parked the ATV in front of Goodsky's photography studio. When he entered, the place seemed empty.

"Hello?" he called.

A young teenager stepped through the curtains at the back of the gallery. Stephen had heard about Goodsky's grandson, who'd come up from the Cities to live on the rez, but he'd never met the kid. He seemed fragile to Stephen and skittish, like a small animal in the forest. He didn't look Stephen in the eye. He held a photograph of Iron Lake reflecting the fall foliage, and when he realized Stephen was looking, he turned the photo so the image was hidden.

"I'm Stephen O'Connor."

The kid said nothing.

"You must be Winston."

The kid nodded, still mute.

"I'm looking for your grandfather. He's expecting me."

"Wait here." The kid disappeared through the curtains.

Stephen strolled the gallery, studying the photographs that hung on the walls. He was no art critic, but he knew what he liked, and he liked very much what he saw. The photographs captured the spirit of the land he called home in moments of stunning beauty. Harmon Goodsky's work was well represented, as were the works of other Native photographers. Stephen had never thought of himself as an artist, but the images on the walls in the little gallery made him wish that he were. Then he found himself thinking he'd probably be no better at art than he was at interpreting visions.

"*Anin*, Stephen."

Harmon Goodsky limped through the curtains, all alone. He held a photograph out to Stephen.

"I snapped this shot of one of the men who was watching Sarah's place, and I blew it up."

The photo showed a man framed in the window on the driver's side of a black pickup spattered with dried, rust-colored mud. He wore a jean jacket over a flannel shirt, and a black stocking cap. His face was broad, ruddy, with a diamond-shaped scar at the corner of his left eye.

"You got a photo of only one of them?"

"They were parked down the street from the Mocha Moose for a while, two of them. I walked down to confront them, but they took off. Not before I was able to snap that. I thought maybe your dad could use it to nail these guys before they cause Sarah or Beulah any trouble."

"I think this'll help."

"They wouldn't have something to do with Phil Hukari's burned-out truck, would they?"

"We're trying to find out."

"What is it they want out here on the rez?"

"We don't know for sure, Harmon."

"Government men, maybe?" He pronounced the word as *guv-mint* and squinted one eye as if taking aim. "Something to do with the senator's plane crash?"

"Might be."

Goodsky looked beyond Stephen, out the front window of the gallery. Across the street was the Mocha Moose, but Stephen understood that it wasn't the coffee shop Goodsky was seeing. In the way he'd earlier sensed a great sickness in the man that wasn't cancer, Stephen felt now an overwhelming sense of anger and anguish, and he understood that Harmon Goodsky had suffered a deep wound that had never fully healed. Stephen had seen Vietnam vets and, more recently, veterans on the rez who'd returned from Iraq and Afghanistan, men in whom he'd sensed a wounding of the soul and a poisonous festering. He'd witnessed the erratic, often destructive behavior that sometimes resulted. It wasn't PTSD, though clearly some were suffering from that condition. And it wasn't the slow debilitation that came from exposure to toxins like Agent Orange. It was a loss of the connection with the Great Mystery, the spirit that ran through all creation and united all things. Those men, Stephen understood, were lost, disconnected from others and from their true selves. Deep inside him, he felt the call to heal.

"Harmon?" Stephen spoke quietly, but the man didn't seem to hear. "Harmon?" he tried again, with no result.

"Grandpa?" Winston Goodsky stood in front of the curtains, looking concerned. "Grandpa?"

Goodsky stirred, returned from wherever his mind had taken him. "What is it, Winston?"

"The television's having trouble again."

"I'll take a look." Goodsky nodded toward the photograph in Stephen's hand. "Tell your father I want to know what he finds out."

"I'll do that."

Goodsky moved past his grandson, and Stephen could hear his heavy, uneven footsteps as he mounted a stairway out of sight.

"He gets that way sometimes," Winston said. "Kind of lost. I have to watch him."

"If you ever need a hand, you call, okay?"

The kid looked down, studied the floor, mute once again.

Stephen crossed the street and found Sarah LeDuc inside the Mocha Moose, wiping down tables. Beulah Love was there, too, helping behind the counter.

"*Anin*, Stephen," Sarah greeted him.

"*Boozhoo*," he replied. "My dad sent me to make sure everything's okay."

"All good here. What's that picture you're holding?"

If he showed her, he'd have to explain that Harmon Goodsky was keeping an eye on her and Beulah, and he wasn't certain how that might go down with her. But he didn't really have a choice.

"Harmon snapped this of one of the men who seem to be watching Ms. Love, and now you."

Sarah studied the photo. "Beulah?"

Beulah Love left the counter and joined them.

"Look familiar?"

"Maybe. It's hard to tell."

"Where did Harmon shoot this?"

"Here in Allouette," Stephen said. "They were parked just down the street."

"*Chimooks* thinking they wouldn't stand out on the rez? They're either awfully bold or awfully stupid." Sarah winked at Stephen. "I know where I'd lay my bet. Can we keep this?"

"I'd like to show it to my dad."

"Sure. I'll get a copy from Harmon. Maybe take him some apple pie to thank him for keeping an eye on us. Tell your dad that Beulah and I are doing fine." She turned to the other woman. "Aren't we?"

"We're fine," Beulah said, but not with any certainty.

Back at the ATV, Stephen sat on the photograph so that it wouldn't blow away. He donned his helmet and headed off, intending to return the way he'd come, along a back road that followed the north shore of Iron Lake. The marina parking lot, as he passed it, was almost empty. On a summer day it would have been crowded with cars. This afternoon, only a couple of vehicles were parked there, one of them a black pickup truck spattered with rust-colored mud.

He swung into the lot and stopped near the concession stand, which, in the fall, was open only on weekends. He dismounted from the ATV, removed his helmet, and set it atop the photograph of the man in the black pickup. Trying not to be too conspicuous, he walked toward the marina docks, past the truck, which was empty. The license plates, both front and back, were so mud-covered they were unreadable. He continued to the docks, where the slips were full of sailboats and launches that, in another month, would be dry-docked for the winter. As nearly as he could tell, he was alone.

He figured that if the two men had a boat, they could linger on the water and with field glasses keep an eye on the comings and goings at the Mocha Moose, only a few hundred yards distant. But Stephen saw no boat. The shoreline was rugged, with a mix of hardwoods and tall undergrowth. He considered the possibility that the men had hidden themselves somewhere in the trees or brush and were surveilling the coffee shop that way.

He took out his cell phone and made a call.

"Stay where you are," his father told him. "I'm calling Daniel. He's at the Blessings' place and can get to you faster than I can. But

I'm on my way. Don't, under any circumstances, approach these guys on your own."

Wait for Daniel. Wait for his father. It was clear he wasn't trusted to handle things on his own.

What kind of man do they think I am?

He started into the trees, moving slowly, carefully, keeping low. He followed the shoreline as it edged Allouette. In the end, he found nothing and turned back, disappointed.

They were waiting for him when he broke from the trees on his return to the marina. They flanked him, coming, it seemed, from nowhere. They were taller and broader than he, wearing sunglasses, and with their stocking caps pulled low.

One of them held up the photograph Stephen had left under the helmet in the ATV. "Who are you?" His voice was like the rumble of distant thunder.

Stephen's throat had gone instantly dry and his heart had begun to leap. Maybe it was the surprise of the men's sudden appearance, or maybe the realization that he was in over his head.

"No one," he replied.

The other man said, "Who are you working for?"

"Nobody."

"Where'd you get this?" They shoved the photograph at his face.

"Why are you so interested in Beulah Love?" he fired back, anger taking over his fear.

The man in the photo grabbed Stephen's jacket in his fist and pulled him up to tiptoe. "Who was the old coot that took my picture?"

When Stephen gave no answer, the man released his grip and gave him a hard shove.

His companion's eyes darted all around. "We need to take this somewhere private." He reached inside his jean jacket and pulled out a handgun. "Let's go, kid."

"I'm not going anywhere."

The barrel of the gun clipped his face and Stephen went down. He was pulled immediately back to his feet and shoved toward the marina parking lot. He tried to resist, and the gun barrel again became a bludgeon across the side of his head. Once more, Stephen went down. This time, things went dark, his vision full of sparks, the world muted.

When he came back to himself, he found Daniel English kneeling beside him.

"Don't get up." Daniel put a hand gently against Stephen's chest.

"I'm okay." Stephen could hear the weakness in his own voice.

"You've got a couple of nasty cuts." Daniel drew a clean handkerchief from his back pocket and folded it. "Here, hold that tight against your head."

Stephen pressed it to a place where he could already feel a goose egg forming.

Daniel pulled out his cell phone and made a call. "I'm with him, Cork. They worked him over pretty good. We need to get him looked at. I'm taking him to the clinic here in Allouette. We'll meet you there."

CHAPTER 31

The cut across Stephen's cheek took three stitches. The cut across the side of his head, four more. Mary Gomes, the PA at the tribal clinic, advised Cork that to be certain the blows hadn't done more significant damage, Stephen should be seen at the Aurora Community Hospital for a CT scan or MRI. Cork's son absolutely refused to go but accepted the ibuprofen the PA offered.

They talked in the clinic parking lot—Cork, Stephen, Daniel, and Bo.

"Did you get a good look at them?" Cork asked.

Failure was written all over Stephen's damaged face. "They were wearing sunglasses, stocking caps pulled low."

"I saw the pickup swing out of the marina lot," Daniel told them. "I didn't know it was important until I talked to Stephen, so I didn't get a plate number."

"You wouldn't have anyway," Stephen said. "The plates were covered with mud."

"What about the photo?"

"They took it," Stephen said. "They wanted to know where I

got it." He eyed his father, as if afraid some kind of accusation was forthcoming. "I didn't tell them."

"I'll get another print from Harmon."

"I blew it." Stephen shook his head angrily. "I screwed up."

"Nothing's happened that can't be fixed." Cork put his hand on his son's shoulder, but Stephen stiffened under the touch.

"All right, here's the plan," Cork said. "Daniel, I want you to take Stephen back to Crow Point. Put him into Rainy's care."

"I'm fine," Stephen insisted.

"Your head doesn't hurt?"

"A little."

"I'm sure Rainy can help with that. You need to stay quiet for a while, just to be on the safe side."

"What about Leah's ATV?" Stephen glanced in the direction of the marina.

"We'll see to that later. Okay, Daniel?"

Cork's son-in-law gave a simple nod, and Stephen, zombielike, followed him.

When they'd gone, Cork said to Bo, "I'm going to see Goodsky, get another print of that photo. Then I'll pop into the Mocha Moose and check on Sarah and Beulah. After that, I'm thinking I'll out head to Crow Point."

"I've got some things to see to myself," Bo told him. "I'll have the people I know run those plates you gave me from the airport, see if we can get a better idea who's involved in whatever's going on up here. When the courier delivers the money for the exchange, I'll give you a call and we can figure where to rendezvous."

"Thanks for your help, Bo."

"Goes both ways."

Cork walked the stone's throw to the gallery, where Goodsky was hanging a photograph. The image was of a soaring eagle silhouetted against a cloud. There were only three colors involved. The black silhouette, the white cloud, the blue sky. It was so simple but so stirring in the emotions it evoked in Cork—freedom, flight, release, all of it somehow accompanied by a sense of peace.

"I want that," he said.

Goodsky smiled. "Not for sale. It's one of Winston's. I just put it up so anyone who comes in can marvel at it. I'm good. My grandson? A genius. Did Stephen give you the photo?"

"He didn't have the chance. The man in it beat him up and took it."

Goodsky gave this somber consideration. "Did Stephen tell this thug where the photo came from?"

"No, but he paid a price for his silence. Three stitches across his cheek and more across the side of his head."

"I'm sorry, Cork."

"Not your fault, but I need another print."

"I'll have one for you in a few minutes. Can you wait?"

"I'll come back. I want to talk to Sarah and Beulah."

"I'll have it ready for you."

The women were fine. Cork felt obliged to tell them about Stephen's injuries, mostly so that they understood fully the risks that might be involved.

"I shouldn't stay here," Beulah said to Sarah. "I'm putting you in danger."

"We're seeing this through together, *nimisenh*."

"*Nimisenh?*" Beulah's eyes teared up. "*Migwech, nishiime.*"

"If we need you, Cork, we'll holler," Sarah assured him.

As he crossed the street to the gallery, Cork thought about what had just occurred. *Nimisenh*, Sarah LeDuc had called Beulah Love. Which meant "my older sister." And in reply, Beulah had called Sarah *nishiime*, which meant "my younger sister." For Beulah, who had separated herself in so many ways from the people of her blood, who'd believed only a day ago that she had no one on the rez to whom she could turn in her time of need, this was a blessing. Once again Cork was reminded of what it meant to be Anishinaabe, a part of this community that, despite its struggle against unrelenting cruelties for generations, had continued to have a strong, welcoming heart. Even in the midst of all the strangeness and menace that had descended on the Iron Lake Reservation, he had witnessed a moment of true beauty.

In the gallery, Goodsky had the print waiting. "These guys mean business."

"I wish I knew what exactly that business is."

"White guys beating up people on the rez. Makes my blood boil. Anything I can do?"

"Just keep an eye on Beulah and Sarah."

"Goes without saying. But I want something in return. When you find out what's going on, who these *chimooks* are, you let me know."

"It's a deal."

In Henry's cabin on Crow Point, Cork found Stephen drinking some kind of tea Rainy had prepared. Stephen looked drained, and there was a sullenness in him that worried Cork.

"How're you feeling?"

"Fine."

"That's surprising," Rainy said. "Those cuts, that knot, most people would be feeling a little pain."

"I've taken a lot more than a little pain before."

"I don't doubt your ability to endure pain," Rainy said gently. "I'm just reminding you that there's no shame in admitting when it hurts."

Cork was pretty sure what hurt Stephen most wasn't his head.

"Where are Henry and Leah and Waaboo?"

"They took Trixie for a little walk," Daniel said.

"There's something we need to discuss."

"That tone always means trouble," Rainy said. "As if we didn't already have enough."

Cork filled them in on the ransom details, at least as they stood.

Rainy looked worried. "Why do they want you to make the exchange?"

Daniel said, "If it is Tom Blessing behind this, it makes a kind of sense. He knows Cork."

"You really believe Tom Blessing would do something like this?" Rainy asked.

"I have to accept the possibility," Cork replied. "If we get the flight recorder back, it doesn't matter who's behind it."

"Why at the town meeting?" Daniel said. "It seems so public."

"The meeting's at the high school. Tom went there, probably knows it pretty well. He may have some special drop site in mind. I like the location. Might be to my advantage."

"How so?"

"Too many witnesses to try something untoward."

"Like shooting you?" Rainy said.

"In a word, yes."

"I should be there with you," Stephen said. "I went to that high school. I know it a lot better than you do, Dad."

"You're staying here. You've already taken enough chances for one day."

Cork saw that this directive didn't sit well with his son, but it was nonnegotiable.

"Tom Blessing." Rainy crossed her arms, clearly unconvinced.

Cork checked his watch. "We'll know in a few hours."

CHAPTER 32

When Gerard answered, he was breathing hard, as if he'd been running or exercising. "Do you have something for me?"

"A question," Bo replied. "Was it your guys who beat up Stephen O'Connor?"

"I've left the locals to you. And why would I have the kid beat up?"

"Exactly. Unless you don't have control over all your operatives."

"You're the only one who ever worries me." Gerard gasped for air. "So, that's it?"

"There's more. It's possible we'll have the flight recorder in our hands tonight."

Gerard was suddenly quiet, as if not breathing at all. Then, "How?"

"O'Connor got a ransom call. Twenty thousand dollars. The exchange is tonight."

"Where's the money coming from?"

"I've arranged for that. My own resources."

"And O'Connor's making the drop?"

"That's right. It's supposed to go down at the town meeting in Aurora."

"I'll have men there."

"Not a good idea. They spot your guys, they might run. Twenty grand isn't much to risk. Leave it to me."

"Right," Gerard said, his voice cold. "And we know how that turned out for you the last time."

Bo ignored the reference to the murdered Argentine kid. "I'll take care of this."

"Who's behind it?"

"At the moment, it's looking like one of the Indians who was on the scene early, a guy name of Tom Blessing."

"Blessing. The one whose mother croaked?"

"Compassionately put."

"Twenty grand. Sounds cheap, even for an Indian."

"Maybe Blessing needs the cash fast. Gambling debt or something."

"Find out."

"Let's focus on securing the recorder first. We can worry about rounding up Blessing later."

"If you get the recorder, there's a bonus in it for you."

A bonus, Bo thought, after he'd ended the call. With Gerard, and depending upon who'd brought him in, that could easily turn out to be a bullet in the brain.

He kayaked to the little island just offshore from Gerard's operations center and downloaded to his cell phone what had been recorded by the voice-activated bug on the window. He reset the instrument, kayaked back to the wooded point where he'd left his Jeep, and listened to the recorded conversations. Mostly they were orders Gerard had delivered to his subordinates and discussions of where to look for what they continued to call the "waves." His name came up. Gerard spoke of him as "our tick on the skin of things up here." That made Bo smile. Then Gerard said something that caused Bo to replay the recording.

"When we get the egg that's dropped, maybe we can shoot down the eagle, too, and close up shop here."

The egg that's dropped. The eagle. These sounded like images straight out of the vision Stephen O'Connor had related, a vision Bo had readily dismissed as Indian voodoo stuff.

He started his Jeep and headed toward the double-trunk birch that marked the beginning of the trail to Crow Point. He needed to talk to Stephen again.

The call came a few minutes later. It was Olympia McCarthy's brother. He informed Bo that he'd just landed at Olson Field.

"I'm on my way," Bo said.

"Look for the chopper. I'm waiting inside."

It was going on four o'clock when Bo had the money in hand, twenty thousand dollars in small bills. Per the extortionist's instructions, it was in a backpack, the kind a high school kid might use to carry books, nothing that would be out of place in a crowd in a high school auditorium. Bo kept the pack on the seat beside him as he continued to the double-trunk birch, then slipped the straps over his shoulders as he began the hike into Crow Point.

He arrived at the old man's cabin to find that all wasn't well. Stephen O'Connor had disappeared. An hour earlier, he'd told everyone he was going out for a few minutes to get some air. He never returned.

"You didn't run into him when you came down the trail?" Cork asked.

Bo shook his head. "And his Jeep wasn't parked on the road either."

"Then he's taken off." Cork was clearly upset.

Meloux, the old medicine man, didn't seem bothered by the kid's absence. "You have put a log across his path, Corcoran O'Connor. He has simply jumped the log."

"It could get him killed, Henry."

"You think he does not know that? And you think he does not understand that you are also willing to put your life in danger? He is his father's son. Would you have him be someone different?"

"Did you try calling him?" Bo asked.

"He's not answering."

"I'm betting he'll be at the town meeting," English said. "With all that bandaging on his head, he'll stand out like a clown. You won't miss him."

"The men who beat him up won't miss him either."

Little Waaboo and his mother sat in the corner of the cabin, the old dog, Trixie, between them. Waaboo looked up from petting the dog. "The monster won't get him. He's too smart."

"What monster?" Bo asked.

"It's a nightmare Waaboo had," Jenny explained.

Which brought Bo back to the reason he'd come to Crow Point. "In this vision your son has, he sees a kid shoot an eagle out of the sky, right?"

"That's right," Cork said.

"And this eagle, as it falls, drops an egg?"

"Yeah."

"The egg has got to be the flight recorder," Bo said. "What about the eagle?"

"I've been thinking it was the senator's plane."

"And the kid?"

"The kid is Stephen," English said.

"And not Stephen," Cork said. "Look, the town meeting's in a couple of hours. I'm heading into Aurora, see if I can track Stephen down before that. Bo, you should probably come with me."

"I'd like to be there, too," English threw in.

Cork shook his head. "I understand, Daniel, but with all the confusion and the disappearances on the reservation, I think it would be best if you stayed. I'd hate myself if I asked you to come and something happened here while we were gone."

"No one knows we're here," English said.

"Maybe. But do you want to take that chance?" He glanced toward Waaboo.

With a nod that was clearly reluctant, English gave in.

Rainy walked with her husband and Bo outside and into the meadow.

"I parked at Crow Point East. That's what we call the parking area nearest Allouette," Cork told Bo. "You came in along the path from the Aurora side?"

"Yeah."

"Let's split up here. I'll meet you at the high school half an hour before the town meeting."

"If you hear anything more, call me," Bo said.

He headed toward the trees where the path to the double-trunk began. Before he left the meadow, he looked back. In the yellow slant of the afternoon light, Cork had his wife in his arms, a long goodbye. Bo felt a deep, painful twist of envy.

CHAPTER 33

Stephen removed the bandaging that covered his cheek. The wound beneath was raw and pink, the stitches black across it. His cheek and eye socket were dark-bruised. Even to himself, he was scary to look at. He'd bought something called Neutrogena Healthy Skin liquid makeup. He tapped a bit onto his fingertip and dabbed the flesh-colored goo over his wound. It wasn't the magic cover-up he'd hoped for, but he did look less like Frankenstein. He applied it to the whole bruised area.

His cell phone rang again. His father. He didn't answer. Next came a text message: *Let me know ur ok*. Stephen replied: *OK*.

He changed his clothes, put on jeans, a long-sleeved T-shirt, a gray hoodie, a black stocking cap. He returned to the bathroom, pulled the hood over his head, and was satisfied. It was hard to tell he'd been injured, and if he kept his head down, hard to tell who he was.

He left the house, figuring that if they were looking for him—his father or the men who put the gashes in his head or the people, whoever they were, who were disturbing the spirits of this place he called home—Gooseberry Lane would be one of their stops. He drove to the Pinewood Broiler on Oak Street, took a seat in a booth next to the window, where he could see who came and went. He had a couple of hours to kill before the town meeting. Coffee and something to eat would do the trick.

"Hey, Stephen."

His waitress was Marlee Daychild, the girl he fell in love with in high school. The only girl he'd ever loved, in fact. Their relationship had been a difficult one, for many reasons, most of them, Stephen knew, because of him, because of all the uncertainty, the restlessness that was such a part of who he seemed to be. Like the town of Aurora itself, Marlee was an element of his life that threatened him because of its comfort.

"When did you start working here, Marlee?"

"Never mind that. What happened to you?"

"Nothing," he said.

Marlee was Anishinaabe and lived with her mother on the rez. Her hair was black and long, tied back in a ponytail. Her eyes were dark brown and warm with concern and caring. More caring than he felt he deserved. She wore a T-shirt with the word RESIST printed across the front.

"You got into a fight?" she asked.

"Just a stupid accident."

"Bullshit." She sat across from him in the booth. "You look terrible."

"Thanks."

"Anything you want to talk about?"

Yes, he thought. But he said, "Let it go, Marlee. It's nothing."

Still, she tried again to break through the shell he'd put around himself. "That stupid accident of yours, it wouldn't have anything do with all the trouble on the rez?"

"Are you going to take my order?"

Her brown eyes became hard and sharp, like little drill bits. "Fine." She stood up and said, "What'll you have?"

"Coffee, a patty melt with fries."

She wrote on her pad, turned on her heel, and left him to his brooding.

When she'd gone, Stephen thought about her T-shirt. RE-SIST. Resist what? But he could feel it inside himself. A stone of resistance. Which was exactly the opposite of the patience and acceptance Henry Meloux had tried for so long to teach him. Stephen wanted to resist everything. What Marlee was offering him. What his father had taught him. The understandings that Henry and Rainy had tried to guide him toward. He didn't want any more visions. He didn't want to sit waiting for answers to come. He had no patience now. He had only questions, and he wanted to track the answers like a hunter and, like a hunter, bring them down.

He stared out the window of the Broiler. Across the street was Ardith Kane's shop, North Star Notions, the display window already full of Halloween decorations. To the left of it, Pflugleman's Rexall Drugs, to the right Finn's Stationery and Office Supply. Rising behind them was the clock tower of the county courthouse. This was all of a piece, a tableau that hadn't changed across the course of his whole life. He felt trapped. In place. In time. In who he was.

"Here's your coffee."

He was startled out of his angry reverie.

"Are you okay, Stephen? Really?" Marlee had put away her own anger, and once again her eyes were soft with concern. "You jumped like you'd been shot."

"I'm fine. Just need some coffee in me."

She smiled gently. "It's not known for settling nerves."

He managed the ghost of a smile. "You're right. Things are a little tough at the moment. I just need some time to think. And maybe a little food in me."

"That I can help with. Your patty melt will be right up."

He lingered more than an hour, as the Pinewood Broiler filled and Marlee got busy with other customers. The sun was just about to set when he signaled her for the check.

"Call me," she told him.

"I will."

"Promise."

And he did.

At the high school, the parking lot was already nearly full. Two State Patrol officers stood at the front door. Stephen joined a small group entering together, and he passed the officers without incident. A loud murmuring came from the auditorium as people gathered, greeted one another, found seats. As with so many of the gatherings that brought Shinnobs into Aurora, the folks from the rez took seats in back. Stephen stood just inside the door, scanning the crowd. He spotted his father in an aisle seat on the far side. Bo Thorson sat not far away. Stephen lowered his head and sat in the dim light of the back row, where he could keep an eye on his father's movements and Thorson's.

A table and two chairs had been set up in the middle of the stage, two microphones on the table. A few minutes after seven, Renée Legris, the mayor of Aurora, and Governor Arne Johnson walked together from one of the wings and took their seats. The audience quieted.

Stephen knew the mayor. Everyone in Aurora knew the mayor. Stephen had served her burgers through the window at Sam's Place. Her daughter had graduated from high school a year behind him. She was a nice enough person, but he'd always felt an uncomfortable energy coming from her, a relentless push. She introduced the governor and offered him the floor.

Governor Arne Johnson was someone Stephen had never liked. His policies had been at odds with so many of the values Stephen held dear. He came from money, not a sin in itself, but it was clear to Stephen that he'd never understood what it was to struggle. Among the policies that Stephen objected to most was Johnson's stand on the undeveloped resources of Minnesota's North Country. He was an advocate for the proposed mine.

The governor opened with an eloquent portrait of Senator McCarthy, which was a very different depiction of her than he'd painted in the past, when their political agendas had clashed, which had been often. He moved smoothly into the issue at hand, the question of granting permits for the proposed mining operation. He defended his own position, which was that moving forward with the mine would be of tremendous benefit to the Iron Range, an area that, in the wake of so many mine closures, continued to suffer economically.

"I understand Senator McCarthy's concerns about sullying the pristine North Country, but I've studied America Midwest Mining's proposal, and I can assure you that there will be multiple safeguards in place, the most modern techniques available to prevent any spillage that might adversely affect the land or the water here. That's my view, but I'm really here to listen, to let you know that your concerns are being heard."

Right, Stephen thought. *In one ear and out the other*.

Mayor Legris opened up the meeting to comments and questions. And there was a landslide. One after another, the residents of Tamarack County gave voice to their fears.

Finally, Dorothy Heinz left her seat near the back of the auditorium and stepped up to the microphone below the stage. She was an old woman, small, white-haired, a little bent, and Stephen knew her well. She'd been one of his Sunday school teachers at St. Agnes. Born in Turtle Lake, Wisconsin, she'd come to the Iron Lake Reservation as a young child to live with her grandparents. During the Second World War, she'd been a member of the Women's Army Corps, and when she came home to the rez, she'd married and become a strong presence in the community. She loved to bake and had taught classes in traditional cooking and in canning, and her berry pies were legendary. When Stephen camped in the Boundary Waters, he still made bannock bread and wild rice leek soup in the way he'd learned from her. She was a strong woman, who could still be found mowing her own lawn on a riding mower, wearing a Twins ball cap. And as she leaned to the microphone and spoke with grace and authority, Stephen thought there was no better voice for her people, the Anishinaabeg.

"I have lived with the beauty of Mother Earth for more than ninety years," she said. "When I was a girl, I went with my grandfather to catch fish in the lakes and the rivers. We plucked blueberries in the clearings where the bears ate them, too. Every fall, we gathered wild rice on Makwa Lake, watched ospreys dive from the trees, listened to the song of the loons coming from the morning mist. Now that I am *nokomis*, a grandmother, I take my eleven grandchildren and my ten great-grandchildren to the places my grandfather took me.

"The earth isn't just rock and dirt and trees and water. It's one thing, one heart, one spirit. It offers us life and beauty and, if we listen, wisdom. And it asks nothing in return, not even gratitude, because giving is the whole reason for its creation.

"And why are we created? To receive, to honor, and to protect. What you talk about here isn't just the wounding of that beautiful, giving spirit. What you talk about here, in your ignorance, is the wounding of the spirit of us all. We are not separate. To kill the water, to kill the fish, to kill the trees, to kill the birds, is to kill ourselves. That is all I have to say."

To great applause, Dorothy Heinz retook her seat.

Then a shout came from the audience: "When I was a boy my father had a job in the Apex Mine, a good-paying job. We drove a nice car and had a nice house. When the mine closed, all that changed. Hell, look around you. The towns on the Iron Range are sliding downhill, and it won't be long before they hit rock bottom. Ghost towns. It was mining built the Range and it's mining that'll save it. We got plenty of ore still in the ground, plenty of minerals, and plenty of men looking for work. Seems to me a match made in heaven. If the governor says the mine's going to be safe, then the mine's going to be safe. I say let 'em start digging. The sooner they get to work, the sooner the rest of us do, too."

Although the wind so far had been against the mine, this spontaneous outburst was met with more than a little applause. From that point on, the comments flew from advocates on both sides of the issue, and Stephen could feel the mounting tension in the air, a taut spring ready to snap.

Then a man leapt up on the far side of the auditorium, Boog Sorenson, someone Stephen had never liked. "We'd've had that mine up and running a long time ago if it wasn't for people like McCarthy," he hollered. "You ask me, that plane crash was the best thing could've happened up here."

Even in a room so contentiously divided, the comment stunned the crowd to silence.

"Sit down and shut up," someone yelled.

"It's a free country," Sorenson asserted. "I've got a right to say what I think."

"And you've had your say." Mayor Legris's voice was stern. "Now sit down and let others speak."

"Let him talk," another voiced shouted. And chaos threatened to descend.

The outburst had drawn Stephen's attention. When he swung his eyes back to where his father had been sitting, the seat was empty. Bo Thorson was gone, too.

CHAPTER 34

When Boog Sorenson began his rant, Cork wanted to stuff his fist down the man's throat. That was generally the response Sorenson elicited from Cork when he opened his mouth. Boog Sorenson had been a deputy under Cork in his first term as sheriff of Tamarack County and was the only officer Cork had ever fired. He took the action after a number of questionable arrests of people of Anishinaabe heritage, and one particularly nasty altercation on the rez, which Sorenson had handled badly and with clear prejudice. In the next election, Sorenson ran against Cork, and much of his platform had been an angry cry against what he characterized as "a blind eye" when it came to policing Indians, on and off the rez. Cork won the election by a landslide, but the bad blood still ran deep between them.

He was tempted to join those shouting down Sorenson, but his cell phone vibrated and the instructions for the ransom drop came as a text: *The gate of the gravel pit. Now. No funny stuff.* It was from the same number as the call that afternoon.

No funny stuff. Straight out of a bad movie. Cork and Bo rose and left while the rant in the auditorium went on. They headed out to Cork's Expedition to pick up the backpack that held the money.

"An access road a hundred yards that way leads right to the gate of the gravel pit," Cork explained. "Unless I get another instruction, looks like the exchange will go down there."

Bo studied the sky. "Getting dark. Hard to see much of anything. I won't be far behind."

"They said no funny stuff. Direct quote."

"Who are we dealing with, the Three Stooges?"

"I'm about to find out." Cork called the number the text had come from but got no answer. Then he texted, *What about my friends?*

A moment later, he got the reply: *Bring the money. You get them and the black box.*

"You're not going to take any chances, right?" Bo said.

"The flight recorder and my friends, that's all I'm after."

"I won't be more than fifty yards away. Anything goes haywire, I'm right there."

Cork shouldered the backpack and walked toward the access road, leaving behind the bright lights of the school parking lot. In the west, the sky along the horizon still held an ice-blue glow, against which the trees were nothing but silhouettes. He crossed the grass of the school grounds and came to the old asphalt of the gravel pit access road. He turned toward the gate, a black mesh of Cyclone fencing that, against the soft blue of the distant sky, reminded him of a spider's web. He saw no one, but that didn't surprise him. He reached the gate and stood alone, waiting for someone to show or to deliver further instructions.

That's when the shot came.

The round slammed into his chest, dead center, knocking him back. He hit the ground and lay still, staring up at a sky sequined with sparkles, none of which were stars.

———

Stephen stumbled onto Bo Thorson first, the man in a crouch, a pistol in his hand.

"Down. Get down." Bo's voice was taut.

"Are you hit?" Stephen said.

"No."

"My dad?"

Bo got slowly to his feet. "Stay here."

"I'm coming."

"Then stay behind me."

Bo loped toward the gate of the old gravel pit, Stephen close enough to be his shadow. In front of the gate, a dark figure slowly stood up.

"Dad!" Stephen leapt past Bo and reached his father in time to help steady him. "Are you okay?"

"Feels like a train ran me down."

Bo came up beside them. "You hit?"

"The vest." Stephen's father put a hand near his heart.

"The shot came from the south." Bo used his pistol to indicate a small grove of birch trees a hundred yards away. In daylight, the leaves would have been golden and the trunks stark white. Now they were just a black clustering. "Shooter's probably already bolted."

The three men stood together in a sudden explosion of light.

"Police! Drop your weapons!"

Bo said quietly, "The cavalry."

Sheriff Marsha Dross held up the armor and studied the place where the bullet had hit. "You could have been killed."

Cork said, "Thanks to Bo, the only hole is in the mackinaw I wore over that vest."

Her glare swung to Bo. "You certainly came prepared. What did you bring to my county besides body armor?"

"A license that makes it all legal."

She set the vest on her desk and slid from it one of the ceramic plates. "You were expecting heavy caliber?"

"Best to be prepared," Bo replied.

She turned her attention to the backpack. "Twenty thousand. That's it?"

"I know," Bo said. "Chump change. Pretty sure it was a setup, just to get Cork in the open."

"A setup by who?"

"Wish I could tell you, Sheriff."

"Bo Thorson." She rolled the name around in her thinking. "Bo Thorson." Then a light came on. "Not the Bo Thorson who saved the First Lady?"

"Yeah, that Bo Thorson."

"No longer Secret Service?"

"Left a while back. Private now."

"Working for whom?"

"That's confidential."

She looked toward Cork. "Do you know the answer to that one?"

"Jerome Hill, Senator McCarthy's father." Cork gave Bo a shrug. "Sorry. Not my client."

"He doesn't believe the crash was due to pilot error?" The sheriff's eyes swung back and forth between the two men.

"He has significant doubts," Bo answered.

"And his hope is that the flight recorder will resolve the issue?"

"At least clarify some things."

The sheriff leaned her butt against her desk, crossed her arms, scowled at Cork. "You never mentioned Thorson. I thought we had an agreement." She reached out and tapped the vest. "Don't you think it would have been appropriate to inform me of this at least?"

"Things moved quickly," Cork said, though that wasn't the whole truth.

Dross looked at Stephen, who'd been mostly silent since they were all brought in. "What happened to your face?"

Stephen had been staring at the floor. He lifted his eyes briefly, then looked down again. Cork wasn't sure what to make of this. Nervousness? Shame? Fear?

"Just clumsy."

"And you just happened to be at the town meeting?"

Stephen's voice was quiet but steady. "I wasn't supposed to be. Dad didn't want me there. I went anyway."

"So you knew about this exchange that was supposed to go down?"

"I knew."

Dross breathed deeply, once, twice, thinking things over. "Okay, Cork. If, as Thorson says, the intent was to take you out, it seems to me it had to be someone who knows you're investigating the senator's crash. Who would that be?"

"My family and some of the folks on the rez."

"What about Gerard?" Stephen said. "He seems to know a lot."

"Gerard?" Dross thought for a moment. "The one who questioned you yesterday, right? Who is he?"

Cork said, "He feels military, but there's more to him than that, I'm sure."

Dross left the desk, began pacing. "I had a visit from Alex Quaker, the number two man in the FBI's National Security Branch. He advised me to keep my nose out of this business. Was this an act of terrorism, Thorson?"

"I can't say at the moment. Maybe that's what the flight recorder would have told us."

"You believe someone has it?"

She addressed her question to Cork, and he brought her up to date on what they knew.

"Do you think it was Blessing who shot at you tonight?"

Before he could answer, the phone on the sheriff's desk buzzed. She picked it up, listened. "Send him in." She hung up. "Quaker's here. This should be interesting."

Two men entered. The one in front had red hair and a prognathic jaw that gave him a relentlessly determined look. The man two steps behind was younger, serious-looking in a religiously zealous way. The chill they brought with them reminded Cork of a storm front ushering in a blizzard.

"Sheriff." A one-word greeting from the man in front. He didn't bother introducing his companion. "Which one is Cork O'Connor?"

Cork said, "That would be me."

"And Thorson?"

Bo lifted a hand.

"And you're the son?" the man said to Stephen.

"Yes."

The man's eyes went across the three of them, and Cork thought of a machine gunner taking aim.

"I'll need an interview room, Sheriff."

CHAPTER 35

Gerard leaned against the deck railing of Bo's cabin, smoking a Cuban cigar and gazing out at the black water of the lake inlet. Lights like solitary stars glittered along the far shoreline. A saffron glow over the treetops pinpointed the place where the moon was about to rise. Bo watched the cigar ember brighten, then dim each time Gerard inhaled. He hated the odor of cigar smoke, especially in this place where the scent of evergreen felt calming and healing to the soul.

"So when Quaker asked about your connection with all this, what did you tell him?"

"The truth. That I'm working for the senator's family."

This was clearly no surprise to Gerard. Bo wondered how long he'd known.

"Did you say anything about me?"

"Silence is one of the things you pay me for."

Gerard fixed him with a cold eye. "I guess it was too much to hope that loyalty might be one, too."

"It's a complicated game we're playing."

"What do you tell the senator's family?"

"Everything I tell you."

"Do you tell them things you don't tell me?"

"I tell you everything."

Gerard considered this, probably weighing its truth. "Quaker will be putting two and two together pretty soon, the stiff-jawed bastard. I'll take care of him eventually, but we need to keep him in the dark awhile longer." The cigar ember bloomed red, and smoke exploded gray above the deck railing. "I wonder if they really have it."

"They?"

"Whoever tried to take O'Connor out."

"If they had the recorder, they wouldn't care about O'Connor. As far as I can tell, we've gotten nowhere. Quaker thinks it's domestic terrorism, thinks the Lexington Brigade might be behind it."

"The Lexington Brigade?" Gerard gave a grunt that passed for a laugh. "Bunch of wackos out of South Dakota."

"The name Cole Wannamaker mean anything to you?"

"He heads up the brigade. He's got himself a compound in the Black Hills."

"Quaker says Wannamaker dropped off the radar a couple of weeks ago. Quaker thinks he might be around here somewhere."

Gerard faced Bo, the cigar ember like a gaping red hole in the center of his pursed lips. "Why?"

"A guy stood up at the meeting tonight and basically hailed the senator's demise. Got some applause among the folks in that auditorium. The guy was Boog Sorenson, commander of the local chapter of the Lexington Brigade. He's got a few followers in the North Country."

"Wacko enough to assassinate a U.S. senator?"

"Think Oklahoma City."

"Why now?"

"Maybe the brigade up here has taken strong exception to the senator's opposition to this mine proposal. Another possibility might be the bill banning assault rifles she was about to introduce. That bill's got a lot of press, and it's looking like it might actually have some good bipartisan support. It certainly has the NRA worried. Or maybe the Manila Accord. The alt right likes it because they hope it'll contain China without America having to confront the Red Dragon directly. The senator made it clear she was going to do her best to defeat the accord."

"How does he think the plane was brought down?"

"Didn't say, but if he's thinking domestic terrorism, it had to be something like a ground-to-air missile."

"The brigade?" Gerard ashed his cigar beyond the railing. "I don't buy it. What about this Blessing?"

"I'll check him out some more, but he doesn't feel right for any of this."

"Did you fill Quaker in about Blessing and the other missing Indians?"

"Yeah. He told me and O'Connor to back off, he'd take things from here."

"You keep doing what you're doing. I'll take care of Quaker." Gerard studied his cigar, which he'd smoked almost to its end. "You're sure there's nothing you haven't told me?"

Bo thought about Stephen's vision and the boy bringing down the eagle, but said, "You know what I know."

When Gerard had gone, Bo made a call. "It was a setup."

"We heard. And we heard that you're okay. The news is reporting it as a flare-up because of the contentious town hall meeting

up there. One shot fired, but not at the governor. No one hurt.
Nothing else official at the moment."

"Alex Quaker is here keeping a lid on things."

"You've seen him?"

"Had a long conversation this evening. His story is that it's the
Lexington Brigade."

"We've suspected that some of the threats Olympia received
came from the brigade."

"So when he puts it out there, it'll be a story that will carry
weight, a good diversion."

"You don't buy it?"

"There are things about it I like. If it is the brigade and they do
have some membership up here, that might explain the disappearance of the Indians. The locals might have the kind of information
that would make it possible for them to locate and grab these
folks." Bo thought for a few moments. "And there've been reports
of white poachers on the reservation. Could be the brigade scoping
out the territory."

"It could be anybody scoping out the territory, even Gerard's people. Bo, is it possible Gerard was behind the setup
tonight?"

"With Gerard, anything is possible. But I don't know how
getting O'Connor out of the picture would benefit him. It could
be someone on the rez who doesn't want him asking questions.
And there are still players involved in this that I haven't identified yet."

"Players?"

"O'Connor wrote down a bunch of numbers from government
plates out at the airport where NTSB is running their investigation. They were all vehicles from a pool, no agency prefixes. I have
a friend looking into who checked them out from the pool. That
might prove enlightening."

At the other end, she sighed. "I'm beginning to wonder if we'll ever know the truth. There's so much smoke."

"I'll do my best to clear it away, I promise."

"I know."

The odor of Gerard's cigar still lingered in the air. Bo moved to the far end of the deck, where the scent of evergreen was strong. "Gerard knows I'm working for the senator's family."

"How?"

"I told him, but it was clear the news came as no surprise. Surveillance of some kind, probably. He might even have somebody on the inside on your end. You be careful."

"I will."

Bo breathed in the scent of pine, which made him feel oddly refreshed, even hopeful. "When will he be arriving for the memorial service?"

"The day after tomorrow."

"He's kept a low profile during all this."

"When we have answers, he'll speak out. You know that."

"And you'll be right there beside him."

"That's where I belong." When he didn't reply, she said, "Is that all for tonight?"

"No rest for the wicked. Still a little cleanup work to do."

When the call had ended, he returned in the dark to the wooded point where he'd sequestered his kayak and paddled to the island offshore from Gerard's command center. He downloaded the most recent recording. Back at his cabin, when he listened, he was more convinced than ever that Gerard wasn't behind the setup that night. In what was clearly a conference between Gerard and a couple of his top people, the suggestion arose of salting the audience with their own men. Gerard nixed that, giving Bo a compliment: "One good man is all I need there."

Gerard was a piece of work, one Bo had never been able to pin down completely. It was clear the man appreciated his abilities, but Bo also understood that if Gerard had to, he'd feed an operative, any operative, to the wolves. The game they were all playing was deadly, and it had no rules.

CHAPTER 36

They'd gathered around the fire ring on Crow Point. The air was still, the moon on the rise, midnight sapphires sparkling on the surface of Iron Lake, only a stone's throw away. Waaboo slept on a blanket on the ground, his little arm thrown over the old dog, Trixie, who wasn't asleep but lay blinking in the firelight.

"Thank God for that vest." Rainy sat close beside Cork, her fingers laced in his and resting on his thigh. He felt her concern in the intensity of her grip. "No more heroics, promise me."

"Nothing heroic about it. I just walked into a setup."

"And you," Jenny said to Stephen. "What were you thinking?"

"That I might be more useful there than sitting around here." His voice remained sullen.

"From now on," Cork said, "nobody acts alone. We're in this together. Clear?" He'd addressed his remarks to them all, but his eyes were on Stephen.

"It wasn't Tom Blessing," Daniel said. "I'd stake my life on it."

"I think you're right. But that probably means Tom's in the same boat as the Hukaris and the Loves, and what boat that is God only knows. There's a clock ticking in my head. I'm thinking that if we don't we get some answers soon, Phil and Sue and Tom and the Loves are . . ." He couldn't quite bring himself to finish, to say the word. *Dead.*

Leah Duling sat next to Henry Meloux, who had said almost nothing since he'd asked for the fire to be built. When Leah had offered a mild objection—"It's late, Henry"—the old Mide had replied, "We are in the dark, and fire illuminates." Now she asked, "Do you sense death?"

The old man looked toward the dark where the forest lay beyond the firelight. "Something is here. It is huge and it is evil and it is meant for killing. That is what I sense."

"The monster at Stephen's back?" Jenny asked.

But Cork was also remembering that Waaboo had had a nightmare of a many-headed monster.

Trixie stood suddenly and eyed the gap in the outcrops where the path from Meloux's cabin came through. In the firelight, the rocks quivered red-orange, the gap between them murky black. The dog gave a low, menacing growl. Cork freed himself from Rainy's grip and stood. Daniel rose, too, reaching for the sidearm holstered at his waist.

What stumbled into sight surprised the hell out of Cork, probably out of them all. Ned Love stood illuminated in the firelight, supporting the weight of his nephew Monkey, whose jacket was black with old blood.

"We're on the dock," Ned explained, "just getting into the canoe to cross Little Bass for some hunting. Cyrus sets up a ruckus like I ain't heard from him in a long while. Then the shot comes, takes out Cyrus. The next shot catches Monkey. I spot two men at the cabin, get my rifle to my shoulder, squeeze off a couple of rounds. I drag Monkey into the canoe and paddle like hell for the far side of the lake. Had to leave Cyrus behind. Near broke my heart."

They were in Meloux's cabin, Monkey Love on the bunk, where the old Mide and Rainy tended to him. They'd opened his shirt to expose the bullet's entry wound.

"I tried to clean that best I could," Ned said. "Put some moss on it, but I knew it needed better looking after. Why I brought Monkey here."

"The wound looks clean, Ned," Rainy said. "That moss was a good idea. But Monkey's lost a lot of blood. We need to get him to the hospital."

"Nope. In a hospital bed, Monkey'd be like a fish in a barrel."

"Did you get a look at them?" Cork asked.

"Not a good enough look."

"Two of them, you say?"

"That's all I saw. Could've been more, I suppose. But if there was, they weren't shooting."

"Two," Cork said. He glanced at Daniel. "Your poachers?"

"Could be."

"Or the guys who did this," Stephen said, pointing to his stitched cheek.

"That bullet's still in Monkey's shoulder," Rainy said. "Ned, we really have to get him to the hospital."

"Ain't going to happen."

"Who knows what damage that bullet's done?"

"I put him in that hospital, I got a feelin' he ain't coming out."

"Ned—"

"Remove his shirt," Meloux said.

Rainy made no move to comply. "Why?"

"Remove his shirt and you will see."

With Ned's help, Rainy stripped off the bloodstained shirt. Monkey Love's torso was like a human game of tic-tac-toe, long scars crisscrossing his skin.

"What happened to him?" Rainy asked.

"Prison fights, mostly," Ned Love replied. "He didn't do so well inside."

"Turn him over," Meloux said.

Monkey, who'd seemed only vaguely aware of things since his arrival, gave a long, painful groan with the repositioning. Like his chest, his back was remarkable for the number of scars it bore. Meloux sat on the bunk and ran his hand lightly over Monkey's back near the right shoulder blade.

"There," he said. "Feel it, Niece?"

Rainy touched where Meloux had indicated. "The bullet."

"We will take it out."

"Uncle Henry, a procedure like that should be done in an operating room."

"You have cut human beings before."

"Minor things. This is way beyond my capability."

"You will not do it?"

"I can't, ethically."

"Fetch my knife, Leah," the old Mide said.

Rainy's dark brown eyes grew huge with surprise and concern. "You're not going to cut it out, are you?"

"I have cut out bullets before."

"I'm not even going to ask about that, but it had to have been in a time when those hands of yours didn't shake."

"I'll cut it out," Cork offered.

"No." Meloux was firm. "This is work for a healer." He looked to Ned Love. "You are his uncle, his closest family. What do you wish?"

"He ain't going to a hospital. He's been sliced up before, and not by anyone who gave a hoot about him. He'll survive another cut or two."

"What about all that lost blood?" Rainy said.

"He is not the first human being to lose blood to a wound.

When the bullet is out, if the wound stays clean, his body will make more blood in time."

"Uncle Henry—" she began but once again was cut off.

"I will take the bullet out," Meloux said.

"No." Rainy turned to Leah. "My medical bag is in your cabin. Could you bring it to me? And, Stephen, I'll need clean towels, lots of them. Go with Leah."

As a public health nurse, Rainy made all manner of calls on the rez, and she always brought her medical bag. She did the same, Cork knew, whenever she visited her centenarian great-uncle on Crow Point. She was a woman always prepared. Now she closed her eyes and steeled herself for what was ahead.

When it was over and Monkey was resting, Rainy said, "I'm going to get some air."

She went outside into the night, and Cork started after her.

"She needs to be alone, Corcoran O'Connor," Meloux advised.

Cork had seldom argued with Meloux, but he said, "I should be with her."

"To tell her that she is a fine healer, that she is loved, that you understand the difficulty in what she has done? Do you think she does not know these things?"

"To comfort her, Henry."

"The comfort of a healer is the healed. Give her the honor of her time alone with herself."

It was hard accepting the advice of the old Mide, but Cork lowered himself back into his chair.

"Who were they?" Ned asked. "Them men who shot my nephew."

"We don't know," Daniel replied. "But we think we know what

they were after. We think they're looking for the flight recorder from the plane that crashed."

"What's it look like?"

"They call it a black box, Ned, but it's really orange."

"Orange?" Ned Love squinched up his face. "A little orange box? I know where it is."

Cork sat suddenly erect in his chair. "You picked it up?"

"Nope, just know where it is. Would have told somebody if I'd known they were looking for it, but we got shoved away from that crash so quick. And nobody came around later to ask us. Then those guys showed up and started shooting."

"Where is it?"

"In the woods by the bog where the plane came down."

"People have been over that area a hundred times, Ned. How come they haven't found it?"

"Them searchers, I'm guessing they were looking at the ground. Me, I hunt squirrels, so I look up."

CHAPTER 37

He woke and lay in his sleeping bag, which he'd unrolled in the tall grass of the meadow on Crow Point. The moon was full and, like a ravenous god, had devoured the stars around it. The two cabins nearby were dark, everyone inside asleep. The breeze was out of the southwest, soft and unseasonably warm. The grass stalks around him swayed, and he could hear the voice of that gentle wind whispering to him. He didn't hear the menace Henry Meloux seemed to have heard the spirits speak. To Stephen, the sound was a hopeful crooning: *Soon, soon, soon.*

It was the vision that had awakened him, the same visitation played out in the same way. His inability to understand its meaning had eaten at him, an acid on his soul. But tonight was different. Tonight there was promise. In the wind. In the voice. In the way the tall grass yielded.

He heard the creak of the door on Henry Meloux's cabin, watched as the old man came his way, bent ever so slightly, like the grass. In the moonlight, the old man was silver.

Without a word or an acknowledgment of his presence, Henry

sat beside him. It was as if, to the old Mide, Stephen was just another of the wild things that grew tall in the meadow.

"It's coming." Stephen spoke in a whisper no louder than the
voice of the wind.

"The great evil?" the old man said.

"The meaning of the vision."

"Ah."

Stephen sat up. The upper half of the sleeping bag fell to his
waist. He wore a long-sleeved T-shirt, which was enough to keep
him comfortable in that fall night. Henry had put on his old mackinaw.

"There's more than evil out there," Stephen said. "There's
promise. The flight recorder Ned Love saw lodged up in a tree, that
was the egg falling from the eagle. I think the full meaning of the
vision is unfolding."

Not far away, the grass shifted suddenly as something darted
through it, an animal who believed there was safety in the night.

"It's been hard, Henry. This knowing and not knowing."

"What in life is not hard, Stephen O'Connor?"

There was another creaking door, this time from Leah Duling's
cabin. Rainy stepped into the moonlight and crossed the meadow.
She was barefoot but wore sweatpants and a light jacket. She sat on
the other side of Stephen. The gray-white streak in her long black
hair gleamed like a vein of silver.

"You were amazing with Monkey Love," Stephen told her.

"I was scared shitless."

"Your hands did not shake, Niece," the old Mide said. "Not
once."

"My heart was doing a tango, Uncle Henry."

"Jameson Love has a spirit of stumbling luck. This wounding
is not the last scar he will bear in his life, I think."

Another voice spoke, and a ghost-white figure appeared beside them. "Monkey's luck may be on the clumsy side, but that spirit of his has got leather in it. My nephew's tough."

"You scared me, Ned," Rainy said. "I didn't hear you coming."

"I learned a long time ago hunting that if I make noise, my supper runs away." He sat beside Rainy. "Thank you for what you done for Monkey tonight. *Chi migwech*."

"He's resting well?"

"Whatever it was Henry here gave him to drink put him out good. Don't know how I'm gonna repay you."

Stephen didn't say it, but he was thinking that the black box was payment enough.

Ned turned to him. "Your dad told me maybe the same guys who shot Monkey gave you that face."

Stephen touched the stitches on his cheek. "Maybe."

"What do they want with that recorder?"

"We think they want to hide the truth of what caused the plane to crash."

"Monkey said it was flying all crooked when it came down this side of Desolation Mountain, like a sick bird."

"Did it look like it had been hit with something?" Stephen asked, thinking of his vision and the boy with the powerful bow.

"Monkey didn't say nuthin' about that."

A subtle cough announced another arrival.

"Couldn't sleep, Cork?" Rainy asked.

"Guess I'm not the only one." Cork plopped down beside her. "I called Bo Thorson. He'll be ready first thing in the morning. We'll be going after that flight recorder, although I didn't tell him that. Best to keep it quiet for the moment."

"The egg that dropped from the eagle," Stephen said.

"That seems pretty clear," his father agreed. "Anything else becoming clear?"

"Not yet, but I think it will. I'm going with you tomorrow."

Cork shook his head. "I've got another mission for you. I want you to head into Allouette and bring Ned's sister out to Crow Point."

"Beulah?" Ned said.

"She's been worried about you and Monkey."

"Monkey, maybe. She never had much use for me."

"We may need to build another cabin, Corcoran O'Connor," Henry said.

They all rose and drifted back to their beds and their blankets, leaving Stephen alone again. He lay under the watchful eye of the moon, thinking about his vision, about the full meaning slowly revealing itself, which was good, except for one thing. The vision always ended with a beast at his back so terrible he couldn't force himself to turn and look at it. Even awake, the idea of facing that monster terrified him.

In the early hours of the morning, long before sunrise, Cork left Crow Point, in the company of Daniel English and Ned Love. Cork had arranged to meet Bo Thorson outside Allouette, though over the phone he hadn't explained why. From there, they'd go to Ned Love's cabin, then walk to the bog where the plane crashed. The site was still closed to the public and periodically patrolled. He was hoping to slip in and out at first light without being spotted.

Bo was waiting for them beside his Jeep. Cork introduced him to Ned Love and recapped the story Love had told the night before.

When Bo heard about the flight recorder Love had seen caught in the top of a pine tree, he said, "I'll be damned." Then he looked up at the sky, which was still full of stars. "I hope you can find it in the dark. They're patrolling the area from dawn to dusk."

"We'll be there at first light and, with any luck, gone before anyone else shows up," Cork told him.

By the time they parked at Ned's cabin, the whole eastern horizon had gone powdery blue. Before they started for the bog, Ned
walked to the end of the dock on Little Bass Lake, whose surface
reflected the image of Desolation Mountain, a hard black shape
against the soft, vague blue of the predawn sky. He knelt and stared
into the water.

"After we get that box, I'm coming back for Cyrus. And then
I'm gonna find the men who shot him and Monkey."

"We'll give you a hand with that, Ned," Cork promised.

"Will you give me a hand shootin' 'em? 'Cause that's what I
intend to do."

"How about we cross that bridge when we come to it?"

The man rose and began to lead the way. They moved
through the woods in the thin, early light. In fifteen minutes,
they'd reached the north side of the bog. Cork saw where the
undergrowth all along the edge and well into the trees had been
crushed by the constant trample of the searchers' boots. They
paused in the cover among the tamaracks, listened, heard nothing. Without a sound, Ned crept around the bog to the place
where, soon after the crash, Cork and Stephen and Daniel and the
men from the reservation had found the broken tail section and
the dead boy still strapped in his seat. Ned walked without hesi-
tation to a red pine whose crown, like many of the others around
it, had been sheared off, leaving only a ragged, white tip of trunk
resembling the end of a broken bone. Cork followed Ned's gaze
upward. Fifty feet above them, a small chunk of plane debris was
caught among the remaining pine branches, and within it was a
dash of orange.

"Damn," Daniel said. "We're going to need climbing spurs or
spiked logger boots to get up there."

"Got anything like that at your cabin, Ned?" Cork asked.

"No use for 'em. When I cut firewood, I bring the whole tree down. Squirrels and possums, when I shoot 'em, they just fall to the ground."

"I'll give it a try," Bo said.

He stepped up to the pine trunk, which had a diameter of roughly three feet, felt for handholds, pressed himself against the rough bark, and tried to find purchase for the soles of his boots. It was hopeless from the get-go. He stepped back, swearing under his breath.

"We'll need to come back with climbing spurs," Cork said.

Bo gave the pine trunk a light kick. "I hate being this close and having to walk away."

"We'll have to wait until dusk," Daniel said.

Cork eyed the patch of orange above them. "At least we know where it is. We're getting somewhere."

Except for the call of birds, the woods were quiet. But from the distance came the diesel rumble of a heavy engine approaching on the logging road.

"That's it for this morning," Cork said. "Let's go before we're spotted."

When they dropped Bo at his Jeep, they made arrangements to meet in the late afternoon. Cork promised to bring climbing spurs. Bo waited until the vehicle was well gone, then made his call.

"I know where it is."

"The flight recorder? You have it?"

"Not yet. Tonight. It's a little tricky." Bo explained about the pine tree. "The recorder might not have any of the answers," he cautioned.

"We'll know soon enough. Thank you, Bo."

He was being paid for his work, but even if he weren't, the sound of her thank-you would have been enough.

CHAPTER 38

Stephen walked with Rainy to the logging road that led toward Allouette. Daniel's pickup truck was parked in a bared pull-off, an area most folks referred to as Crow Point East. They drove the three miles into town, and Rainy dropped him at the marina, where he'd left the ATV side-by-side the day before. The plan was for him to use the little machine to take Beulah Love back to Henry Meloux's cabin. Rainy stuck around only long enough to make sure there was no problem with the ATV. As soon as Stephen kicked the engine over successfully, she headed to the clinic, just to check in.

It was still early and Allouette was quiet. Stephen pulled up in front of the Mocha Moose, where Sarah LeDuc and Beulah Love waited for him inside. The café smelled of sweet, freshly baked dough.

"*Boozhoo*, Stephen." Sarah greeted him with a smile and a white pastry bag. "Donuts to take back to everyone on Crow Point."

"How is Jameson?" Beulah asked, her face pulled tight with worry.

"He's doing fine, you'll see."

"And Ned?"

Stephen filled them in on the mission of the men that morning.

"It's all about a black box stuck up in a pine tree?" Sarah said. "That's why Monkey was shot? Any more word on Sue and Phil and Tom?"

"Dad's still working on that, Sarah."

"Let him know that everyone on the rez is willing to beat the woods to find them."

"If Dad knew what part of the woods to beat, I'm sure he'd say go for it."

"I heard you were at the town meeting with the governor last night when somebody fired shots."

"Only one shot, Sarah. And I heard it was just a couple of rowdies." The lie he'd sworn to tell. "No one hurt. You ready, Ms. Love?"

"Call me Beulah."

Across the street from the Mocha Moose, several teenagers from town had gathered where the bus would pick them up and take them to the high school in Aurora. Stephen spotted Harmon Goodsky's grandson, Winston. He stood apart from the other kids. Stephen wondered if that separation was his choice or theirs. The kid had been looking at the ground. Now he lifted his eyes and they locked on Stephen. There was something about him that set a hook in Stephen's thinking. Maybe it was that Stephen, too, knew what it was to be different.

Beulah settled herself beside him in the ATV. "I've never been in one of these before."

"Here, put this on." He handed her a neon yellow helmet and grabbed the other for himself. "The ride's a little rough, but it'll get you there."

A mile outside Allouette, Stephen swung off the pavement

onto the dirt road he would follow back to Crow Point East. The ATV kicked up a rooster tail of red dust. A few moments later, he felt prickles climb his spine, and he glanced back. Nearly cloaked in the dust behind him and closing fast was a black pickup.

"Hold on!" he hollered to Beulah.

He gunned the ATV and began a rapid calculation. Half a mile ahead was the cutoff for a logging road unused for years and overgrown. If he was able to keep ahead of the pickup, he figured he could swing onto that track, which would take them into low hills, where he might be able to lose whoever was dogging them.

Although she'd buckled into a harness, Beulah held to the roll bar for dear life. Her eyes were riveted to the road ahead, and when Stephen looked her direction, he saw that her lips were moving. A prayer, he figured. What could it hurt?

He slowed, took the turn, and plowed into undergrowth two feet high. The trees were close on both sides. He shot a quick look over his shoulder. The cutoff was choked with a swirl of red dust, and a dim black shape flew past. They'd missed the turn, but only for a moment, Stephen knew. As soon as they broke from that dust cloud, they'd double back.

The little ATV bounced along the narrow track, leaving a clear trail of crushed vegetation behind. There were hundreds of old logging roads in the woods of Tamarack County, and this was one Stephen had never traveled. He had no idea where exactly it would take them, but at least he'd bought some time. Beulah was still praying up a storm.

Then they hit a dead end. The track simply stopped. Tall pines boxed them in on three sides. The only way out was the way they'd come. Stephen had no time to consider options. He pulled off his helmet and threw it down.

"Out," he shouted to Beulah.

Her face was a mask of horror and she didn't move.

"We have to get into the woods. Now!"

He reached out and unbuckled her harness, then leapt from the ATV. She was slow to follow, as if dazed. Stephen grabbed her arm and pulled her into the woods. In the quiet after he'd killed the engine, he heard the grind of the big truck engine coming. He ran through the pines with Beulah in tow. They were among hills with lots of gneiss outcrops. Stephen made for a low rise with a crowning of rock where he hoped they'd leave no footprints. They struggled up and made the summit just as the black pickup roared up behind the ATV. Stephen yanked Beulah down beside him and they lay prone. Through the pines, he watched two men exit the truck. He recognized them as the ones who'd beat him the day before. They were dressed for the North Country—jeans, flannel shirts, boots, ball caps—and carrying rifles. They checked the ATV, then scanned the woods. One of them walked in a slow circle, studying the ground. He said something to his companion, and they started in the direction Stephen and Beulah had fled.

"We have to go," Stephen whispered.

He slid back, staying low until he was sure the rise hid him. Beulah followed suit. He began at a lope through the woods, searching for good cover somewhere ahead. Beulah did her best to keep up, but she wasn't a woman used to running, especially in the wilderness. Twice she fell, tripped by underbrush. She didn't say a word of complaint, simply pulled herself up and ran on. Stephen made for a long ridge whose gray-white rock stood out through the trees. When they reached it, he glanced back, looking for the men on their tails. He didn't see them, but that didn't mean they weren't coming.

Beulah stared hopelessly at the rock face, which rose thirty feet above them. "Climb?" she said, as if that would be asking the impossible.

"Not here. This way."

Stephen led her north fifty yards to a place where a natural crease cut up the ridge at an angle. It would still require a climb, but one he hoped Beulah could handle. "Follow me."

Good shrub cover grew in the crease, Juneberry bushes whose leaves had gone red with the season. Beulah used the thin branches to help pull herself up. They'd made it halfway to the top when she cried out and fell and lay holding her ankle.

"Twisted," she said through gritted teeth.

Stephen crouched beside her. The men had topped the rise where he and Beulah had first hidden themselves and stood surveying the woods.

"Stay down and keep still," he told her.

He hoped the men would come no farther into the forest. But his hope died almost immediately as they began in the direction of the ridge.

Stephen wore light green khakis, a tan chamois shirt, a brown, quilted vest. Not bad camouflage for the woods. Beulah was another story. She had on blue jeans, a red jacket, and was still wearing the neon yellow crash helmet he'd given her in the ATV. Because of the red leaves on the Juneberry shrubs, the jacket might be okay, but that helmet had to go.

The men veered south. Although Stephen hoped that they wouldn't follow the ridge to the crease with the Juneberry thicket, he decided hope wasn't enough.

"Give me your helmet. Stay here and stay quiet. I'll come back for you," he promised.

"No." Beulah grasped his arm, her eyes wide with fear. "Don't leave me."

"I have to. You'll be fine if you just lie still." He pulled free. "Go ahead and pray," he advised before he left. "But silently."

He slid down the crease to its base and jumped into the open. The men were bent, focused on studying the ground. Stephen loped in the opposite direction along the rock face until he was well away from the crease. Then he stood tall, donned the bright yellow helmet, and waited until the men spotted him and leapt to the chase. Although the place where a bullet once lodged in his back burned like a forge on which every step hammered out pain, Stephen put his whole body into running, and his heart as well.

On their way back to Crow Point, Cork and Daniel made a stop in Allouette at the home of Dennis Vizenor, a man who'd logged timber all his life, and they left with a pair of spiked logger boots. When they reached Meloux's cabin, Cork was surprised to find that Stephen hadn't returned with Beulah Love. He called Sarah LeDuc, who assured him that his son and Beulah had left together a couple of hours earlier. Rainy also hadn't returned from checking in at the clinic. He called her cell and was relieved when she answered.

"I'm sorry, Cork. I got held up here. They were a little overwhelmed this morning, so I stayed to give a hand."

"Have you seen Stephen?"

"Not since I dropped him at the marina. Why?"

"He and Beulah have gone missing."

She was quiet on her end, then spoke the words Cork had thought but hadn't said. "Like all the others."

"I'm going to find them," Cork vowed. "But Daniel and I are coming to get you first. I don't want you traveling back to Crow Point alone."

"If you're looking for my sister, I'm going with you," Ned Love insisted.

Henry Meloux, who had listened to all the conversations without comment, offered this as they departed: "What your head believes you are looking for is not always what your heart is seeking, Corcoran O'Connor."

Which, Cork thought with frustration, was no help at all.

They double-timed it to Crow Point East, where Cork had parked his Expedition, then followed the logging road that ran along Iron Lake into Allouette and rendezvoused with Rainy at the clinic. They split up—Daniel and Rainy to the safety of Crow Point, and Cork and Ned to the Mocha Moose, where Sarah told them that the last she'd seen of Stephen and Beulah, they'd been headed back to Meloux's cabin.

As they left Allouette behind, Ned said, "If I was going to bushwhack 'em, I'd do it somewhere down that logging road toward Crow Point. Not much traveled, so less chance of anybody seeing what they're up to."

Cork sped to the logging road cutoff, but as he headed toward Crow Point, he began to go more slowly. Several other tracks led off into the woods, old logging accesses, but nothing caught his eye.

"There," Ned finally said. "See them wheel marks?"

Cork turned onto the cut into the woods, a narrow track he'd never followed before. The tall weeds had been pressed down along several lines; multiple vehicles had recently passed this way. They came to a dead end, and there sat the ATV, abandoned. One of the crash helmets lay on the ground in the tall grass. Cork scanned the woods, but saw no sign of his son or Beulah.

"Over here." Ned had moved to the far side of the ATV and was studying the ground cover. "A bunch of folks went this way."

Cork saw where the wild grass had been trampled, and he and Ned followed the trail into the trees. Cork had always been a hunter and wasn't a bad tracker. But for most of his life, Ned Love had fed himself on wild game, and he could follow a track as if it had a voice and called to him. Cork followed Ned to a rocky rise and then beyond, where they paused.

"They separated here. A couple of 'em went that way." Ned pointed toward a place where the gray-white rock of a low ridge was visible through the trees. "And a couple took off that way." He pointed toward a line that went a bit to the south.

"Let's check the ridge," Cork said. "That's where I'd go if I was trying to lose somebody."

"I'm with you on that one."

They went another hundred yards, then Ned stopped abruptly and studied the ground. "Another trail crosses here. Looks like the two who headed south changed their minds and cut north, going fast."

"Which trail do we follow?"

Ned considered, gave a nod toward the low ridge, and moved on. At the base of the rock face, Ned turned north, moving quickly and confidently, until he came to a fold in the ridge full of June-berry bushes, where a small voice stopped them.

"Ned? Is that you?"

"It's me, Beulah. You can come on down from there. You're safe now."

"I can't," she said. "I think I've broken my ankle."

"Hold on," her brother told her. "We'll come get you."

She lay in a place well concealed by the thicket, and when they reached her, she offered them a huge smile of relief.

"Stephen?" Cork asked.

Her smile vanished. "He led them away hours ago. He promised he'd come back for me, but he never did."

"Them?" Ned said.

"Two men. They chased us here."

"Did they come back?" Cork asked.

"I haven't seen them since they took off after Stephen."

"We're going to get you to safety, Beulah," Cork promised her.

Using a two-man chair carry, they carted her to the Expedition and drove her to Crow Point. A vehicle like Cork's was a rare sight in front of Henry Meloux's cabin. When people came to Meloux, they made that pilgrimage on foot. The big SUV seemed so out of place that as he parked, Cork felt a little sacrilegious. They carried Beulah Love inside and Cork explained the situation. Daniel and Ned both insisted on returning with him to search for Stephen.

It was well into the afternoon by the time Ned Love picked up Stephen's trail at the crease in the rock face and followed it north, where it was joined by the trail the two men had left. For a mile or so, Cork could easily see the signs. Then they came to a bare, rocky slope and Ned paused.

"They split up here. Only one kept after Stephen."

"The other?" Daniel asked.

"Headed back toward where they left their truck."

Cork studied the ground but saw nothing. "Which way did Stephen go, Ned?"

Ned gestured toward the top of the broad, barren rise. "He's staying north. Smart boy."

"Why smart?" Daniel asked.

"Bunch of rock rises for the next half mile. Me and Monkey, we call this area the Hungry Hills. Never can track deer here. We always go home hungry. It'd be hard for anyone to follow Stephen in these rocks, me included."

"We've got to try," Cork said.

"Yeah, we gotta try." But Ned's voice held little promise.

They spread out and moved separately, yards apart. Wherever there was soil between the rocks, Cork looked for prints. On the stone itself, he searched for patches of lichen that might have been scarred by boot soles. He found nothing. Ditto Ned and Daniel.

"We could maybe keep going north," Ned said. "But once Stephen hit this area, he coulda took off in most any direction. Me,

I'd circle back, but maybe Stephen done something different. You know him better, Cork."

The honest-to-god truth was that Cork didn't have a clue. He couldn't put himself inside his son's thinking, particularly in this uniquely terrible situation. He felt deficient, like there was something essential lacking in him, especially as a father. Christ, why didn't he know his son better?

Daniel said, "We have a good hour of sunlight left. We can keep looking. But there's the flight recorder."

Cork stood on the rocky ground, which had yielded nothing, thinking for a hopeless moment that his son, like the others, was gone.

Then he remembered Henry Meloux's advice, which he'd discounted as nonsense: *What your head believes you are looking for is not always what your heart is seeking.*

"Let's get the flight recorder," he said, turning back.

"What about Stephen?" Daniel asked.

Cork walked ahead of the others, saying as if it were a prayer, "Stephen can take care of himself."

CHAPTER 39

"You just left him out there?"

Jenny looked stunned. In Meloux's cabin, they all looked a little nonplussed. Except perhaps for Meloux. The lines on his face gave away nothing but the fact that he was practically as old as creation itself.

"Dad, you can't just abandon him." Jenny was furious.

Daniel said, "We didn't have time to search anymore. We need to get the flight recorder." He looked out the window at the setting sun, which was balanced on top of a distant pine like a yellow ball on the nose of a seal. "And your dad's right. Stephen can take care of himself."

"Like Ned and Monkey?" Jenny threw back at him. "Like Sue and Phil and Tom?"

"This is different," Daniel said. "Stephen was on the run."

"On the run? How far do you think that gimp leg will get him?"

Ned spoke up, a little hesitantly, as if unsure he should intrude. "He's not alone out there."

Jenny turned her anger on him. "No, he's out there with men who probably want him dead."

"That's not what I meant."

"I made my decision, Jenny," Cork said. "It's too late to go back now. It would be too dark to see anything."

"You're going after that damn recorder in the dark."

Daniel said, "It'll only be dark if we don't leave right now."

"Fine," Jenny said. "I'm going to look for Stephen."

Meloux said, "Ned is right. He is not alone out there."

Probably because it was Meloux who'd spoken, Jenny took a deep, calming breath. "I don't understand what that means."

"Monsters," Waaboo said fearfully.

Meloux reached out and placed a reassuring hand on the boy's shoulder. "Not monsters, Little Rabbit. Spirits. Energies. Guides."

"That's sorta what I meant," Ned said. "If you know the woods, you pick up on things. Spirits maybe, but I was thinking more about things like that Juneberry patch Stephen hid my sister in."

"We just stumbled onto it," Beulah said.

"Might've seemed that way to you," Ned said. "I look at it different."

"If we're going to get that recorder, we have to go now," Daniel told them.

"Stay here, Jenny," Cork said. "We don't need you lost out there in the dark, or maybe running into the men who are after Stephen."

He could tell there was more his daughter wanted to say, but it was also clear that he'd gotten through to her.

Meloux walked the men out and looked deeply into Cork's face. "You found what your heart was looking for."

Cork eyed the solid line of trees at the edge of the meadow to the north. Stephen was somewhere in the wilderness a few miles beyond, and the dark would soon be descending. He looked back at Meloux and repeated, as if it were a mantra, "He can take care of himself."

"And," Meloux added, "he is not alone."

———

Bo Thorson was waiting for them in the place where they'd met that morning. He had a pair of climbing spurs with him. "Bought these this afternoon. I'm ready."

Daniel held up the spiked logging boots. "We borrowed these this morning."

"Then let's go get some answers."

They parked at Ned Love's cabin and began their hike to the crash site as the light in the sky was fading. When they arrived at the bog, the area was deserted.

"Like I told you," Bo said. "They only patrol dawn to dusk. They've become a little predictable. That's good for us."

They quickly made for the tall red pine where they'd spotted the flight recorder caught in the high branches. At the base of the tree, they gazed up. Cork saw the green of the needles, the brown of the branches, the pale blue of the sky beyond. But nothing orange-colored.

"Where is it?" Daniel asked.

"Wrong tree?" Bo scanned the nearby pines.

"This is the tree," Ned assured him.

Cork ran his hand over the bark. "Holes from climbing spurs. Someone beat us to it."

"Who knew about this tree but us?" Daniel said.

Cork, Daniel, and Ned eyed Bo Thorson and the pair of climbing spurs he'd brought.

Bo said coolly, "We've got some talking to do."

Henry Meloux insisted they build a fire. It was dark night, and the blaze in the fire ring illuminated the rock outcrops with a dancing yellow glow. Except for the convalescing Monkey Love and Leah, who'd offered to stay with him, they were all gathered there, even little Waaboo, sitting on cut sections of log. Meloux had smudged and said a prayer, asking for clear minds and clear hearts and true tongues. And now they were silent, listening to the pop and crackle as the flames consumed the wood.

Cork chewed on anger, on doubt, on guilt. The recorder was gone. Phil and Sue Hukari and Tom Blessing were still missing. Stephen was out in the wild with God knew what—assassins maybe—and Cork was beating himself up for not continuing the search for his son. He doubted everything now, especially his trust in Bo Thorson.

Thorson continued to insist that he wasn't responsible for the missing flight recorder, but what did Cork really know about the man? When Thorson was Secret Service and Cork was sheriff of Tamarack County and they'd worked together on security, Thorson had seemed not just competent but accomplished. And trustworthy. But that was years ago, and people could change. He didn't really know who Thorson might be now. His sense had been that the heart of the man was still good, still decent, but at the moment, he wasn't sure he could trust in his own sense of anything.

Meloux said, "Speak the truth." He was looking at Thorson.

"I didn't take the flight recorder. That's the truth. All of it."

"What'd you do today after we split up?" Daniel asked.

"Picked up that pair of climbing spurs."

"Took you all day?"

"I made my report to the people who hired me."

"Who exactly is that?" Daniel said.

"I've already told you."

"Olympia McCarthy's father. Would you object if we called to check that out?"

"You can call. I doubt that he'll admit to it. It's a delicate matter, a man in his position questioning the veracity of the NTSB and the FBI."

"How can we be sure you're not working for Gerard?"

Bo said, "Cork, do you really think I might be working for Gerard?"

Cork gave the question serious weight, and finally shook his head. "I still think you're one of the good guys."

"Thanks," Bo said. "Now let me ask a question. Did you tell anybody about the flight recorder?"

"Only the people around this fire," Cork said.

Beulah Love, who'd been carried to the fire ring because of her swollen ankle, said, "Ummmm."

Ned cocked his head. "Something to say, Beulah?"

"When Stephen came to get me this morning, he told Sarah and me about the recorder in the tree."

"Sarah LeDuc," Cork said. "Christ. So much for secrecy. I'm sure the whole rez knows by now."

"Are you suggesting someone on the rez is working with those goons, Cork?" Rainy gave him a doubtful look.

"Unless Bo told someone."

"I didn't say a word to anyone," Bo protested. "But there's another possibility."

"What's that?" Daniel asked.

"Bugs," Bo said simply. "Maybe in the Mocha Moose or someone's phone's been tapped or there are a dozen other ways of listening in. The technology of surveillance would amaze you."

"The bottom line," Cork said with a dismal sinking of his heart, "is that we're right back where we started."

Trixie, who'd been lying at Waaboo's feet, lifted her head and gave a little woof. Henry Meloux's face went intent as he listened. "Maybe things have moved farther ahead than you think, Corcoran O'Connor."

In the next moment, a figure stumbled between the rock out-croppings and into the firelight, a stranger in ragged pants and with his hands tied behind his back. Then another figure appeared.

His heart singing, Cork said, "Good to see you back, Stephen."

Bo listened with the others as Stephen O'Connor recounted his ordeal. He'd been chased by the two strangers and had headed north from the low ridge where he'd hidden Beulah Love.

"Why north?" Ned Love asked.

"I don't know. It's just the way I went."

"If you wanted to lose those guys, north was the way to go."

"I found that out when I reached all that rock."

"The Hungry Hills," Love said.

Stephen described how he'd mounted the rocky slope and had hidden himself and watched as the two men who came after him stopped to talk things over. One headed back and the other continued trying to find Stephen's trail.

"My leg was killing me, and it was pretty clear he knew how to track, so I decided my best shot was to take him out."

"With what?" Jenny said.

"The thing those Hungry Hills has the most of. A rock. I was lying low behind a big boulder. He was studying the ground, walked right past me. I caught him in the back of the head. As soon as he was down, I pulled the gun from his holster. He had a knife on his belt, and I took that, too."

"How come his pants are all raggedy?" Waaboo asked.

"I cut strips so I could tie his hands."

"Any ID on him?" Cork asked.

"I didn't look."

"Stand up," Cork ordered the stranger. He checked all the pockets, found nothing, and shoved the man back down to the ground.

He turned back to his son. "We looked for you at the Hungry Hills."

"We didn't stay there. I thought his partner might come back, so I pushed him north across all that rock. When I thought we were clear, I cut west, then finally south, making for Crow Point."

"So," Cork said to the stranger, whose hands were still tied with strips cut from his own pant leg. "Who are you?"

The man's eyes flicked toward Cork, then back to the flames, and not a word came from his mouth.

Bo, who so far had been silent, said, "Gerard sent you?"

The man showed no sign of recognition.

Cork said, "Rainy, Jenny, Waaboo, join Leah and Monkey back at Henry's cabin. We'll be along shortly."

Jenny stood, took Waaboo's hand, and walked away between the rocks with Trixie at their heels. Cork's wife had risen, but she didn't follow. "What are you going to do, Cork?"

"Question him."

"I know how you question people."

"We need to know what he knows, Rainy, especially if he knows about Sue and Phil and Tom."

"You're going to hurt him."

"Only if necessary. The choice is his."

"Cork—"

"Stay, Niece," Meloux interrupted her. "Sit." He said to the stranger, "My niece is a healer. It may be that you are going to suffer much. When we are finished with you and you have told us what you know, we will allow her to do what she can to ease your pain."

In the firelight, Rainy's face was a blaze of surprise. Or was it dismay?

"Sit, Niece," Meloux said again.

Bo had been studying the stranger, who'd seemed unmoved

until the old man spoke. The way such menacing words came so soothingly from those ancient lips made them even more chilling. The man eyed Meloux, then the others, and Bo saw cracks in his stolid veneer. He'd begun to understand what even decent people might be capable of when protecting those they cared about.

"I am Ojibwe," Meloux said to the stranger. "Do you know what that word means?"

The stranger made no response.

"In the language of my people, it means 'to pucker.' Do you know where that name comes from? I will tell you what I have heard. It comes from the way in which my people have been known to treat their enemies. We roast them until their skin puckers." The old man waited for his words to sink in. "There is no glory in giving a man pain. There is also no glory in hurting those who have done nothing to you." His dark eyes held the stranger's gaze. "There is only one thing we ask. What has become of the people we care about? Have they been harmed?"

Although the stranger didn't speak, Bo could see that his brain was working, worrying itself over the old man's words.

"Bring me fire," Meloux said to Cork.

"Wait," the stranger said. "We weren't supposed to hurt nobody, just bring them in."

"What about these stitches?" Stephen said.

"You'll heal," the stranger said, as if the beating were nothing.

"You shot Monkey Love," Daniel pointed out coldly.

"Wasn't me. There's others out there."

"You killed people's dogs."

"The dogs got in the way. And they was just dogs."

"Just dogs?" Ned Love rose, huge and menacing. "I'll pucker you, you son of a bitch."

"Hold on, Ned." Cork stepped between Love and the stranger.

"Let him talk. You said you brought them in. Brought them where?"

"The Op Center."

"Where's this Op Center?"

The man stared into the fire. "I want immunity."

"What?"

"I want immunity. I don't want to go to jail. I remember when you was sheriff, O'Connor. I figure you still got some clout."

"Immunity," Cork said. "All right, I'll do what I can."

The stranger looked up at Cork. "Then I guess I'll tell you."

CHAPTER 40

The stranger's name was Wes Simpson. Once they got him talking, he told them much. He came from Yellow Lake, a community fifteen miles south of Aurora. He was a member of the Lexington Brigade mostly because his cousin had recruited him.

"Axel says our country's going to hell in a handcart. The government's been taken over by big money and special interests. He says a war's coming, but it ain't going to be between us and the Russians or the Arabs. It's going to be us against the government. He gets real worked up. Me, I kinda like the maneuvers we sometimes go on during weekends. Get to pretend we're at war for a while, then have us some steaks and brews. Honest to god, I never thought we'd be tapped to do anything."

He claimed he didn't know much about what was going on. He and his cousin had been called up a day before the senator's plane went down. That's when he met Cole Wannamaker for the first time.

"I knew about him, course. We all got pictures of him. But meeting him in person, that was something. I mean, he's a celebrity."

"Was he the one giving orders?"

"Yeah, him and Boog Sorenson. He's our local colonel."

"I know Sorenson," Cork said, with an unpleasant taste in his mouth. "You were called up before the senator's plane went down. What for?"

"Boog put Axel and me at a barricade on the road to Desolation Mountain. Gave us hard hats to wear, like we was working road construction. Told us to keep anybody out who was headed toward the mountain that afternoon. He spread the others out in them aspens up there on the mountain. Said a plane was going to be coming down somewhere around there. When it crashed, our job was to get rid of the barricade, get to the wreckage along with the other guys, and pull out the flight recorder. He showed us a picture of what it would look like. Told us it would be somewhere in the debris of the tail section."

"Did you know whose plane was going to crash?"

"Not until after, when I heard it on the news."

"But you didn't get the recorder," Bo said.

"Didn't have no chance. That plane came down way past where any of us was. When we got there, them Indians was already all over the place. By the time we assembled ourselves enough to maybe run 'em off, fire trucks and police cars and you name it had showed up, and we had to get our asses out of there."

"Did Boog tell you to round up the people from the reservation?" Cork asked.

"Them orders came from Wannamaker hisself."

"Your cousin, was he the man with you when you went after my son?"

"Look, I'm sorry about that beating, kid," he said to Stephen. "That was Axel's doing. He's always been on the impulsive side."

"What about my dad?" Stephen said. "Someone took a shot at him. Was that you?"

"Not me. Nels Jensen, one of the other guys in the brigade. Boog's orders."

"Why me?" Cork said.

"Boog was real worried about you interfering. You know, you being this hotshot investigator and all. Plus, I guess he's never liked you much. Jensen was supposed to take you out at your house, but he blew it."

"The break-in," Daniel said.

"After that, you were bouncing around so much, we couldn't get a bead on you. Wannamaker suggested Boog set you up somewhere Jensen could take a good, clean shot. Boog came up with the ransom idea. Guess he didn't count on you wearing body armor."

"Why'd you and your cousin split up today?" Stephen asked.

"Got a cell phone call from Boog. Surprised the hell out of me that we could even get service out here. Something big was going down. He wanted us all back at the Op Center. By then we figured the woman must be hiding somewhere behind us. Axel went to look for her. I kept after you. He was supposed to come back for me. The son of a bitch musta just took off. Or maybe he was under orders."

"Something big?" Cork said. "Did they tell you what it was?"

"Uh-uh. Just ordered us to come back."

Cork saw a look in Bo's eyes that told him they were both thinking the same thing. It was Bo who spoke. "They have the flight recorder."

"Where's this Op Center?" Daniel asked.

"Bout five miles west of Aurora on a little lake called Celtic."

"Because the water's green," Cork said. "I know the place. An old hunting lodge, the only structure on the lake. Pretty well isolated. Used to belong to Casper Ferguson before he died. Don't know who owns it now."

Rainy spoke for the first time since the questioning of Simpson had begun. "What about the people from the rez you rounded up?"

"Got 'em locked in an old smokehouse at the Op Center."

"They're okay?" Cork asked.

Simpson was slow to answer. "The men, their faces are going to look kinda like your boy's. Nothing that time won't take care of."

"What's the plan?" Bo said. "Any idea what they're going to do with those people?"

"I don't know."

"Think about it for a moment, Wes," Bo pressed him. "Those people were kidnapped. That's a felony, maybe a capital crime. If they can identify you and the others, that's prison, at the very least, for all of you."

"Not me. I got immunity promised."

"My point is this," Bo said. "Now that they have what they wanted, they can't just let those folks go."

"Kill 'em?" Simpson said, as if it was the first time the thought had occurred to him. "Naw. Axel is a little hotheaded, but he wouldn't just kill somebody."

"Maybe not him," Bo said. "But the others. Wannamaker or Sorenson or that Nels Jensen who took a shot at Cork."

Simpson mulled it over. "Yeah, I guess I could see Wannamaker or Boog or Jensen doing something like that. Or maybe even one of the other guys. They really buy this resistance shit."

"How many are there?"

"Seven locals and Wannamaker."

"We need to get our people out of there now," Cork said.

Daniel spoke the unthinkable. "Maybe it's already too late."

Henry Meloux, who'd been silent for a long while, staring into the fire and listening, said, "And maybe it is not. There is only one way to know."

———

Before leaving Crow Point, the men discussed bringing in Sheriff Marsha Dross, but Cork was deeply concerned that every passing minute placed the prisoners in greater danger, especially if the brigade had the flight recorder in its possession. If the sheriff was brought in, too many agencies would want a hand in mounting an assault, and the time it would take to mobilize them might make it too late to save the Hukaris and Blessing. At the very least, it would be wise to confirm the truth of the things Simpson had told them before bringing in the authorities.

It was well after midnight when they got to the cutoff to Celtic Lake. The moon was up, casting shadows. Cork pulled the Expedition off the road and into a grove of aspens. Simpson's hands were bound with duct tape substituted for the strips cut from his pant leg.

"Just keep away from the road and you should be good," Simpson advised. "About that promise?"

"I'll make sure you get immunity," Cork said, a lie that fell easily from his lips.

On foot, they paralleled the lane through the forest, keeping their distance because of the motion sensors Simpson had claimed were placed along the way. In the moonlit night, it took them fifteen minutes to reach the lodge, which was perched on a rise overlooking the small lake. A light shone in a window on the first level; otherwise the building was dark. Several vehicles had been parked in front.

"Yep, Axel's there. See that big black Ram pickup? That's mine. We was driving it today."

Cork said, "Where's the smokehouse they've got our people in?"

"Among them trees to the right of the lodge. Can't really see it in the dark like this."

"Is it guarded?"

"Just locked. But the brigade's got itself an armory," Simpson cautioned. "Heavy-caliber stuff. They hear us coming, they'll cut us down in seconds."

Cork prayed they could do this thing without any shots being fired. Bo had drawn his Sig and Daniel his service sidearm. Ned Love carried his rifle. But from what Simpson said, this was nothing compared to the armaments inside the lodge.

They moved slowly, carefully. The building was surrounded by birch trees whose leaves were so newly fallen that they'd created a soft bedding on the ground, which muted the men's footfalls. At the edge of the birch trees lay a wide, barren space, the parking area for the brigade vehicles. Some twenty yards to the right, just as Simpson had said, stood a squat log structure, dappled with silver moonlight breaking through the branches of the trees. The men made their way around the yard to the smokehouse. Again, just as Simpson had said, the door was padlocked.

"Who has a key?" Cork asked.

"Wannamaker and Boog. That's it."

"We'll need to pry that hasp loose."

"I got a crowbar in the toolbox in the back of my truck. I can get it," said Simpson.

"No, I'll get it," Cork told him.

"There's a combination lock." Simpson gave him the numbers.

He stole across the yard to the big Dodge Ram and climbed into the bed. He unlocked the toolbox and dug as quietly as he could for the crowbar. Just as his hand wrapped around the cold metal, the door of the lodge swung open, and a man stepped onto the porch. The opened door allowed light to spill across the yard, and Cork was no longer in the dark. He froze, pressed himself against the back of the cab, the crowbar clutched in his hand. The man walked to the edge of the porch, a figure black against the light from inside. There was something odd about the silhouette. Then Cork understood he was carrying a rifle on a strap, and the long barrel was like a single antenna jutting up from his shoulder. The man struck a flame, illuminating his face for a moment as he lit a cigarette. Cork didn't recognize him. The man smoked for a while, then flicked the butt and its ember onto the ground.

"Time to take care of business," he mumbled to himself, but loud enough that Cork heard.

Business? he thought. His hand tightened around the crowbar. He calculated quickly. If the man headed to the smokehouse, he'd have to be taken out, and taken out quietly. It would require a leap from the truck bed and a sprint, a significant risk, but one that couldn't be avoided.

The man moved across the yard toward the smokehouse. He brought the rifle off his shoulder and cradled it with both hands. Cork tensed, ready to leap.

Then the man stopped. He set the rifle on the ground. Cork heard the sizzle of a zipper being lowered, followed by the dull sound of urine on dirt, a sound that went on for a while. The man zipped back up, lifted his rifle, and returned to the porch, where he paused, eyeing the night one last time before he slipped back inside, closing the door behind him.

Cork loped to the smokehouse.

"Thought he was coming this way for sure," Daniel said, his firearm in his hand.

"Keep those guns ready," Cork said. "This might be noisy."

He worked the teeth of the crowbar between the hasp and the wood of the door, which had softened with age. He wedged the two teeth deeper until he got some force behind the pry. The wood gave a loud creak. He stopped, waited. Nothing from the house. He resumed the prying and in a minute, had broken the hasp free. He opened the door, and the smell of burned wood washed over him. There was no sound from the utter dark inside, and he tried to prepare himself for the worst. Bodies, maybe. Or maybe nothing. Because if you killed someone in the North Country and you wanted to get rid of the evidence, there were plenty of bogs that would swallow a body whole.

He slipped out his cell phone and used the light to illuminate the dark.

They sat on the dirt of the smokehouse floor, their backs against the wall. Sue Hukari was positioned between her husband and Tom Blessing. Her eyes were white circles of fearful anticipation. Her hands, and her husband's and Blessing's, were bound at the wrists with disposable plastic restraints.

"It's Cork O'Connor," he whispered. "We're getting you out of here."

Ned Love and the others joined him, and they cut the restraints. They helped the prisoners to their feet and, because their ordeal had weakened them, offered support.

In half an hour, they were back at the Expedition, and Cork made the call.

"Marsha, we've got a situation."

CHAPTER 41

"I had to bring Quaker in, Cork. Domestic terrorism is out of my jurisdiction. Quaker made that abundantly clear to me."

They waited with Marsha Dross at the Tamarack County Sheriff's Office—Bo and the O'Connors and Daniel English. The others—Wes Simpson, Ned Love, Phil and Sue Hukari, and Tom Blessing—were all still being questioned by the FBI. Assistant Director Alex Quaker had come and gone, taken with him the information they'd supplied, as well as diagrams of the exterior and interior of the lodge that Wes Simpson had sketched. Quaker assured them that agents were preparing an assault at Celtic Lake. Dross had put a call out to all her deputies to assemble and stand by.

"They better get there soon," Cork said. "If those lunatics see that broken hasp on the smokehouse door, they'll scatter like flies." He stood at the window of Dross's office, staring where the streetlights of Aurora shone in bright circles on the empty thoroughfares.

It had been a long day for Stephen O'Connor, who sat in the common area visible through the door of Dross's office, his feet propped on a table, eyes closed and, despite all the activity around him, napping. English had gone outside to talk to his wife on his cell phone.

Bo sat in a hard wooden chair in front of the sheriff's desk, drinking bad coffee from a cardboard cup.

"The Lexington Brigade shot down Senator McCarthy's plane." Dross sat at her desk, looking as tired as the others, her words sounding leaden. "I would have said that's nuts, except for Oklahoma City and Ted Kaczynski and the bomb at the Atlanta Olympics."

Bo could have offered other examples of patriotism gone horribly awry, many of which were completely unknown outside a relatively small circle of D.C. national security experts.

"What did they hope to accomplish?" She spoke more to herself than to the others.

"Maybe they'd finally had enough of her political agenda," Bo said. "It certainly ran contrary to everything the brigade espouses. But there's still the question, why now?"

"The mine?" Dross offered. "It's generated a lot of anger up here, from all sides. And Senator McCarthy was outspoken in her opposition to the project. Maybe Wannamaker convinced Boog Sorenson this was the time to make a stand."

Cork was still looking through the window at the dark night. "A stand. Shooting down a civilian plane? Now there's true American heroism for you."

Bo said, "If they were the ones who got to the flight recorder before us, I'd love to know for sure how they understood where to look. The rez telegraph you talk about, Cork?"

Cork looked over his shoulder. "No telling who's tapped in."

"Boog Sorenson is a horse's ass," Dross said bluntly. "But he's got a lot of feelers out there in Tamarack County, and some of them, I'm sure, extend into our Native community. And, Cork, somebody must've let the brigade know you were involved and helped set you up for that shot at the town meeting."

"There are lots of people with Native blood who share the brigade's distrust of our government," Cork said. "But I have trouble believing they'd go along with any of this. I'm inclined to think Bo was on the right track. Someone bugged us."

"The brigade?" Dross said.

"If they have the flight recorder, I guess it had to be them." Cork put his hand to the window glass as if trying to touch the night outside. "We'll know in a while."

Not long after, a sudden commotion arose in the common area, and Alex Quaker entered the sheriff's office, flanked by two men looking just as grim as he. Daniel English and Cork's son came in behind them, escorted by another agent.

"Close the door," Quaker ordered one of the agents.

It was a crowded room now, and Quaker moved to the center. Dross said, "Well?"

Quaker focused on Cork. "Tell me again what went down while you were out there."

"We arrived at Celtic Lake and proceeded to the lodge, then to the smokehouse, where I pried off the hasp. We freed our friends, left the scene. I called Sheriff Dross and brought everyone back here."

"You were armed?"

"Bo, Daniel, Ned, they had firearms. No one else."

"What kinds of firearms?"

"A Sig Sauer, a Glock, a hunting rifle."

"Did you discharge them?"

"Are you kidding? From what Simpson told us, they had an arsenal in that house. If we'd fired a shot, they would have cut us down. What's going on? When are you going to make your assault on the lodge?"

"The operation is finished."

"Finished?" Dross sounded astounded. "So soon?"

"We encountered no resistance. What we found were seven bodies inside the lodge. They'd been lined up and executed."

"Wannamaker?"

"He wasn't among them."

"Boog Sorenson?"

"Dead, like the others."

"What about the flight recorder?" Cork asked.

"We retrieved the flight recorder."

"Executed," English said. "By whom?"

"That's the question, isn't it?" Quaker sat on the edge of the sheriff's desk. "It's going to be a while before you folks go home."

They were all interrogated again and, as the sky began to show the first light of day, finally allowed to go. The Hukaris and Tom Blessing had been taken to the Aurora Community Hospital to be checked over before they were officially released. Wes Simpson was being held, pending charges. The others piled into Cork's Expedition and headed toward the reservation. They were silent, drained, each lost in thought or in the drowse of exhaustion. They arrived at the place where Bo had left his Jeep the evening before, and they prepared to separate.

"Guess that's it," Cork said.

"Are you kidding?" Bo gave a short laugh. "The press is going to descend on you. You're heroes."

"I don't feel like a hero," Stephen said.

"As I understand it, heroes seldom do," Bo told him. "I don't know about the rest of you, but I need some shut-eye."

"Thanks for your help." Cork extended his hand.

"Any time."

Bo stood on the roadside and watched as the Expedition

headed toward Allouette and beyond that the dirt road that would take them all back to Crow Point East. He believed that for them, this incident was over. He still had miles to go before he slept.

She was quiet on her end.

"Quaker will release an official statement soon, I'm sure, at least outlining the operation and what came of it," Bo told her.

"The Lexington Brigade. Fanatics. And all this death." She sighed, a sound like a hand smoothing satin. "What about Cole Wannamaker?"

"If what Wes Simpson told us was correct, he was at the lodge earlier. But he wasn't among the dead. The speculation at the moment is that he executed them all."

"Why?"

"A case could be made, I suppose, that he was just trying to cover his tracks."

"Or he was just as crazy as he's always sounded."

"They'll grab him. Maybe not right away, but he can't stay underground forever. Once they have him, they'll get the whole story."

"Remember Jack Ruby? Someone arranged for him to kill Oswald before the man could talk."

Conspiracy theory, he thought. But she, of all people, was entitled to believe in conspiracies.

"How did they do it?" she asked.

"What?"

"Bring Olympia's plane down?"

"Quaker said they found a couple of Stingers among the armaments at the lodge."

"A Stinger?"

"A manually operated ground-to-air missile system. Looks like a fancy bazooka. Quaker believes that the flight recorder and the NTSB investigation will verify that's what brought the plane down."

"So. End of story."

"Maybe. I'm not letting go yet. There are still some loose ends."

"Like what?"

"Like how the brigade knew where to find the flight recorder."

"Didn't you say that word got out on the reservation?"

"That's one possibility. It's also possible someone involved was bugged."

"But you're not buying it?"

He waited a moment, then, "Who did you tell on your end?"

"You still think Gerard might have somebody on the inside here?"

"I'm just trying to consider all the possibilities. Who did you tell?"

"Olympia's father, that's it."

"Who did he tell?"

"I don't know."

"Ask him."

"All right," she agreed, but she didn't sound happy. "What about you? What are you going to do?"

For the first time since she'd brought him into this situation, he wondered if he should tell her the truth. "Get some sleep, then get back to work."

Bo brewed himself some coffee, sat at the table in his cabin, and as the sun began to peek above the trees along the inlet on Iron Lake, listened again to what he'd just downloaded from the recorder hidden at Gerard's command center. It was nothing but static, which could have been the result of defective equipment. Bo sipped his coffee, watched the sun ease itself into the day, and didn't for an instant think that defective equipment was the reason.

CHAPTER 42

The news, when it broke the next day, was big, and Aurora swelled once again with media people thick as summer tourists. Just as Bo Thorson had predicted, the O'Connors and the folks on the reservation became the targets of significant and unwanted attention. When Cork attempted to reopen Sam's Place, reporters descended like locusts, and he shut down again. Stephen tried to return to his classes at the community college but was dogged even there by reporters and barraged with questions from his classmates, so he stopped going. He'd begun texting regularly with Marlee Daychild and found her company, even in a virtual way, comforting. Mostly, the O'Connors hid out on Crow Point, waiting for things to quiet down.

Allouette was overrun. Phil and Sue Hukari took off to stay with relatives in Oregon until things died down. Tom Blessing muddled along in the preparations for his mother's funeral. Ned and Monkey Love, whose cabin was nearly impossible to find, were the only lucky ones.

Although the FBI had reported that the flight recorder recovered in the lodge on Celtic Lake was wiped clean by the brigade, word had leaked that the NTSB's investigation confirmed the senator's plane had, indeed, been shot out of the air by a missile. A national manhunt for Cole Wannamaker was under way. Members of the Lexington Brigade were being rounded up and questioned. The president, in a news conference, praised the work of the FBI and vowed that protecting the nation against terrorism, both domestic and from abroad, was a top priority. At the Capitol, the Senate prepared to begin debate on the Manila Accord.

The nightmare should have been over. But Stephen's vision continued to plague him.

Three days after the rescue of the Hukaris and Blessing at the lodge, Stephen sat with Henry Meloux, Leah Duling, and Beulah Love on the shoreline of Iron Lake. It was a perfect morning, the lake a mirror reflecting the powder blue of the sky and the trees along the shoreline full of autumn fire. Beulah Love had shown no inclination to return to her home in Allouette or to her former existence. A woman Stephen had always seen as cold and aloof had undergone a remarkable transformation. She'd formed a deep friendship with Leah Duling and was constantly expressing her appreciation for Stephen's heroic effort in saving her from the men of the Lexington Brigade. She'd just finished weaving a wreath of wildflowers, and she leaned far forward and studied her reflection in the mirror of the water.

"I used to make these when I was a girl. A long, long time ago."

"Before boarding school?" Leah said.

"The end of my childhood," Beulah noted with sadness.

"But you have found again the child in your heart," Henry told her.

"I would never have thought something good would come from all this."

"I think there is still more good on the horizon," Henry said. "More good before the storm."

"Storm?" Stephen turned his gaze from the far islands that lay like sleeping dogs on the mirror of the lake.

"These woods," the old Mide said. "They still speak of a great evil."

"The monster at my back," Stephen said.

"Maybe at the backs of us all."

"You're scaring me," Leah said.

"And me," Beulah chimed in. "Are you afraid, Henry?"

"Unsettled." To Stephen, the old man said, "I would like to see this monster that does not show itself to you. When you face this thing, and I think you will, I would like to be with you."

Stephen was torn. If he ever confronted this terrible thing, he would like his old mentor at his side. But he was also afraid for Henry, who sometimes seemed so frail that a strong wind could blow him over.

"It might show itself when you're not with me, Henry."

The old man thought about that. "Then I will stay with you."

"I'm not sure that's feasible."

"Then we must flush this beast from its hiding."

"I'd love to. Any idea how?"

"I will think on it."

Henry rose slowly and began to make his way back to the cabin. Beulah stood and followed, but Leah remained seated beside Stephen. "I'm afraid for him," she confessed.

As the old man moved away, he seemed to grow smaller. Stephen said, "So am I."

That same day, Daniel and Rainy returned to work. Daniel took his truck, but Stephen shuttled Rainy in his old Jeep. In Allouette, he dropped her at the clinic, then passed the stop where the kids from the reservation waited for the school bus. Winston Goodsky wasn't among them. Stephen parked and went into Harmon Goodsky's gallery. The place felt empty. He prowled, admiring the photographs on the walls, and came to one of a familiar scene, a gray-green outcrop crowning a hill of stone. Desolation Mountain. The photo made the rock outcrop look like a castle keep, a foreboding structure against a threatening sky, a powerful and disturbing image.

Harmon Goodsky stepped from the curtains that closed off the back rooms. "*Boozhoo,* Stephen." He walked like a man teetering at the edge of a precipice, doing his best not to fall. Looking at him, the healer in Stephen understood that he was beyond the help of even Henry Meloux. "What can I do for you?"

"Just looking. I like this photograph. Did you take it?"

"One of Winston's. My grandson's got a natural eye for drama. I forgot about that one." He removed it from the wall.

"You should leave it up. It's good."

"He's shot better."

"I didn't see him at the bus stop this morning."

"Isn't feeling well. I've been keeping him home. Things okay with you and your family now? That was some big stuff went down."

"Not quite back to normal, but we're headed there."

Stephen left, but Winston Goodsky's photo had nudged him in a direction he hadn't thought of in a while. He decided to make a visit to the place where everything had begun.

The road to the base of Desolation Mountain was clear and empty. Stephen hiked the path that most people took to the top and made his way through the ring of aspen trees. The path was blanketed in fallen gold leaves. He walked in stillness until he came to the end of the aspens and stood at the edge of the wide, bare apron of rock that lay around the base of the crowning outcrop.

It was a golden day. The sun sat atop the mountain like a king on his throne, and Stephen shielded his eyes against the brilliance. Under the shade of his hand, he saw a figure fifty yards up the slope. The figure was turned toward the mountain crest. To Stephen it appeared as if one of the figure's arms was pointed toward the crowning outcrop, and the image shook loose a startling recognition.

At the sound of Stephen's approach, the kid spun, his face full of surprise and fear.

"Easy, Winston," Stephen said. "Just me."

The kid held a camera, to which was affixed a long telescopic lens.

"I thought you were sick," Stephen said. "That's why your grandfather's keeping you out of school."

The kid looked down at the hard rock beneath his feet. "He wants me to stay home for a while, until everything settles down."

"Does he know where you are?"

Winston shook his head. "I told him I was going to shoot along the lakeshore. He doesn't want me coming up here."

"Why?"

"He's afraid."

"Of what?"

"I should go."

"Wait. I'll make you a deal. There's something I want to tell you about this place, something that might sound pretty strange. If it makes sense, you tell me why. Okay?"

"Really, I have to go."

"It's important."

The kid let a few seconds pass. Stephen wondered what he was weighing in his thinking. Then the kid gave a simple nod.

Stephen told him about the vision in which they both played a part. When he finished, he said, "I see this night after night. Does it mean anything to you?"

The kid looked away from Stephen. His eyes settled on the outcrop that topped the mountain. "There's something you should see."

He tipped his camera and, in the shade of his own shadow, studied the LCD display screen as he scanned through images. He stopped and handed the camera to Stephen. The image showed the crown of Desolation Mountain, that outcrop like a castle keep. But to the right was something else, something smaller and squarish in design. Stephen squinted but could make out only that he was looking at a vehicle of some kind. "I don't understand."

The kid took the camera, zoomed in on the image, and returned it to Stephen. Now what Stephen saw was a military-looking truck painted in camouflage. From the open bed in back rose a huge device that, with its hood and forked tongue, reminded Stephen of a cobra about to strike. Three men seemed to be attending to the device.

"What is it?"

"I don't know," Winston said. "But look at this."

He shifted the focus on the LCD display to a bird in the sky above the vehicle and zoomed in even farther on the display. Now Stephen could see that it wasn't a bird at all.

"Is that Senator McCarthy's plane?"

Winston didn't reply, but his face said it all.

CHAPTER 43

The final meeting with Gerard went, as Bo had suspected it would, with all the emotion and formality of an exchange of chips at a casino window. He was paid in cash for his services, and Gerard didn't even bother to shake his hand. It took place at Bo's cabin, and as Gerard headed toward the door, Bo said, "What about my bonus?"

"Bonus?" Gerard turned back. "What bonus?"

"You told me if I got the black box, there'd be a bonus in it."

"The FBI got it in their sweep of the lodge on Celtic Lake."

"Ah, but how did it get there?"

"Search me."

"That wouldn't do any good. You'd be clean as a new bathtub." Bo was sipping a beer, Leinenkugel's. He lifted the can in a toast to himself. "I didn't do a bad job of sorting out the players. NTSB and FBI, they were obvious. I tracked a lot of vehicles up here back to DoD, several different departments. The Lexington Brigade, of course. Elements of the Ojibwe community. But I still have no idea who hired you."

"Is that important?"

"The FBI may have the black box, but the information that was on it? That went to whoever brought you in. Then you wiped the recorder clean."

"The Lexington Brigade wiped it clean."

"That's certainly the story."

"I know another story, Thorson. One about a man hired to do a job. Then he sells himself out to another employer. What do you think of a man who'd do that?"

"Like everything that happens in the world, Colonel, it all depends on the reason."

"In this story, if I were a romantic, I'd say the reason was affection."

"Maybe you wouldn't be entirely wrong. But the truth is more complicated."

"Truth?" Gerard's face was a gray slate on which nothing was written. "We float on a sea of lies. There is no solid ground called truth."

"What poem is that from?"

"No poem. Just the way it is."

"And that's where we differ."

Gerard turned back toward the door. "I'll expect you to leave this county today."

"Always a pleasure dealing with you, Colonel."

For the next couple of days, Bo lived out of his Jeep, staying off Gerard's radar, avoiding communication with everyone. Communications had clearly been monitored. He was almost certain that, from the beginning, Gerard had known about *her*. The bug, he suspected, was probably on her end the whole time. Without knowing it, she had been compromised from the get-go, or Olympia McCarthy's family had been.

Although the man had made it quite clear that Bo was not to stick around, Gerard himself made no move to leave, which led

Bo to believe there were still loose ends to be tied up. The knots Gerard used to tie up loose ends were often of a lethal kind. Bo was concerned about the safety of the O'Connors and the people on the reservation. He was also concerned about getting to the truth. A U.S. senator had been assassinated, and her family killed along with her. As corny as it sounded, Bo wanted justice for them.

He practically hijacked Cork O'Connor. He'd been waiting half a day near the double-trunk birch that marked the path to Crow Point. When Cork finally showed and began the hike, Bo stepped from the cover of the trees.

"Jesus!" Cork jumped back and tensed as if for a fight. "What the hell, Bo? I thought you were gone."

"We need to talk."

"I'm heading to Crow Point. Why don't you join me? You'll be welcome there."

"Maybe not after you hear what I have say. There's something I need to explain."

Cork waited. Everything around them was quiet. Bo felt as if the forest, too, was listening. After all he'd heard the old Mide say, he'd come to accept that the forest might have eyes and ears and spirit. That it might already know the truth.

"That ransom I told you about, Cork? The Argentine diplomat's son? It was Gerard who brought me in. I've worked with him a few times over the years."

Cork looked stung, then wary. "Why didn't you tell me sooner?"

"It's complicated."

"Were you working for him up here?"

"Yes. And no. After the senator's family contacted me, Gerard did the same. I knew if he was involved, something definitely wasn't right. I accepted his offer, thinking that what I learned from him, I could pass along to the senator's family."

"Like some kind of double agent?"

"More or less."

"And you couldn't tell me?"

"Safer for you and for everybody if I didn't. I'm sorry about that, but I hope you understand."

"So who is this Gerard?"

"An operative of sorts for the government. A kind of fixer."

"A fixer?"

"He's brought in to manage delicate situations."

"Like the assassination of a U.S. senator?"

"Let's walk," Bo said.

As they made their way toward Crow Point, Bo explained to Cork about the bug he'd placed at Gerard's headquarters and that Gerard had eventually discovered and disabled.

"They talked about looking for bear tracks on Desolation Mountain and looking for waves on the beach. Code, of course, but code for what?"

"The flight recorder," Cork said, as if it were obvious.

"Bear tracks? I don't know. And waves on the beach? I get a different feel."

"Maybe he's talking about evidence of the brigade's missile attack. Bear tracks could, I suppose, refer to the trail they left up on the mountain."

"What about waves on the beach?"

Cork thought for a bit. "Got me."

"Waves," Bo said. "It sounds electronic to me."

"So how do you want to proceed?"

"I'm not sure. Mostly I wanted to warn you. Gerard hasn't left Tamarack County. If I were a betting man, I'd lay odds that he got to the flight recorder ahead of us. I think he downloaded the info he wanted from it, wiped it clean, then planted it at the lodge on Celtic Lake."

"Planted it?" Cork stopped and stared at Bo. "Are you saying Gerard killed all those men?"

"I wouldn't put it past him."

"How did he know about them?"

"I don't know if he was aware of them from the beginning, or if he picked up that information along the way. There are still a lot of unanswered questions. But one of the reasons I wanted to talk to you was just to alert you to the fact that he's still around, maybe still monitoring you and your family and those folks on the reservation. Be very careful what you say and who you say it to. And keep watching your backs. There must still be some loose end, and until he's tied it up, Gerard won't leave."

They'd come to the creek Cork told him was called Blood in the language of the Ojibwe. Bo paused there.

"Don't tell anyone you saw me. But, Cork, if you learn anything of value, anything that might point us toward some answers, let me know."

Cork studied him, and Bo knew that he was making a difficult decision. The man understood the whole truth now and had no reason to trust him.

"A call?" Cork finally said.

"That's fine. But let's use a code word to let me know without saying it."

"*Migwech*," Cork said.

"*Migwech?*"

"It means 'thank you' in Ojibwe."

"All right. *Migwech* it is."

"If we need to meet, how about the fire ring on Crow Point? A good, safe place."

The two men shook hands, and as Cork walked away in the early afternoon shadows, Bo looked after him, thinking how wrong

Gerard had been. In every sea of lies, there were always islands of truth.

On his return to Crow Point, Cork found Jenny and Daniel at Meloux's cabin. Daniel seemed in a particularly good mood.

"We finally tracked down those two we thought were poachers," he told Cork. "Tom Blessing reported them at Bourbon Lake again, near the otter lodge. They were still out there when I arrived."

"Thought were poachers?" Cork said. "They weren't?"

"They were pretty reluctant to talk, but when I threatened them with the poaching charge and told them it could carry a sentence of up to two years in prison and a ten-thousand-dollar fine each, they spilled the beans."

"Two years in prison? Ten thousand dollars? And they bought that?"

Daniel laughed. "Clearly not hunters."

"So what are they?"

"They call themselves 'prospecting geologists.'"

"Prospecting for what?"

"They were hired to find the limits of the Duluth Complex, this mother lode of heavy metals."

"On the rez?"

"They think the bulk of the resources may be under reservation land."

"Who hired them?"

"A company called PolyOre Exploration. They were supposed to keep this on the QT. That's why they were so elusive."

"PolyOre Exploration? I'm thinking we should know more about these people."

"I already do. As soon as I finished interviewing the geologists, I got on the Internet. PolyOre Exploration is a subsidiary of Intercontinental Minerals Inc., which, if you follow the difficult track back, is owned by America Midwest Mining."

"What do they think? That in the end they can mine anywhere they want? That land belongs to the Anishinaabeg."

"All of the Black Hills belonged to the Lakota once," Jenny pointed out.

"Did you keep them in custody, Daniel?"

"No reason. They weren't poaching."

"Where is everybody?" Cork asked, because except for his daughter and son-in-law, Crow Point was deserted.

"Rainy's still at the clinic," Jenny replied. "Henry, Leah, Beulah, and Waaboo are out gathering herbs. Trixie trotted along with them."

"Stephen?"

"We haven't seen him since he left with Rainy this morning. He should have been back by now."

Bo's warning—*Keep watching your backs*—returned in a powerful rush.

"Try his phone, Jenny."

She used her cell, waited. "He's not answering."

"He could just be out of cell phone range," Daniel said. "Hit and miss out here. But if you want to look for him, I parked my truck out at Crow Point East. I'll drive."

The two men moved quickly down the path that headed east from Crow Point and along the lakeshore. Cork went over in his head all the safe possibilities: Stephen was, as Daniel suggested, out of cell phone range; his phone was out of juice; he was involved in something important and had simply missed the call. At the same time, he had to consider the more dire possibility: just as Bo Thorson had speculated, there was more going on in

Tamarack County, and Stephen was caught in some deadly, new threat.

"Cork," Daniel said, pulling him out of his dark reverie. "Listen."

They stopped near a copse of birch. A stiff wind shoved through the trees, and at first Cork heard only the loud liquid sound of the leaves rustling in its passage. Then he heard what Daniel's younger ears had already picked up, the sound of an approaching vehicle. With all the uncertainty that had been the norm of late, they took to the trees to wait. In half a minute, Stephen's dusty old Jeep appeared, carefully following the narrow path. Stephen wasn't alone, and the kid in the passenger seat was quite a surprise to Cork. He and Daniel stepped into the open.

"You've been gone a long time," Cork said, approaching the driver's side. "And you aren't answering your phone."

"Sorry, Dad. It's on vibrate, hard to feel in the Jeep." Stephen took the phone from the pocket of his jacket and made the switch.

"Afternoon, Winston," Cork said.

The kid stared down at his feet.

"What's up, Stephen?"

"Dad, there's something you've got to see. Show him, Winston."

The kid had a camera in his lap, a fine-looking Nikon with a powerful telescopic lens affixed. "You . . . you need to come over here," he said.

Cork moved around to the other side of the Jeep. The kid held out the camera in a way that made the display screen visible. What Cork saw appeared to be a military vehicle mounted with some kind of dish being operated by men in camo.

"What is this?"

Stephen answered: "Winston took that on Desolation Mountain the day Senator McCarthy's plane crashed. Show him what's in the sky, Winston."

The kid took the camera, shifted the image on the display, enlarged it, and handed the camera back to Cork. After a long moment, Cork said, "We've got a lot of talking to do, son."

Fresh in his mind was Bo's warning of the possibility of surveillance bugs everywhere, even in the cabins on Crow Point, and Cork herded everyone to the safety of the fire ring to hear Winston Goodsky's story. The young man was clearly uncomfortable with such a large gathering. Cork suspected he would be uncomfortable regardless of the size or makeup of the group. He was like an animal of the forest, a deer maybe, harmless, whose best defense was stillness and second best was flight.

"After school, I went to take some pictures on the mountain. My granddad lets me use his truck as long as I don't leave the rez. I couldn't get to the mountain that day. There was some work going on and the road was closed."

"Roadwork?" Daniel looked to Cork and Stephen. "Wes Simpson and his cousin at the barricade."

"Let him finish," Cork said.

"I know lots of old logging roads, so I drove around to the north side, and parked near Little Bass Lake and hiked up from there. I wanted to get some pictures of those rocks at the top against the clouds. I thought it was, you know, a dramatic setting."

"I saw one of your photographs of Desolation Mountain at your grandfather's gallery today," Stephen told him. "I thought it was awesome."

The kid's face lit up at the praise. "What I wanted to do was make a series across the whole fall, then winter and spring and summer. My granddad said I should call it the Desolation Series."

"Go on," Cork said.

"I was standing just where the trees end, that ring of aspens, you know. I liked the long shot up the bare slope, nice foreground stuff. I put on my AF lens." He tapped the powerful attachment on his camera. "I did a couple of shots, then that truck or what-ever showed up. It parked at the top of the mountain and those guys started working with that thing in back. They ruined the whole scene. But I thought what the heck and kept shooting anyway."

"Did they see you?"

"Not then. I was still in the cover of the trees. But I heard the plane coming and then, it was really strange because the sound of it cut out. Like the engines just died. I could see it starting to fall from the sky and I took shot after shot. I got so caught up that I moved out of the trees to follow it as it fell. That's when they saw me."

"What did they do?" Cork asked.

"I don't know. As soon as they saw me, I ran. I got down to my granddad's truck and took off and went back to Allouette as fast as I could."

"Did you tell your grandfather what happened?"

The kid nodded. "And I showed him the pictures. He told me not to say anything to anyone until he decided what we should do. Then everybody started disappearing on the rez, and he got real scared for me. He made me promise never to say a word. And never go to the mountain. But I've sneaked back a cou-ple of times and watched them searching. I never could figure what for."

"I saw you there," Stephen said.

"I know. When you came into the gallery, I was afraid you would recognize me and tell my granddad." The boy looked at the others in a guilty way, thinking, perhaps, that what he'd revealed to them was a breach of his promise.

"You've done the right thing," Cork assured him.

What he didn't say was that he understood now Bo Thorson's concern regarding Gerard. Winston Goodsky was the loose end that needed tying up.

CHAPTER 44

The call came much sooner than Bo had expected.

"Just wanted to say thank you for all your help, Bo. In the language of the Ojibwe, that would be *migwech*."

"No problem, Cork. You folks up there in Tamarack County, you take care of yourselves. I'm sure our paths will cross again someday soon."

He turned his Jeep around and headed back to the double-trunk birch, then along the trail to Crow Point. It was late afternoon when he found Cork and the others gathered around the fire ring. With them was a teenager he'd never seen before.

O'Connor introduced Winston Goodsky and explained all.

"Let me see the picture."

Winston showed Bo the image on the camera display.

"EW, I'm guessing," Bo said.

Cork gave him a look of incomprehension. "EW?"

"Electronic warfare. A weapon that fires an electromagnetic pulse, an EMP. They're designed to take out electronic systems. Shooting planes out of the sky is one of the potential uses." He glanced at the kid. "Which might explain why you heard that plane's engines go suddenly quiet." Bo studied the image again. "I've only seen pictures, so I don't know for sure. I have a friend in the Pentagon, a guy who used to work Secret Service with me. He might be able to help us out. Can I get a copy of this?"

"I'll have to download it first," Winston said. "My laptop's at my granddad's."

"We need to talk to your grandfather," Cork told the teenager. "He should know all of this."

The kid didn't look happy about it.

"Okay if I go along?" Stephen addressed this to Winston, not to his father.

The kid looked so relieved he almost smiled. "Thanks."

In the end, it was Bo, Winston, Cork, and his son who headed into Allouette. Stephen led the way, ferrying the Goodsky teenager in his old Jeep. Cork and Bo followed. On the way to town, they went over the pieces, trying to fit things together.

"An EW, that would be a military weapon, right?" Cork said. "So, how did the Lexington Brigade get its hands on something like that?"

"They sure as hell didn't buy it off the Internet," Bo said. "Stole it, maybe."

"If it was an electronic weapon that brought the senator's plane down, why is the word from NTSB that a missile was responsible?"

"This sounds like that rare bird, multiple agencies of the government actually working together, in this case to cover up the truth."

"Which brings us to Gerard," Cork said. "If he's this fixer, who's he working for and how does he fit in?"

"He keeps the hands of important people clean. Very important people. Who is that in this case? You could cover him in red-hot coals and he wouldn't tell you."

"Might be a good man to have on your side," Cork noted.

Although he couldn't disagree, Bo added, "But one hell of an adversary."

On the way to Allouette, Winston was quiet, staring straight ahead as if looking into a dismal future.

"Don't worry," Stephen told him. "My father will square things with your granddad."

"He worries about me. A lot." The kid sat slumped, as if under a heavy burden. "He won't talk about it, but everybody knows he's dying. He's worried what'll happen to me when he's gone."

Not an unreasonable concern, Stephen knew. Across the course of his life, living so near the rez and being of mixed heritage himself, he'd seen the frightening pitfalls of the foster care system firsthand, especially when it came to Native kids.

"No family left on the rez?" he asked.

"No one interested in taking me." Winston's hands gripped his knees, as if trying to hold himself down. "I grew up in the city. Feels strange on the rez. I'm not like the other kids there. And I'm not like the kids in town."

Not Ojibwe enough for the Ojibwe or white enough for the whites, a feeling Stephen knew well, one that had plagued him, too, for most of his life. And he thought about his vision and Winston's part in it. *Him and not him.* Kindred spirits, he understood.

In Allouette, Winston lingered in front of the door to his grandfather's gallery, gathering strength to face the music.

"It'll be okay," Stephen assured him.

Stephen's father put his hand on the boy's shoulder. "Telling us was the right thing."

"Convince my granddad of that," the kid said hopelessly.

Inside, Winston led them through the curtains into the back

area of the gallery, where his grandfather sat at a bench, building a frame of lacquered birch for one of his photographs. Goodsky looked up from his work, clearly surprised to see his grandson in all that company.

"What's going on, Winston?"

"Okay if I explain things?" Cork asked, and Winston looked grateful.

When he'd finished the story, Cork said, "It's a good thing he told us, Harmon. There are still people out there trying to track him down."

"And they're the kind of people who won't stop until they find him," Bo added.

Goodsky stood up. In the wake of his conversation with Winston, Stephen was struck by how all the man's ailments threatened to topple him. "Go on," Goodsky said to his grandson. "Put that photo on your laptop. I want a few words with these men."

Winston headed upstairs.

"Wish you didn't know any of this," Goodsky said. "A secret never keeps long on the rez." He looked toward the ceiling. "I fear for him."

"With good reason," Stephen's father said. "But maybe the best way to protect him is to make sure the right people hear what he knows."

"And who would that be?"

"Why don't we start with talking to the sheriff?"

"I don't want to talk to the sheriff." Winston stood at the bottom of the stairs. He held his laptop and a cable connection. "Can't you just show them the picture?"

"It's on the laptop now?" Bo asked.

Winston nodded and handed over the computer. They spent a couple of minutes together, transferring the image to Bo's cell phone.

When they'd finished, Bo said, "What do you think, Cork? Once we get confirmation about the EW, we can take everything to Sheriff Dross. I think in the meantime we could leave Winston out of this." He eyed the boy. "You understand that you'll have to tell your story eventually."

Winston looked as if he were suffering from a toothache.

"We'll be there with you," Stephen assured him.

The rest of the day they waited on Crow Point. Dusk came, and still no word from Bo's contact at the Pentagon. After dark, Stephen walked out into the meadow, unrolled his sleeping bag, and lay down, staring up at the stars. Daniel and Jenny had erected a big tent next to Leah's cabin, where, until the craziness in Aurora had passed, they would sleep with Waaboo. Cork and Rainy shared the cabin with Leah. Bo Thorson had accepted the loan of a good thick blanket and had thrown it out in the meadow near the tent. Stephen, too, preferred to bed down under the open sky, but he'd moved far away from the others. He should have felt satisfied because at last he'd been able to divine much of the meaning of a vision in time for it to be useful, at least where protecting Winston Goodsky was concerned. He understood the element of *him and not him* now. Winston, a kid of mixed heritage, unsure of his future, whose eyes saw the world in a way others did not, and who was somehow able to capture that vision with his camera. Stephen, who often felt like an outsider, too, and had his own unique way of seeing. But there were still two significant elements of the vision that remained a mystery. He didn't understand the part he'd played—or may have yet to play—in the bird shot from the sky. And, maybe most important, he had yet to face the monster at his back.

Dog-tired from another long day, he was asleep before he knew it. And the vision visited him again.

He woke with a start and sat up. A glow came from beyond the rock outcrops where the fire ring lay. He slipped from his bag, put on his boots, and headed toward the fire. Except for Henry, all the men were there: his father, Daniel, and Bo Thorson.

"What's up?" Stephen said.

"We thought you were sound asleep," his father told him.

"I was. What are you all doing here?"

"I got a message from my friend in the Pentagon," Bo said. "He's onto something. I'm waiting for the next communication."

"We're all waiting," Stephen's father said. "Have a seat."

Stephen sat between Bo and Cork and stared into the fire.

"I've been meaning to ask you about this vision of yours," Bo said. "I know the general outline, but I don't know the specifics. Mind going over it with me?"

Although he'd told it many times now, Stephen told it again in detail.

"The eagle shot from the sky? You think that's the senator's plane?"

"What else?"

"Hmmm." Bo tossed a stick onto the fire. "Why, in this vision, does Winston shoot the eagle out of the sky? It wasn't him operating that electronic weapon on the mountaintop."

"I don't know."

"Tell me about this eagle."

"It's just an eagle. Except there's something odd about its tail."

"Odd how?"

"It's not like a regular eagle's tail, which is all white. This one has other colors mixed in."

"What colors?"

"Blue and red."

Bo looked at him, wide-eyed. "Red, white, and blue? The eagle's tail is red, white, and blue?"

Stephen said, "I've been thinking that must be because the plane was carrying a U.S. senator."

Bo pulled out his cell phone, keyed in something, then said, "Does your bird look like this?"

The image was of an eagle in flight, wings spread, talons sharp, as if preparing to grasp some prey. The tail feathers, like those on the bird in Stephen's vision, were red, white, and blue.

"That's it," Stephen said.

Bo tapped in something else on the phone and showed Stephen the screen again. This time the eagle was part of a commercial logo.

"American Byrd Industries," Stephen read aloud. "Never heard of it."

"The name William Byrd doesn't mean anything to you?"

"William Byrd?" Cork said. "As in the Black Bird?"

"The Black Bird," Bo confirmed.

Stephen said, "Wait a minute. Who's this Black Bird?"

"William Byrd, a very wealthy Kansan with a finger in a lot of pies," Bo replied.

"What does he have to do with my vision?"

"You don't know anything about him?"

Stephen gave a shrug. "I don't pay a lot of attention to the news."

"This guy's a heavy hitter in American business and has bullied his way into politics. His family made its fortune manufacturing drilling equipment early last century. During World War Two, they shifted to military production of all kinds, including weaponry. Which made them even richer. After the war, they got into mineral extraction, agribusiness, railroads, trucking, you name it. William Byrd has an interest in more commercial enterprises than you can imagine, but he's still heavily invested in developing weapons for the U.S. and building much of the expensive armaments that we supply to our friends overseas."

"Why did you call him the Black Bird?"

"It's how he refers to himself."

Bo tapped on his cell phone again and showed Stephen an image of a man with a dark complexion and a thick mane of hair the color of an obsidian knife.

"His mother was Italian, I think. Maybe even Sicilian. That's probably where the dark skin comes from. Byrd's somewhere in his eighties, but he keeps that hair as black as coal dust. His nickname probably comes from that. But I've had a couple of brushes with him, and it also describes the color of his heart. Calls himself a patriot, but if you ask me, what he stands for is what's good for William Byrd."

"What kind of brushes?" Stephen's father asked.

"The first was up here, back when you were sheriff and I was Secret Service. He made a visit to the vice president at his vacation home on Iron Lake."

"I don't remember him coming."

"It was very hush-hush, at Byrd's insistence. The man was an asshole, behaved abominably to everyone, including the vice president and his family."

"What about the second brush?" Cork asked.

Bo shook his head. "That one I can't talk about. It's the only job I ever walked away from."

"How would he be involved in what's gone on up here?" Stephen asked.

"For starters, the Senate begins debate on the Manila Accord next week. That's an agreement Senator McCarthy was leading the charge against. Passage would facilitate trade with much of Southeast Asia. It's aimed at taking away some of China's economic influence there. Byrd Industries would certainly benefit from that. But a lot of the accord is about selling military armaments to these nations as well. I'd bet my bottom dollar there's plenty of money earmarked for Byrd Industries. So that's a possibility. I've got to tell you, the Black Bird's a man who feels privileged right down to the marrow of his being. If he wanted someone dead, no matter the reason, he'd see that it was done." Bo gave Stephen a long look of careful appraisal, one that made Stephen uncomfortable. "I've had my doubts about all this vision stuff. But like the man said, there's clearly more in heaven and earth than I've dreamed of in my philosophy."

"You really think Byrd might be behind all this?" Cork asked.

Bo said, "I'm hoping my friend at the Pentagon can enlighten us." Once again, his eyes settled on Stephen. "But you know that monster at your back in the vision? If there are real monsters in this world, William Byrd is one of them for sure."

The night wore on, and the men finally split up and returned to their sleeping places. Stephen sat cross-legged on his sleeping bag in the meadow and thought about the eagle shot from the sky in his vision. He was relieved that it wasn't a sacred eagle, but instead an evil thing that had taken an eagle's form. He used his cell phone to explore further the monster named William Byrd. He wondered what could turn a man's heart to such darkness. He wondered if there was any ceremony that could heal that damaged spirit. He might have spent the rest of the night caught up in the electronic web, which offered him information but no answers, except that his phone chirped at him and shut itself off, and he realized he'd emptied the battery.

Probably for the best, he decided. He lay down and gazed up at the stars, which were beautiful but, like the Internet, gave him no answers.

CHAPTER 45

The text from Bo's contact in the Pentagon came in the dark hours long before dawn.

This is big. Meet contact 0400 hours. Fly silent. Code word: Eagle. The GPS coordinates followed.

In the meadow not far from where Stephen O'Connor was sleeping, Bo threw off his borrowed blanket. He couldn't see the young man, the grass was so high. It had been a long time since Bo had spent a night like this, under the stars. Hiding out from Gerard, he'd slept in his Jeep. Under the night sky, it was as if something wonderfully clean and whole had been shared with him, a feeling he couldn't recall experiencing since his days on the farm down in Blue Earth, when he was a delinquent teenager trying to become someone better.

He tapped at the door of Leah Duling's cabin. Cork opened up.

"My friend at the Pentagon finally got back to me."

"What did he say?"

"Nothing except that it's big. He's set me up with a meeting, one of his people. I'm on my way."

"Where?"

Bo gave him the coordinates, then said, "When I map it, that's the junction of County Roads Eight and Seventeen."

"South end of Iron Lake. Reasonable if he's coming up from the Cities," Cork said. "Want company?"

"I'll take this one alone."

"Be careful."

"You sound like someone's grandmother."

Bo had parked his Jeep near the double-trunk birch. When he reached it, he was still an hour away from the meeting time. The headlights of the Jeep illuminated a tunnel in the dark, and as Bo headed toward the rendezvous, he considered again the players in this game.

NTSB, FBI, DoD, the Lexington Brigade, maybe William Byrd and Byrd Industries. And Gerard. Were they working at odds with one another, Bo wondered, or in concert? The most recent word from NTSB had confirmed that the Stinger found in the brigade's lodge was probably what had brought down the plane, so all the official lips were saying the same thing. But Winston Goodsky's photograph told a different story.

Bo came back to Gerard. He was pretty sure the man's job was to keep a lid on the truth, to eliminate any evidence that contradicted the official story. Why? Who needed protecting? Gerard was a floater. He and his team worked for no one, and for everyone. So, who was he working for this time around?

Bo's contact at the Pentagon, Max Freeman, had begun his career in the Secret Service, training with Bo. Then he'd moved on, taken a position with DSS, the Defense Security Service, and been assigned to the Pentagon. They'd remained friends and in touch. But this was the first time Bo had tapped Max for something more than a few beers together whenever his own work took him to D.C. He hadn't been certain Max would be willing to help but was grateful his friend had come through. As Bo approached the rendezvous point, he was still puzzling, hoping the information from his contact might help.

He was still a few minutes early and parked well shy of the junction of the two isolated county roads. He checked his Sig Sauer, slipped it back into the holster on his hip, and got out. He kept to the trees that edged the road. The moon was a deflated yellow balloon but gave enough light for Bo to see his way. There was no sign of anyone at the lonely intersection, and he hunkered among the trees, as still as one of the trunks, waiting.

The vehicle came slowly, two bright eyes in the distance, then a broad beam of headlights that illuminated the crossing. An SUV, dark blue or black. It pulled to a stop on the shoulder. The engine died, then the headlights. A door opened, closed. A figure separated itself from the vehicle and moved to the middle of the intersection. Bo couldn't tell a thing about it in the faint moonlight.

Then the figure struck a match and lit a cigar and Bo understood.

He didn't even turn when he heard the click of the cocking hammer at his back.

"The Colonel would like to see you." It was a woman's voice, as cold as he'd ever heard.

The smoke Gerard blew was dark gray against the waning moon. The cigar ember was a third eye low in his face. Two of his people were with him—one just behind Gerard, and the woman with the weapon still in Bo's back.

"I'll take it from here, Lieutenant Craig," Gerard said, and Bo sensed the woman retreat a step or two. Gerard held up a photograph, and Bo didn't have to look to know what it was. "You should be more careful who you trust, Thorson."

"So much for friends," Bo said.

"In our business, friendship is a luxury we can't afford. Which is too bad. In a different world, I think you and I might have had something."

"That's a world I can't even imagine," Bo replied.

"I offered you a chance to get out of this cleanly. That was partly because of our relationship. Not exactly friendship, but about as close as I ever come."

"What's your relationship with the Black Bird?"

"I have none."

Bo thought about this, then said, "You're a fixer. You were called in to fix a fuckup. His?"

"William Byrd has always been a shrewd businessman, but in his old age, he's chosen to wade into areas well beyond his expertise. He used to be satisfied just giving a shitload of money to both sides of the aisle in Washington, currying favors, which we both know is pretty much the norm. But the Black Bird is a little cantankerous these days and impatient with Congress. He finally decided to take things into his own hands."

"And get rid of Senator McCarthy?"

"Not a bad idea when you think about it, with the Senate poised to debate the Manila Accord and Senator McCarthy the very vocal leader of the opposition. And then there's that pesky assault rifle legislation she was about to introduce. If she's out, your governor steps in to fill her shoes, and he's made his own sympathetic views on the accord and his opposition to gun control quite clear. There's one other interesting intersecting consideration here, probably not even on your radar. That mine that's got everybody so worked up in these parts? If you follow the very convoluted trail of ownership, who do you think it leads back to?"

"William Byrd."

"Turns out all those heavy metals in the ground under our feet are necessary to the production of sophisticated military weaponry. A kind of beauty in the synchronicity of all this, if you look at it in the right way. Do you know your Keats? 'A thing of beauty is a joy forever.' "

"Byrd brought in the brigade to do his dirty work?"

"Not exactly. You remember General Buck Cushing? Well, if you don't, he was removed from his command in Iraq because of his very public criticism of how our commander in chief was conducting things over there. After Cushing's forced retirement, Byrd, whose sympathies were much in line with the general's, hired him to head up research and development in Byrd Industries' military weaponry division. Now, guess who was Cushing's chief adjutant. Colonel Cole Wannamaker. He took retirement along with Cushing and got himself a ranch in South Dakota, where he raises horses and continues to play at being a soldier with the Lexington Brigade."

"Cushing supplied Wannamaker with the weapon in the photograph?"

"Cutting-edge electronic warfare, Thorson. It's the Vulcan N-17X, still in the test phase. It has the capability of sending out a powerful EMP, yes, but it's also a neutron cannon."

"Which is what?"

"Remember the neutron bomb? Kills a whole city without damaging any of the superstructure. This is a big gun that does the same thing. It fires a directed neutron beam. Imagine being able to take out a whole cadre of terrorists deeply embedded in the buildings of a city block without reducing that block to rubble. Humanitarian in its way. Keeps homes and businesses intact for the return of the citizenry. Think what most of Syria might be today if we'd been able to use it there. The beauty of employing it to assassinate the senator is that everyone on board was dead before they hit the ground. No chance of survivors telling a tale."

"Senator McCarthy and her family weren't deeply embedded terrorists."

"Of course not. No one would ever consider what the Black Bird and Cushing did a reasonable action. But the kind of weaponry Byrd Industries is developing, now that's worth protecting."

"Have you known it was him from the beginning?"

Gerard blew smoke toward the stars. "Pretty much. Three weeks ago, someone inside Byrd Industries leaked to the Pentagon that one of the N-17X prototypes had gone missing from Byrd Industries' test facility in Utah. That kind of weapon doesn't just go missing. None of this was ever made public, of course. When the senator's plane came down, I was sent to check it out. Hell, everyone was sending someone to check it out. It was a mess of bureaucracies stumbling over one another. Nobody was sure of all the details. That's where you came in. You and your friends up here, you've been very helpful. I didn't know the territory like you do. I didn't have the local contacts. Once you gave me the lay of the land, I passed that along and things finally began to be coordinated. From very high up."

"How high?"

"You have no idea, Thorson."

"All to protect the Black Bird?"

"If you blow that photo up enough, what you see is that one of the men operating the N-17X prototype is Cushing himself, no doubt acting on orders from Byrd. If I could, I'd just put a bullet in those nutcases. But Byrd Industries is important to our national security."

"What happened to the N-17X?"

"Two days after the plane crash, some of my people intercepted it on its way back to Utah, along with Cushing. He claimed they'd done a field test in Wyoming and denied any involvement in the senator's death, but what we got off the black box was pretty damning. We thought that was it, the end of it. Then you and O'Connor led us to Wannamaker, and he told us about the photographer on the mountain. If that photo of Cushing and the N-17X ever got out, there was no controlling the damage." Gerard smiled around his cigar. "Thanks to you, that's not a problem now. Cushing and the prototype have been returned safely to the Utah test facility. The NTSB's report, when it's finally made official and public, will confirm the Stinger story."

"You planted the Stingers and the flight recorder?"

"It's what I do."

"And the massacre of the brigade, that was your work, too. What about Wannamaker? Did you kill him, dump his body somewhere he'll never be found?"

Gerard gave his head a shake. "He still has work to do."

"And me? I'll just disappear?"

"Not quite yet." Gerard threw the butt of his cigar to the ground, crushed the ember with the heel of his boot, and said, almost sadly, "I need some answers from you first. Then I have another massacre to arrange."

CHAPTER 46

Trixie barked.

Cork, who was in a sleeping bag with Rainy on the floor of Leah Duling's cabin, woke in the dark. The old mutt was up, teeth bared, growling at the door. Cork's first thought was that a black bear had come prowling. Then another possibility set in, and he rose quickly, but too late.

There was no lock on the door. Meloux had no need of locks in his little piece of paradise. The door was thrown open and banged against the wall. Cork crouched, his hands empty but fisted, ready to throw blows. The light from the doorway blinded him.

"Hold it right there, O'Connor, or I'll shoot you where you stand!"

Rainy had risen and stood shoulder to shoulder with her husband. She was dressed in gray sweatpants and a blue T-shirt and held herself tense. Behind them, bunk springs creaked.

"What's happening?" Leah said.

"We need you folks to come with us."

You folks, as if this were a friendly invitation, but the voice was icicle sharp.

"Who are you?" Cork demanded.

"Everything will be explained."

"Let me put on something warmer," Leah said.

"We've got a fire going. It'll be plenty warm."

Trixie continued to growl and bare her teeth, the hackles on her neck raised. No one moved yet.

"Maybe this will help," said the voice behind the blinding light.

Little Waaboo, looking confused and scared, was shoved into the beam of the flashlight. Cork lunged for him protectively, but a black-gloved hand grabbed the child and pulled him back into the dark.

At that Trixie, in full protective mode, gathered herself and launched her old body with a youthful vigor toward the source of the light. But the automatic rifle barked several times. Trixie fell short of her mark and lay sprawled on the cabin floor, perfectly still.

"No!" Rainy cried and tried to move toward the dog.

Cork held her back because the barrel of the automatic rifle was trained on his wife now. But Waaboo somehow broke free and ran to the dog and laid himself on Trixie as if trying to protect his beloved pet from further harm.

"Get the boy," the voice behind the beam ordered. "Get him up and let's get going."

Cork eased Waaboo gently from the still body. "She won't feel any more pain, little guy. Trixie's with the angels now."

The T-shirt his grandson had slept in was stained with blood, and tears streamed down little his cheeks. Waaboo turned toward the light beam and growled, "Monster!"

They were ushered outside, where they joined Daniel and Jenny, who'd already been rounded up. Jenny hugged her son to her. "Oh, God, I heard the shots and was so afraid."

"Trixie," Cork told her, his voice as sharp and jagged as a saw blade. "She tried to protect our little guy."

They stood in a loose group and watched as Henry Meloux was brought from his cabin. Although the old man walked slowly, his back was straight, his shoulders squared. When he was with the others, he said to the men who surrounded them, "Weasels and thieves come in the dark."

"It's clear you've never been in a war, old-timer." The man who spoke wore camo and his face was painted shades of black and dark blue. "Okay, folks, move out. Follow the flashlight."

Cork and Rainy walked directly behind Jenny and Daniel, with Waaboo between them, each holding one of his hands. They were all barefoot, the ground cold against their soles. Cork's brain was going a thousand miles an hour, trying desperately to figure a way to bring a moment of chaos into this situation, some ploy that might help those he loved break free. But the men who herded them held all the cards. It was clear they were disciplined. From the very first order delivered in the cabin and reinforced by Trixie's death, Cork understood that whoever was in charge had given permission to shoot to kill.

They were taken to the fire ring, where flames from the earlier blaze had been rekindled. Another man with an automatic rifle was already there. Seated with his back against one of the rock outcrops that isolated the ring was someone Cork recognized immediately from all the recent news stories: Cole Wannamaker, national leader of the Lexington Brigade. His hands were cuffed with a plastic restraint, and duct tape sealed his mouth. His eyes followed Cork and the others as they were paraded past and, like him, seated with their backs against the rocks.

There were four guards in all. Cork watched as they spoke quietly among themselves, then he asked, "What now?"

One of them responded simply, "Now we wait."

———

Far out in the meadow, Stephen crouched. He'd watched the lights play across the cabins and the tent, had heard the angry voices, the shouted orders, the shots. He didn't know what was happening but understood that something terrible was going down on Crow Point. He slipped his boots on and began to crawl on all fours through the high meadow grass toward the two rock outcrops that sequestered the fire ring. East of the rocks, he crept among the birches along the shoreline of Iron Lake, where the moon created a yellow path across the surface of the black water. He darted from the cover of one white birch trunk to the next, until he could see the fire ring.

Four men with powerful-looking rifles stood guard over his family and Henry Meloux and Leah Duling. It took Stephen a moment before he recognized the man seated with the others: Cole Wannamaker, whose face had been all over the newspapers. What he was witnessing made no sense to him. But he understood that there was nothing he could do alone that would change the situation.

He carefully retraced his steps to the meadow and took the cell phone from his pants pocket. He tried to turn it on, then remembered to his profound dismay that his Internet search earlier that night had drained the last of its power. His phone was dead.

He looked back to where the glow of the fire rose above the rock outcrops. He could put together no plan to save his family and the others. He had nothing to match the automatic weapons. His only hope, he decided, was in Allouette. He dug into his pants pocket and made sure he had the key to his old Jeep, which was parked at Crow Point East. Then he began to run.

He'd reached the edge of the meadow and was just about to

take the path that led along the lakeshore when, in the dim glow of the waning moon, a figure stepped from the shadow of the trees and blocked his way. He couldn't see the figure clearly. What he could see was the rifle the figure held and the long barrel that was pointed at his chest.

CHAPTER 47

When Bo Thorson stumbled into the flickering light around the fire ring, Cork saw the damage that had been done to him, at least the damage that showed. His face was a bloody mess. Because it was hard for him to walk, he was supported between two of Gerard's people. They threw him roughly against the rock wall, and he slumped beside Cork, his chin on his chest, his breathing labored.

Gerard strode into the firelight. He looked down the line of all those who'd been taken prisoner.

"Craig," he snapped. "Where's the kid?"

"This is everyone," the woman told him.

"No." He stepped to Cork and leaned down. "Where's your son?"

"I don't know."

Gerard spoke to them all, "Anyone care to answer?" When no one did, he moved to Waaboo and crouched in front of the boy. "Do you know where your uncle Stephen is?"

"You're a darkpoople," Waaboo threw at him.

"A what?"

"You're a . . . a muggymonster."

Gerard smiled. "That sounds about right. Now, son, I need to know something. I need to know where your uncle is. It's important to me."

"I don't care."

"I understand. But if you don't tell me, this is what I'm going to have to do. I'm going to have to hurt your mommy. I don't really want to do that. But I will if I have to."

"You hurt my mommy and I'll kill you."

"He was sleeping in the meadow." Bo raised his head wearily. "I doubt he's still there."

Gerard gestured to two of his men, who headed into the dark.

Gerard pulled a photograph from under his jacket, the photo Winston Goodsky had shot and Bo had sent to his friend in the Pentagon.

"I want to know who took this." When no one responded, Gerard nodded to another of his people. "Bring Thorson."

The man yanked him to his feet and marched him to where Gerard stood.

"I asked Thorson the same question I just put to you," he said to Cork and the others. "This is what his silence got him. Crude methods, but in the field, you do what you have to." He clapped Bo on the shoulder, as if they were comrades. "Thorson's a tough son of a bitch, I'll give him that. I didn't get an answer from him." His gaze shifted to Cork. "One by one, I'll question your family, O'Connor. Even little—what do you call him? Waaboo?"

"Gerard," Bo said. "I'll make you a deal."

"I don't think so." Gerard hadn't taken his eyes off Cork. "I think I'll get what I want."

Meloux said, "These woods have eyes and ears and spirit."

Gerard shifted his attention to the old Mide. "You're the shaman, right?"

"I am just an old man. But old men understand many things younger men do not."

"Like who took this photograph?"

"I was thinking more that among human beings there is sometimes a sense of order that is not true."

Gerard looked interested. "I have time, old man. Explain."

"One thing leads to another. Is that how you believe it works?"

"That's how it's always seemed to me."

The old Mide gave his head a single shake. "All things happen at the same time. What was, what is, what will be. Nothing comes before. Nothing comes after. Everything is."

"This is important to me how?"

"The spirits of these woods are part of the eternal. To a man who knows how to listen, they speak. Of what was, what is, and what will be."

"You're talking nonsense, old-timer."

Meloux's face was cracked and hard. Like the ancient rock that crowned Desolation Mountain, Cork thought.

"Nonsense only because you do not understand. But you are about to." Then Meloux smiled almost beatifically. "Things fall apart. The center cannot hold."

Gerard was clearly taken by surprise. His eyebrows lifted, he studied Meloux and added, "Mere anarchy is loosed upon the world."

"Yeats," Jenny murmured.

Gerard stood pondering this as the two men he'd sent to look for Stephen returned. Cork felt a flood of relief to see that all they brought with them was Stephen's sleeping bag.

"Well?" Gerard said.

"This was it. No kid."

"He's out there somewhere. This time don't come back until you find him. Take Craig and Edwards with you."

Before any of them could act on his order, a shot splintered the quiet. The sound of it came from somewhere along the lakeshore. It kicked up dirt at Gerard's feet. Gerard and his men scattered like roaches into the dark at the edges of the firelight.

"Stephen?" Rainy asked.

"Maybe," Cork replied. "Where's your Winchester, Henry?"

"It was hanging on the wall in my cabin." The old man spoke calmly, as if none of this was surprising to him, and Cork thought: *What was, what is, what will be.*

Another shot cracked the night. This one came from a different direction.

"If it's Stephen out there," Daniel said, "he's not alone."

With the fire ring deserted by Gerard and his people, Wannamaker pushed himself up and made a run for the lake. He hadn't gone but a few steps before a burst of automatic weapon fire from the dark cut him down.

Cork had been considering the same thing but thought better of it now. He stayed where he was seated, waiting to see how this sudden turn of events played out, wondering if it was Stephen out there with the rifle, and if not Stephen, then who?

For half an hour there were no more shots, then Gerard stepped suddenly into the firelight, pushing someone before him as a shield. Monkey Love. Gerard held the barrel of a big pistol pressed to the back of Monkey's head.

"You out there!" he hollered. "Come into the firelight or I'll put a bullet through this man's head."

Monkey looked at Cork and the others. "Sorry," he said.

"Shut up," Gerard snapped. "You out there! You have two minutes before I shoot!"

Gerard was the only visible member of his squad. The others

were still out there, looking for the second shooter. Because it was Monkey whom Gerard had snagged, Cork knew the other shooter had to be Ned Love. How they had come to be on Crow Point, God only knew.

"Did you hear? Two minutes!" Gerard called out.

Another rifle shot came from beyond the rocks, followed by the staccato of an automatic weapon. Then silence, broken only by the crackle of the fire in the ring.

"One minute!"

Cork watched as Monkey Love pulled himself proudly erect. His arms were every bit as long and awkward-looking as they had always been, but there was a noble aspect to him in this moment as he prepared, Cork understood, to die.

"Gerard," Cork said.

"Shut up, O'Connor." Gerard hollered toward the night, "His death is on your hands!" He cocked the hammer on the pistol. "Ten seconds!"

Into the firelight from the direction of the lake stepped Ned Love. In front of him was one of Gerard's people, the woman, Craig. Ned carried a rifle with the barrel pointed at her back. "You okay, Monkey?"

"Put the rifle down," Gerard ordered.

"Let's barter," Ned suggested.

"You have nothing to barter with."

"This woman's life isn't important?"

"Lieutenant Craig is a soldier. Dying is what soldiers do."

"Colonel?" the woman said, clearly not on the same page.

"How about you call the others in and we do some dealing?" Ned said.

"I don't have to call."

At the edges of the firelight, his men appeared. They ringed Ned, weapons trained on him from every direction.

"Winning hand," Gerard said. "Put your rifle down."

Ned hesitated a breath or two, then lowered his rifle to the ground.

Gerard holstered his sidearm and shoved Monkey. "Both of you over there with the others."

Ned and Monkey sat against the rock, and Cork thought how they were all lined up now, as if readied for an execution.

Gerard walked to where Wannamaker lay dead and stared down at the man, a disgusted look on his face.

Bo said, "Can't use him now. A second massacre perpetrated by a man with a dozen bullet holes, that just won't fly."

Gerard spun, crossed with a determined step to Waaboo, lifted the boy in a rough grasp, and hauled him toward the fire. He held up Waaboo with the boy's bare soles only two feet above the flames, his little legs kicking ferociously at Gerard.

"Who shot the photo? Ten seconds before the boy burns."

Bo said, "Do this and you become everything you claim to fight against."

Gerard seemed not to hear. There was a demonic blaze in his eyes that had nothing to do with the reflection from the fire, and Cork made his own desperate calculations: ten feet to Gerard; knock him and Waaboo away from the fire; if he was lucky, he might make it before he was cut down; if he wasn't lucky, maybe it would create enough distraction that someone else could grab Waaboo.

"Five seconds."

"Winston Goodsky," Jenny shouted. "He shot the photograph. Now put my son down, you bastard."

But Gerard didn't seem inclined to keep his promise. He lowered little Waaboo so that his kicking feet were only inches above the flames. "Who is Winston Goodsky?"

"No," Jenny screamed.

"Winston is my grandson, and a better man than you'll ever be, you son of a bitch."

The words were spit out from the dark beyond the firelight.

The moment Gerard looked in that direction, Daniel and Cork both shot up, launching themselves toward Gerard and Waaboo. Cork hit the man and spun him away from the fire. Daniel grasped his little son and wrested him from Gerard's grip. Gerard stumbled to the ground with Cork all over him, and they grappled. Gerard was made of iron, a soldier. But Cork was full of bitter fire, and the blows he threw were fast and angry.

"It's over, Cork!"

He felt hands pull him off Gerard, and he stood breathing hard, glaring down at the man. Gerard slowly brought himself into a sitting position. The blaze in his eyes had died, replaced by a cold understanding of his situation. His people made no move to help him, because they were in need of help themselves. Behind each one of them stood at least two Shinnobs from the Iron Lake Reservation, who had emerged from the dark, holding hunting rifles.

Harmon Goodsky strode fully into the firelight. Stephen flanked him on one side, Winston on the other. Cork smiled at his son, then turned slowly, recognizing all the faces of these reservation folks he'd known his whole life. Sarah LeDuc was there. And Tom Blessing. And Clyde Kingbird, with the mole above his lip like a blackfly. And Isaiah Broom and Sonny LeBanc and Dennis Vizenor and so many others. Some were his cousins by blood, others he simply called by that name.

"*Chi migwech, niijikiweyag,*" he said to them. Thank you, my friends.

CHAPTER 48

They sat around the fire ring, the O'Connors and Bo. Little Waaboo, exhausted, lay sacked out on his mother's lap. Sarah LeDuc had stayed, but the other Ojibwe had gone. The sun was little more than a promise on the horizon, creating a long ribbon of pink sky. Sheriff Marsha Dross was with them, too. Her people and Quaker's agents had taken Gerard and his squad and had removed Wannamaker's body. The FBI's initial round of questioning had been completed, but there would be others. A mountain of paperwork was waiting, yet Dross had taken this time to be alone with the O'Connors, who were more to her, Bo understood, than just constituents. Like so many others in Tamarack County, she was a good friend, one far truer than the last friend Bo had chosen to trust.

"When I ran into Ned and Monkey Love lurking out there at the edge of the clearing, my cell phone was dead. And you know Ned and Monkey," Stephen was explaining. "They live outside the twenty-first century. So no cell phone with them. Taking my Jeep into Allouette for help was the only option."

"What were they doing out there?"

"Ned told me he and Monkey had been keeping tabs on Crow

Point since the raid at Celtic Lake. With Cole Wannamaker still at large, they were concerned about our safety."

"So they just lurked around here?"

"Pretty much."

Cork looked to Meloux. "Did you know?"

"There is little about these woods that I do not know."

Which made Bo remember how calm the old man had seemed in the face of all Gerard's threats. And he remembered the old man's words: *These woods have eyes and ears and spirit.*

"Why didn't you say something, Uncle Henry?" Rainy asked.

"Because I am a better keeper of secrets than some around this fire." He didn't look at anyone particularly.

Stephen went on: "Ned told me that he and Monkey would do their best to keep Gerard and his people busy until I came back from Allouette with reinforcements."

"And then you ran the whole way to the Jeep, all two miles to Crow Point East, with that leg?" Jenny said this as if it were a kind of miracle.

Stephen shrugged it off. "I didn't have much choice."

"Didn't it hurt?" English asked. "Your leg?"

"Are you kidding? It hurt like hell. But I wasn't alone out there."

"The spirit of the woods?" Bo smiled when he said this.

Young O'Connor looked at him steadily. "The spirit of all things. It's all connected."

In this, Bo heard wisdom, the kind he might have expected from the old Mide, and although it would be a long time before he fully accepted that there were mysteries which could never be solved, in that moment, in that intimate circle around the fire, he was willing to embrace the truth of Stephen O'Connor's words.

"What happens from here?" Rainy asked.

Dross said, "It'll be complicated, I'm sure. There are still a lot of missing pieces. It's clear that much of what's gone on was manipulated from high up."

"They'll get nothing from Gerard or his people," Bo said.

"But the truth will come out, yes?" Rainy looked to him with hope.

Bo spoke carefully. "There will be a lot of smoke. There will be a lot of accusations designed to misdirect, obfuscate, confuse. There will be a lot of finger-pointing that will get no one anywhere. It's how our government operates when all the disparate heads are trying to cover their asses. It's never about getting to the truth."

"The many-headed monster of Waaboo's nightmare," Jenny said. She ran her hand gently over her son's cheek. "Maybe you're not the only one who has visions, Stephen."

"But *we* know the truth," Sarah LeDuc insisted. "We can speak out."

"Who takes the word of an Indian seriously?" English said bitterly.

"Marsha knows the truth," Stephen said.

"I'll do what I can," the sheriff promised, then, after a pause, added with a dour note, "But they've taken all the evidence."

"What about Winston's camera and laptop?"

Bo said, "By the time the sun is up, Quaker's people will have confiscated that, too."

"There's your cell phone," Cork pointed out. "You used it to send the photo to your Pentagon friend."

Bo shook his head, which still hurt from the beating he'd taken when Gerard tried to get information from him. "They grabbed that when they nabbed me at the crossroads."

"They can't just make Wannamaker's body disappear," English said.

"He was a dangerous, wanted man, a domestic terrorist. They

caught him. He tried to run. They shot him." Bo shrugged. "Who knows? In the end, Gerard might end up the hero of this story."

"They beat you," Jenny said.

"That's my story. Did any of you see it happen?"

"You sound like one of them," Sarah LeDuc said.

"Believe me, I'm not, Sarah. But I know how they work."

"They can't just cover all of this up."

"They've done it before," Bo told her. "This won't be one of Gerard's finer moments, but whenever you try to pin him down, he's like an eel. And he'll get all kinds of protection from above." He threw a stick into the fire, watched it burn. "Doesn't matter who's in the White House, the truth about our government, any government for that matter, is that protecting its citizens is never its first priority. Its first priority is protecting itself."

Around the fire, the mood had taken a sour turn. It was the old man, Meloux, who lifted their spirits.

"This is not a time for heavy hearts," the Mide said. "Death was our shadow, but that shadow is gone. Justice? We will pray this comes with the light of day. In this moment, here and now, we celebrate the spirit of what is good in each of us and in those friends who stood with us in the dark and chased away death's shadow." He lifted his eyes to the night sky. "We give thanks to the Creator and we pray that in the battle between love and fear, which is always raging in the human heart, love will triumph." He lowered his eyes and, one by one, fixed each of them around the fire with his steady gaze. When he came to Bo, he smiled. "Love will win," he said gently, as if the words were meant for Bo especially. "In the end, love always wins."

CHAPTER 49

The memorial service for Olympia McCarthy and her family was held in the Twin Cities at the Cathedral of St. Paul on a rainy autumn afternoon. The broadcast was carried live on all the local network stations. The governor was there and other politicians. A number of the senator's colleagues from D.C. had flown in to attend. The huge sanctuary was packed, every pew filled shoulder to shoulder. During the service, the governor spoke. He praised the work of the FBI and never mentioned Gerard's name when speaking of the death of Cole Wannamaker, a man he called a wild-eyed, misdirected fanatic. Gerard's name, in fact, had never come up in any of the journalistic accounts of what occurred in Tamarack County. Wannamaker's death was always attributed to very nonspecific "U.S. security personnel."

Alone in his condo in St. Paul, Bo watched the service on the television. Every so often the camera angle shifted to the cathedral's front pew, where Olympia McCarthy's father sat, along with other members of the family. With them was the most illustrious of the memorial's attendees: former President Clay Dixon. His wife, the lovely former First Lady, sat at his side.

The media had made much of the fact that Olympia McCarthy and Kathleen Jorgenson Dixon had been college roommates and lifelong best friends, and how, after the tragedy, the former First Lady had been with the senator's family constantly, offering her support. She didn't speak at the service, but Bo could still hear her voice, the sound of her soft breathing, like wind across tall grass. He thought about how she'd kept their conversations from her husband, so that, should things go south, he could claim plausible deniability. He wondered what she intended to do with the photo he'd sent her from his cell phone, moments after he'd sent that same photo to the man he'd believed was his friend in the Pentagon. It had been his last communication with her before Gerard nabbed him and beat him and prepared to stage another massacre. Bo never told Cork O'Connor or his family about that final communication. He didn't want to raise their hopes only to have them dashed on the rocks of some necessary political cover-up.

When the service had finished, under an awning erected outside the cathedral to protect the podium from the rain, former President Clay Dixon, as promised, addressed the media. He was flanked by his wife and by Olympia McCarthy's father. In a surprise move, he opened his remarks by displaying a photograph, which he said had been taken by a young Native American atop Desolation Mountain the day Olympia McCarthy died.

Cork sat with Rainy in front of the television in the house on Gooseberry Lane. They'd watched the service, had heard all the lauding of a woman who, in the end, had sacrificed everything in her fight for the ideals she believed in. They'd both shared their story with reporters, but they'd never seen any of the truths they told make it into print.

Waaboo and Jenny came from the kitchen, bringing coffee and cookies.

"A little something to brighten a dark day," Jenny said.

Waaboo settled himself on the sofa next to his grandfather. He lay his head against Cork's shoulder. "I miss Trixie, Baa-baa."

"She died trying to protect us. A good death."

"Do dogs go to heaven?"

"Why wouldn't they?"

"They're not people."

"Do you think only people are in heaven?"

Waaboo took a bite of the chocolate chip cookie in his hand. "I guess I'll find out someday."

Cork put his arm around his grandson. "That day is far, far away, little guy."

On the television, the service had finished and former President Clay Dixon was stepping up to a microphone under a canvas awning that dripped rain, preparing to speak.

"Just for once," Jenny said, "I'd like to hear a politician say something meaningful and true."

"Give the man a chance," Cork said and reached for a cookie.

It was night and Stephen was alone with the old Mide. They sat before a fire burning in the stone ring at the edge of Iron Lake. The sky had spit rain all day, and there was still a brooding overcast, so that the only light came from the dance of flames in the fire ring.

"He told the truth," Stephen reported. "In front of television cameras, he showed the photograph Winston Goodsky took, and he told what happened up here."

With a nod of approval, the old man said, *"Debwewin."* Which, Stephen knew, meant "truth" in the language of his people. "One of the gifts of the Seven Grandfathers." Then the old man said,

"I hear that you have befriended Winston Goodsky." He nodded in approval. "He is a young man who will need guidance and a friend."

"He knows his grandfather's death isn't far away and he's afraid of what will come after that. It's important for him to know he won't be alone."

Small drops of rain hit lightly on Stephen's face. He had come to the old man with a heavy heart and he hadn't spoken yet the real truth that brought him. He summoned all his strength of spirit. "Henry," he said. "I had the vision again."

The old man waited. The fire popped. Embers flew like glowing bits of a shattered dream toward the black night sky.

"This time I found the courage to look at the great, terrible thing at my back. It had nothing to do with what happened on Desolation Mountain."

The old man turned his face to Stephen, his skin cut by the lines from a century of erosion, his eyes like ancient stones. "And what did you see?"

Stephen looked long and deep at this man who had taught him so much about life, whose spirit was the truest he had ever known.

He said at last the words, which nearly broke his heart: "I saw you dead."

Henry's smile was comforting. His old hand when he placed it over Stephen's was more warming than the fire. He let silent moments pass before he spoke in the soft voice of acceptance, "I know."

About the Author

William Kent Krueger is the award-winning author of seventeen previous Cork O'Connor novels, including *Sulfur Springs* and *Manitou Canyon,* as well as the novel *Ordinary Grace,* winner of the 2014 Edgar Award for Best Novel. He lives in the Twin Cities with his family. Visit his website at williamkentkrueger.com.

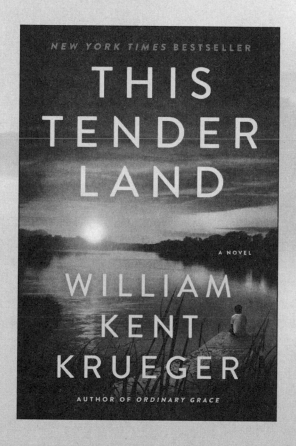